BRAVO FOR THE BRIDE

BRAVO FOR THE BRIDE

Elizabeth Eyre

St. Martin's Press
New York

Library of Congress Cataloging-in-Publication Data

Eyre, Elizabeth.
Bravo for the bride / Elizabeth Eyre.
p.   cm.
ISBN 0-312-11756-6
1. Italy—Court and courtiers—Fiction.   2. Renaissance—Italy—Fiction.   I. Title.
PR6009.Y74B7   1995
823'.914—dc20   94-35469   CIP

First published in Great Britain by Headline

First U.S. Edition: January 1995
10 9 8 7 6 5 4 3 2 1

To
Ella Watson
For old times' sake.

Contents

The People in the Story

In Borgo
Galeotto, Prince of Borgo
Ariana of Altamura, Prince Galeotto's bride
Prince-Bishop Gioffré, Abbot of Borgo
Lady Leonora ⎫
Lady Zima ⎭ Prince Galeotto's mistresses

In Venosta
Duke Vincenzo
Duchess Dorotea, his wife
Ristoni, a rich merchant
Madonna Ristoni, his mother
Mario Marietti, an engineer
Rodrigo Salazzo, a brigand

In Altamura
Duke Ippolyto
Duchess Violante, his wife
Lord Andrea and Lady Camilla, their children
The children's Nurse
Lord Tebaldo, cousin to the Duchess
Bonifaccio Valori, the Duke's chief counsellor
Tristano Valori, Bonifaccio's son
Polidoro Tedesco, a philosopher

Atzo Orcagna
Cola Borsieri } his pupils
Onorio Scudo
Poggio, dwarf to the Duchess
Nuto Baccardi
Stefano Cipolla } landlords of lodgings

In Transit
Pietro Brunelli, an architect
Master Valentino, a doctor
Pyrrho, a professional
Sigismondo, a soldier of fortune
Benno, his servant
Biondello, a dog

Chapter One

A complete Quintilian

'And a man died for this?'

'Men have died for very much less, as you well know, my son.' The Abbot's long fingers hovered over the page, not quite touching the parchment, as if he blessed the elegant writing, the coloured rondels along the borders illustrating the narrative. The fingers descended beside the book to tap the table. 'Do you know how much this cost, my son?'

'Apart from a man's life?' The speaker's voice was deep, amused. He shrugged broad shoulders. 'I have no idea, my lord, except that in your judgement it was worth the price.'

The Abbot sighed and stood back. A bird in the tree outside the window burst into sudden celebration of the warm morning, and he lifted his head to listen. 'Who can say what is to be valued? I do what I can with the resources at my disposal. The Prince is not interested in the abbey library. Duke Vincenzo of Venosta, now, has no care for books but he'll pay for them, the rarer the better.'

'To show that he can?'

'I imagine so.' The Abbot's smile transformed his austere face. He tapped the table again. 'He has a manuscript I would − not kill for, but perhaps die for,

1

God forgive me. Found by one of his collectors in a monastery in south Germany. A Quintilian. *Complete!* The only one I have ever heard of, Sigismondo.'

A long, thoughtful hum greeted this. 'A complete Quintilian, my lord, must be measured by more lives than one. Who died for *that*?'

'You think too much in terms of death, my son. It's natural to you, but do not let killing occupy your thoughts nor blood stain your mind.' The Abbot was severe, but he softened as the shaven head opposite bent in acknowledgement of the reproof. 'You are a devout man, as I have seen during your stay with us. I know that you do not take pleasure in killing, as some do. Yet we must remember that those who live by the sword, die by the sword.' He shut the heavy book with care, secured the silver clasps and permitted himself to caress the crimson velvet cover. 'No, the Quintilian, as far as I know, was purchased by money only. Duke Vincenzo is a secretive man. Brother Ursino was in Venosta a few days ago on business to the Duke's librarian, and he was allowed a glimpse of the Quintilian – no touching!' The Abbot snatched his hands from the velvet book in illustration. 'For ten minutes only . . .' He sighed again and turned to look out of the window. 'How hard it is in this world not to long for other things than God.'

Down in the courtyard, two monks, their robes kilted up to their knees, dug in a centre bed of earth where herbs grew. Others walked in the shadow of the colonnade, silent, eyes down, hands under their scapulars or in their sleeves. In a sunny corner, on a stone bench, sat a small bearded man, trying to teach a very small woolly dog with one ear to walk on its hind legs with a stick in its mouth. One of the monks was paying more attention to this than to his digging, and the Abbot frowned. Sigismondo, however, smiled.

'Has your man — Benno, isn't it? — profited at all from your stay here?'

The small dog took several steps on his hind legs before dropping to all fours and depositing the stick on the ground, but Benno clapped.

'I think, my lord, that he's succeeded in some things.'

The Abbot glanced at Sigismondo's smiling face and remarked, more tolerantly, 'St Paul teaches us that we must suffer fools gladly. I do not think your Benno as much of a fool as he looks, but that, like your subtlety, my son, is between him and God.'

A bell, slow and sonorous, rang out in the square tower of the great church, a small part of whose outer wall formed one side of the courtyard. The monks below stopped still for a sign of the cross and a prayer; the Abbot and Sigismondo above in almost exact synchronicity.

'It is getting late. I must go and prepare myself.' The Abbot looked round regretfully at the tall shelves with their heavy volumes, at the Livy in its crimson velvet on the carved cypress-wood lectern. 'The wedding couple are to hear a Mass in the abbey once the Lady Ariana has arrived and been received by the Prince.'

'The Duchess Violante comes as well?'

'You know her? Yes, she escorts her stepdaughter and will be here for the week of the festivities. Duke Ippolyto honours us in sending his wife as well as his daughter—'

An outburst of clapping in the courtyard drew the Abbot's attention. Both gardening monks, abandoning their spades, were applauding the little dog which advanced triumphantly across the cobbles, stick askew in his mouth, forepaws paddling the air.

The bearded man was the first to glance up, and in a

moment the monks were scrambling for their spades. The Abbot turned from the window and extended his hand to the tall man facing him, who went down swiftly on one knee to kiss the ring. 'We must bid you farewell, Sigismondo. It has been pleasant to see you again. When I taught you in Paris, those years ago, I did not think to see you in such a fashion here.'

'I believe you didn't think to see me ever again, in this world or the next.' Sigismondo was smiling broadly and the Abbot, responding almost gravely, inclined his head.

'I shan't ask you how you escaped hanging at that time. I hope only that you sought and received absolution for the blood you shed . . . Go in peace now. I do not adjure you to shed no more, because I am not so unworldly as to think you could obey. But may you have no occasion to shed blood during your stay in our fair city.'

Sigismondo bowed and the Abbot was gone, having voiced a wish doubtful of fulfilment.

Chapter Two

The omen

'I do love a good wedding.' Benno, his beard disgracefully greasy with vestiges of a pork fritter, beamed round at the street as they made their way along. People were already gathering in groups to secure places on the wedding procession's route. Almost any princely wedding will be a popular occasion, with such opportunities for feasting and carousing, but this one, their Prince Galeotto marrying Duke Ippolyto's daughter Ariana, was particularly pleasing to Borgo's citizens: it was good for trade, binding a neighbour state in the alliance of marriage.

Also gratifying was that Ippolyto of Altamura was not the only one to seek an alliance: Duke Vincenzo of Venosta had, everybody knew, offered his eight-year-old daughter to be Galeotto's bride. It was, all the gossips agreed, wholly sensible of their Prince to prefer the fifteen-year-old Ariana. You didn't get heirs on girls of eight without waiting around for longer than might be safe. The Prince's previous marriage had not been useful. Three daughters needing dowries were the only survivors and could not be considered a benefit. Principalities with no heir have a vulnerability no prince can afford.

'A good wedding? You sound like an old grandmother, Benno. Haven't you seen enough weddings?'

'Only two,' said Benno, aggrieved. 'I mean two royal ones.' Picking up his small woolly dog, he held him under his beard, which at once got licked with enthusiasm. 'Biondello likes a good wedding, don't you? This Prince Galeotto's done well for himself, hasn't he? Getting Duke Ippolyto's daughter. What's she like? You seen her?' Benno paused, with a clean beard and a feeling of anxiety. He might have overstepped the mark. His master had a prejudice against questions and Benno, although weak on mathematics, rather thought he had just asked three.

'Mm'mm. What she's like is what everyone here has been asking too. They seem at least to know that she has red hair.' Sigismondo pointed towards an arch that spanned the street they were climbing.

It was an ingenious structure, the framework interwoven with ivy, box and myrtle and laurel so that it looked as if it had decided to grow across the street of its own accord. Its true glory, however, was the pair of wooden figures tied into the arch at either side, facing each other. They were lifesize if not lifelike, and evidently their devisor had been at pains to represent the Prince and his bride, both of whom wore crowns of gilded wire twined with bay and flowers. The figure of the bride wore a dress of finest muslin embroidered with rosebuds, which Benno was sure was already bespoke, at some expense, to adorn a body of flesh rather than wood once the ceremonies were done. The crown had been fastened carefully to a wig of brilliant red silk whose ringlets had been teased out into a cloud upon the figure's shoulders. The people of Borgo were determined that, even if they hadn't got the shade exactly right, their new Princess should see they knew about her beautiful red hair.

6

As Sigismondo and Benno regarded it, the figure trembled almost as if it lived, and a man, halfway along the arch, checking the lashings that held the figure in place, put a wreath of flowers over one of the outstretched hands, and climbed down, slowly and carefully. The wooden face, large eyes painted black and small mouth red, stared at the wooden face of the Prince across the way.

The people of Borgo were confident in their representation here. The Prince's hair was but a pale shadow of his bride's, of ginger silk, only reaching to just below his wooden ears. The face was rounded, with even a suggestion of the turnip in its proportions, the nose large, the eyes small, the lower lip a generous blob. Benno stared, astonished, and turned to Sigismondo.

He breathed, 'He looks *awful*. He can't look that bad, can he?'

'Wait till you see him,' was the reply, following a long, derogatory hum. Benno reflected that, even if the Prince's effigy understated his actual appearance, it argued that his people were not so frightened of their ruler that they had to flatter him unduly. That could mean either that the Prince had a kindly nature or that he was weak.

In fact, the populace was counting on the known fact that their Prince was shortsighted, and that none of his courtiers was likely to risk injury by describing the effigy to him.

While Sigismondo and Benno contemplated his likeness, Prince Galeotto was getting dressed. What Nature takes away with one hand, she bestows with the other. The accident of birth had given Galeotto his face and figure; neither would have won him much admiration had they not come along with other gifts of birth: the principality of Borgo and its overflowing coffers. True, he was not as rich as Duke Ippolyto whose daughter he was marrying, but he was rich enough to afford the quantity of rubies, diamonds and sapphires tastefully incorporated into the embroidery of his doublet. On the ginger hair, which was already retreating as if in despair at the features below, he wore a large scarlet velvet hat trimmed with bullion that glittered as he turned his head to and fro to judge the effect in a mirror held up by a page.

He was satisfied, seeing not his looks but his wealth. In the right hands, it could be made to last a lifetime, which looks never can. It did not cross his mind that his bride might be disappointed. She had received his portrait in the course of the marriage negotiations, as he had received hers. Although the freckles had been left out on hers, his showed him as he had been in his late teens, two stone lighter and two chins less, the ginger hair in thick supply − more a Platonic ideal of himself than the real thing. All the same, daughters of dukes can no more be choosers than beggars can; the Lady Ariana was marrying money and should be glad to get it.

After a moment's thought, Galeotto pointed to a large brooch with a pendent pearl the size of a quail's egg lying in the coffer held open before him by a page. Another pinned it to the Prince's hat, where its weight pulled the velvet into a pouch over one eye, in harmony with those beneath. The Prince straightened his shoulders and beamed round. He was ready for his bride.

His bride was certainly ready for him. The Lady Ariana had already entered the city, welcomed with her stepmother at the Prince's Gate by the chief citizens of Borgo, fifty men, solemn in identical gowns of purple and scarlet to which their Prince had treated them. A forest of purple bonnets came off in a simultaneous gesture that had taken lengthy rehearsing. One elderly citizen muffed it and fumbled his bonnet to the ground, fixing a glazed limit to the bride's smile. There were the usual trumpets and Latin speeches which the grand folk were supposed to understand and the common folk took as a useful rest in which to stare at the Lady Ariana. They had been right about the hair; it was red, copious, and fluffed out to make it seem more plentiful – 'locky' was the fashionable mode – and they were gratified to find that she was, in spite of freckles that showed under rice powder, pretty. Duchess Violante was beautiful, but everybody knew that. Both ladies shimmered in cloth of silver and gold brocade and the crowd was deeply satisfied with the spectacle.

The Lady Ariana spoke briefly in Latin thanks and the Duchess spoke fluently. More trumpets, and the ladies and their train (got up in matching dresses of green satin) moved on, among loud cheers, at a dignified pace on their white palfreys towards the arch bearing the effigies of the bridal pair. Advancing towards them, with well-timed slowness, accompanied by a troop of courtiers in brown velvet and gold chains, came Prince Galeotto, straining his small eyes for the first sight of his bride. Could she live up to her picture, though he didn't?

Sigismondo and Benno had secured an excellent place on the route, firstly by early arrival and then because of Sigismondo's commanding build and presence. They stood right by the arch with the bridal figures, under which the real pair were to meet. Again there would be a fanfare, and a group of trumpeters either side of the arch was fidgeting in readiness. Their trumpets, bannered with the arms of Borgo worked in gold on scarlet, rested on their hips.

9

The Prince was to give his own Latin speech, a short one because his Humanist secretary had found it impossible to get him to memorise one of any length; the trumpeters were to time their fanfares both before he took the hand of his bride and began his speech, and after he had finished and was wheeling his horse to ride at her side towards the palace. As Prince Galeotto was inclined to mumble, they were terrified of cutting him short, not realising how grateful he would be.

Amid cheers, the two parts of the procession came slowly nearer to their moment of union. Twelve girls in white silk, chosen, amid brutal competition, from the maiden daughters of the richest men in town, had met the Lady Ariana and sung her praises, promising her the blessings of Venus and Ceres in a nicely mingled allusion to love and fertility. Now they walked before the white palfreys, scattering rose petals from gilded baskets. When they reached the green arch they divided ranks and, six a side, drew back to allow the bridal pair to meet under their likenesses. Benno, delighted to have a pretty girl backing onto his toes, kept Biondello from licking her neck and reflected that if the girls hadn't got out of the way they might well have been crushed between the two processions, hardly the best of omens for a wedding.

There was an omen worse than that to come, in fact.

Prince Galeotto's horse, a magnificent grey chosen for looks rather than manners, was growing restive at being held to the ceremonial pace and, tossing its head, was further irritated by the gold tassels and bells on the bridle. The groom at its head, suddenly threatened by its teeth, flinched aside; Galeotto in consequence was having to give his attention not to staring out for his bride but to controlling his horse, and so he luckily missed the vivid look of disappointment on his bride's face when she

10

came near to him. A moment later, everyone's attention was distracted.

She had arrived a little prematurely under the arch and under, as had been arranged, her own image. The crowd was pleased to see they had not been far out in their choice of colour for the wig, as there was little to choose between the red silk above and the red tresses below. Even the expressions, now that the Lady Ariana's schooling in diplomacy had returned to her, were almost identically wooden as the bridegroom drew near. The trumpeters raised their trumpets and waited.

It was Sigismondo, under the arch, who first caught the sound under the shouting of the crowd: first a thud, and then a cracking, tearing sound growing louder. He seized the shoulders of the girl in white silk pressed against him and put her aside but he was, as he came forward, too late.

With a rending crash the effigy of the Lady Ariana left the arch and tried to join its original on her palfrey. She had luckily just raised her hand to the wreath of flowers which the ebullience of her hair had begun to unsettle. The shift of her weight made her palfrey sidestep in obedience. The effigy struck its quarter only a glancing blow and then slammed to the ground behind, splintering and shedding limbs. The wig lay like a splash of blood.

Chapter Three

After the fall

Screams and shouts turned to uproar. The front ranks gasped and cried out in shock, those at the back whose view had been obscured shouted to be told what had happened. Those under the arch looked upward and crowded back. Galeotto's horse had reared and he was battling with it as its hooves struck out at all around. He had no time to spare for his bride.

Not for nothing had the Lady Ariana been put on a horse's back at the age of three. Her palfrey bucked, then wheeled and made a try at dashing back the way it had come but she brought it under control, with the help of a man who had emerged from the crowd to add his considerable strength to holding the bridle.

She gave the creature's neck a couple of reassuring thwacks as it shivered and sweated and trampled, and she looked down at the man, Roman nose, shaven head, black broadcloth, and saw an angel in disguise and breathed her thanks.

'Sigismondo!' The Duchess Violante had recovered control of her own mount – which had taken into its head that the end of the world had come – and rode up. She was not daunted by the happening. Danger was her favourite drink. Her startling blue eyes sparkled, her blonde braids looped with pearls were beginning to slip their moorings; her exhilarated smile might be relief at her stepdaughter's escape, but Sigismondo knew better. Duchess Violante enjoyed life and she was not averse to a bit of death either, even close to. She was definitely not the woman to have hysterics at any dire event. Almost, from her glowing face, one might think she had arranged the whole business as a superior entertainment to any the citizens of Borgo could offer.

'Your Grace. Excuse me . . .'

It is not commendable behaviour, for a man whose livelihood depends upon the great, to desert a duchess who has done you the honour of recognising you, but Sigismondo wove a swift way past the trampling horses, among the squealing ladies who now surrounded Ariana, and back to the arch, where he found Benno reluctantly surrendering a swooning girl to the care of a neighbouring matron. Benno had caught her and his proximity, acting as the strongest smelling salts, had restored her to consciousness in seconds. He now watched, gaping, while Sigismondo climbed the arch with its lone figure and almost disappeared among the greenery, making the structure tremble so that the rest of the crowd screamed and backed, confusedly.

Out on the processional route, Prince Galeotto had finally got command of his horse and the situation. He knew bad omens must be countered with a show of confidence. He rode forward, with a summoning gesture at the trumpeters, who managed a ragged fanfare short of one who had dropped his trumpet when the statue fell past him. Galeotto took his bride's hand and kissed it with ceremony. Stuff the speech in Latin!

His presence of mind paid off. The crowd roared approval, and clapped like a hailstorm, their noise purging the nasty fright they had had. The wedding, the feasting and the serious drinking were after all to come; if the bride had been brained by, in a manner of speaking, her own fall, everyone would have missed the lot.

The only people in the crowd still terrified were those responsible for the decoration of the arch. The figure's fall might be interpreted as an Act of God — and much would be whispered about that — but the punishment of those who had put it up would undoubtedly be an act of the Prince. Hanging could be thought altogether too good for the incompetents who had nearly killed their future Princess, and the professionals would think up things better than hanging; or worse, depending which side of it you were.

After all, if the Prince had been a bit quicker off the mark, he might have been crushed too. The citizens of Borgo suspected that, once short of a prince, they might rapidly have acquired a duke and become Venostans.

Meanwhile the show must go on. As the hubbub calmed, and the remains of the wooden lady were hurried from sight, the fifty citizens in scarlet and purple adjusted their coats and hats, thanked God privately that they still had a prince, made the sign against the Evil Eye inside their velvet sleeves and resumed their slow pacing behind the cavalcade. The ladies attending the bride pulled themselves together and assumed bright smiles. The bride herself, a becoming greenish white, rode onward at the side of her uninviting bridegroom; she had all the normal superstitions but she was a girl of determination and spirit. It occurred to her that her effigy had collapsed at almost the moment she caught sight of the Prince and she had to master a wild desire to giggle. Her palfrey had been carefully examined for damage by the pages at her stirrup, and proved to have been barely bruised, the heavy silk and the gilded leather

15

of its caparison having protected it; it too resumed its usual pace, persuaded that the sky would not fall again that day.

At Duchess Violante's stirrup walked the man who had helped the bride to control her horse. A border of white shirt with black embroidery showed, but he wore black doublet, hose and boots; he had a sinister look that interested the crowd. The shaven head did not really suggest a priest, for it was total, not a tonsure; he looked, in fact, uncomfortably stripped for action. Either the Duchess feared for her life, which was not very friendly of her in a neighbour state about to be linked to her husband by this marriage; or she had brought her own private assassin with a view to taking someone else's life – even less friendly. As the Duchess rode to the Prince's right, while all his attention was naturally for the bride on his left, he did not notice his guest's unusual page.

When they came to the palace – more a forbidding castle than a palace, but now softened by the hanging and flying banners of Borgo and Altamura in gold and silk – Prince Galeotto led the Lady Ariana up the long wide curve of steps, formally welcomed her and the Duchess (relieved at needing no Latin here), kissed his bride's mouth to polite applause from the assembled courtiers and dignitaries, and surrendered her to the care of her ladies. They had the task of changing her gown and tidying her up in general after the variegated disasters of the morning, not least of which in her opinion had been Prince Galeotto's kiss. She wished the night further off. The next, and immediate, public engagement was Mass in the abbey church, conducted by the Abbot, Prince-Bishop Gioffré of Borgo, a Mass which could be usefully dedicated to thanksgiving for God's mercy in saving life in that frightful accident.

'Accident?' Sigismondo was answering a question of the Duchess Violante at the entrance to the abbey church as they went in. 'No, your Grace, it was no accident.'

Chapter Four

Meant to kill

'Now is surely not the time, madam, to talk of misfortune.'

Prince Galeotto, lower lip protruding even further than Nature had provided, stared at his stepmother-in-law with growing dislike. Duchess Violante was beautiful, and Heaven only knew he appreciated beauty in women; she was high-spirited, and he was all for a reasonable amount of that; but he also liked women to keep their place and not interfere. This was no time to start rumours.

'It was not a misfortune, sir. Ask him.'

Prince Galeotto squinted at the tall stranger in black, leaning at his shoulder. He had no wish to waste his time on people from nowhere telling him things he didn't want to hear. He had enjoyment in hand − now this feast, later his bride. He drank with slow deliberation from his gold cup before saying, 'Well?' at his surliest.

'Highness, the effigy that fell had its lashings cut almost through beforehand.'

Prince Galeotto snorted, expelling some wine. 'So why didn't it fall before?'

'It needed a blow to tear the last shreds and make it fall.' The stranger's voice was deep and confident. He was offering information with no effort to persuade of its truth. What he was saying was, however, absurd.

'A blow? And who gave it a blow?' Half the Prince's attention was on the larks wrapped in forcemeat to which his page was helping him from the other side of the table. He had to make sure the boy gave him enough. 'Did you see anyone give it a blow?'

'No, Highness. I heard the blow.'

Galeotto slewed in his seat to stare. 'You *heard*? An invisible man delivered it?'

The stranger had a disconcerting gaze, with dark eyes completely steady. 'Probably slingshot, Highness. I heard the thud of it before the figure fell.'

Galeotto popped a lark into his mouth and crunched it. Delicious. He reached for another and waved at the stranger dismissively. 'You could have heard anything. Anything. All that noise. The men who put the figure up will be flogged, then hanged. I've given the order. Damned carelessness. An accident.' He turned to his bride, busy deciding between larks and chicken pasty with raisins and almonds. He directed the page to give her both, and patted her hand with his rather greasy one. 'Nothing shall go wrong on this auspicious day, dear one!'

The Prince's major-domo, directing the feast, and alert as always to his master's wishes, put his gold-tipped staff between Sigismondo and the Prince's chair, a signal not hard to read. The Duchess Violante's eyes flashed, but she nodded at Sigismondo as if to say, Wait, and turned back to the table and the inquisitive glances of the guests. The gold and jewelled pomegranates on her dress glittered; the dark shadow drew away behind her. What had her private assassin, or bodyguard, been saying to the Prince? Had he received a commission? Or, as the Prince had not looked pleased, was he reporting a failure? It was true he did not look like an incompetent, guilty of an assassination that had not come off; he had an air of confidence. Yet the guests had no idea how close they were to the truth.

In any case, such dire matters did not occupy their minds for more than an instant that evening. The Prince's cooks were out to impress. Neither money nor effort had been spared. A gilded statuette several inches high stood before each diner at the high table, outstretched hands holding scented flowers and trailing fronds of ivy – symbolic of fidelity and so particularly apt at a wedding. A lady whispered mock-pious hopes that no more statues would fall, others hushed her and giggled.

The statues did make a little difficulty each time the damask cloths were removed between courses and replaced, but nowhere was this refinement more necessary than at the high table where Prince Galeotto's enthusiastic appreciation of his food led to a generous distribution of it around his plate, especially when he offered titbits to his bride. The Lady Ariana pleased him more and more. Not only did she look as appetising as the food, with that creamy skin peppered with freckles, and the hot spicy red of her hair, but also she displayed an excellent appetite. He was not to know of Ariana's decision to eat and drink so much at the feast that, with any luck, she might be able to pass at least some of the night in a stupor no matter what else was taking place. Besides, it was easier to take the gobbets offered on the two gold prongs of the Prince's fork than to bear the close proximity of his slobbered face. Conversation was clearly not required of her. A bride was supposed to be modest, to smile a little, say less; so when she was not submitting to having her face stuffed by the Prince, she

21

simply looked down at her food or straight ahead at the entertainment.

Of course this, like the food, was spectacular. A Florentine, highly recommended by the Duke of Nemora, was in charge of the occasion and was determined not to let his reputation down. He had at least four nights of festivities to provide, not to mention the various amusements that would be expected by day in this summer weather.

Tonight demanded the bravura presentation: always dazzle to start with. In delicate compliment to the bride, Venus made an entrance in a chariot, gilded, wreathed with the ubiquitous ivy and drawn by a unicorn whose gilded and slightly unsteady horn gave it a puzzled, cross-eyed look; Venus threw flowers at the Lady Ariana – actual, costly flowers, not merely symbolic leaves and herbs. She was to have worn a red wig, in further compliment, but after the fate of this morning's effigy, it had been very hastily decided that gold silk would be more tactful now.

The seven Virtues accompanied Venus, in a happy mixture of Biblical with classical. They wore thin layers of silk which their dancing movements caused to waft about revealingly, prompting speculation as to what the seven Vices might have worn. The Prince for a moment forgot to attend to his food.

The Florentine had been put in a quandary over the cornucopias borne in by youths in white silk sewn with myrtle leaves. Originally they were to have spilled out a medley of fruit, so abundant at this season, before the high table. In rehearsal, the dancers who came next complained loudly of apples and pears rolling treacherously underfoot, of tripping on melons, of slides on squashed grapes. The Florentine thought again. To have the bounty swept up would create the wrong impression. So now the youths advanced with the gilded horns held high, pointing towards the coved ceiling, to the music of harp and cithern, and then, when the high table was reached, the horns were lowered to pour out sweetmeats, candied fruit, and nuts around the feet of the golden statuettes.

One expects pageant at a wedding, but there must also be comedy. The Florentine knew he would be fortunate if these elaborate entertainments ended without comedy he hadn't planned for and a hall full of guests laughing their heads off at a grand effect gone catastrophically wrong. Once, in a city state he had not visited ever again, he had brought on the youths with the cornucopias and for a particular flourish had organised flames coming from them – that made the company give that 'Aaah!' of applause every impresario works for – and one idiot youth needs must get too close to the one in front and offend the guests' nostrils with the stench of burning silk, followed quite rapidly by the worse stench of burning youth. Such a fuss! The Florentine preferred now to send on a trio of jugglers, who at least were professionals, and who would at first pretend to make a hash of their act and get nuts and chicken legs thrown at them, and would then triumphantly incorporate these items into a skilful and brilliantly fast exchange for which they might get gold coins. Their faces were painted, their wigs absurdly tousled, so that no guest was in danger of taking them seriously. To underline the point, they wore bells sewn at random onto their clothes and one of them was a dwarf.

Another dwarf, who had come in the Duchess Violante's train, watched with a critical eye. Pratfalls were all very well, but to work properly they had to be done with dignity. The laughs this lot were getting could have been doubled if he'd had the training of them. He stood between two of the servers against the tapestry by one of the side tables, and snatched a glance under someone's elbow at the Duchess Violante. He was glad to see she wasn't laughing.

In fact she wore a look he knew well. She was furious. Because he had only just come in — there were pickings between here and the kitchens — the dwarf had no idea why the Duchess should be furious. Surely she was pleased at the Lady Ariana's marriage?

The Duchess was furious but she was also anxious. Galeotto was a fool. She'd suspected as much from the start; too much of a fool to heed a warning from a man who did know what he was talking about. If Sigismondo believed the effigy had been meant to kill, whom was it aimed at? The thing had nearly hit Ariana but then she, Violante, had been riding beside her and Galeotto was only a few yards away. Such a thing as the fall of an object was probably difficult to get exact. Had the assassin got it wrong? More importantly, when was he going to try again?

Chapter Five

A corpse in her arms

'Which dress, Highness?'

Ariana looked blearily at the choices held up before her by deferential ladies-in-waiting. The only thing she was pleased about this morning was the title of *Highness*. God knew, she deserved it. The first instalment of the price of being Princess of Borgo had been paid last night, and Galeotto's drunkenness had not done as much to mitigate things as she had hoped; nor had her own feasting stupefied her nearly enough. There would be another banquet today as well, and Galeotto was not going to vanish like the conjurer's doves last night.

Better wear the pink. The green, which became her more, was a little too close to the way she felt. And with the pink, she would wear the silver brocade sleeves lined with pink, and one of them sewn with pearls; and the belt of linked pearls and rubies, gift of the bridegroom. The collapse of her effigy might not have been a good omen for one side of her marriage, but she had received enough presents so far to make her appreciative of the material benefits.

'You will wear the Prince's bracelets, Highness?'

Stupid woman, of course she would. And they were the Princess's bracelets now. Galeotto had clasped them on her arms this morning, mumbling compliments and

25

pressing his revolting kisses after them. The workmanship alone was excellent: little gold leaves and tendrils entwined sapphire and pearl flowers dewed with diamonds; and they were nearly a hand deep. She held out her arms commandingly now, and two ladies hurried to put the bracelets on them. It had been sad to take them off a short time ago when Nurse wanted to wash her. Perhaps after all it had been a mistake to insist on bringing Nurse, even though she could be so useful.

She moved her arms about, admiring the bracelets, while her ladies held up the skirt of the pink dress ready to drop it over her head.

'I don't suppose there are any bracelets quite like these anywhere in the world.'

'I don't know, your Highness. I'm sure I have seen the match to these somewhere, quite recently. Now where could it have been?'

The lady who appeared to be racking her memory was not one of the Princess's ladies, those chosen by the Prince from the great families in the state to wait on her. Her own, the ones who had come with her, already had been made to feel out of place here; most of them were in any case to return to Altamura with her stepmother Violante at the end of the festivities. No, this lady, more finely dressed than most of them, had come independently to pay her compliment to the bride and to bring a present of ten yards of pretty blue brocade. Ariana stared at her.

'A match to these?' She looked down at the glitter of the diamonds, the gold tendrils entrapping the sapphires, the rubies. 'Oh no. The design must be unique.'

'Ah! I have it!' The lady had a reasonably attractive face for someone who, Ariana judged, must be at least in her late twenties, if not her *thirties*; it was suddenly illumined. 'I know where it was – a pair exactly like these.'

Ariana noticed that the other ladies of Borgo were exchanging glances, were drawing away very casually from the speaker as if her presence were danger. Here was something the Princess was not supposed to know about, and would not like to hear. Ariana hadn't grown up at court for nothing.

'And where was that?' Whatever she was told, she would show them she was their Princess now.

'Why, I believe . . .' The woman was milking it, finger to lip in an effort to recall what she was intent on telling anyway. The ladies had moved together, a defensive group, eyeing her, distancing themselves from her. *They all knew.* The woman smiled suddenly, looking round at them, bringing them in. 'You were there too. At the Villa Brunetta. The Lady Zima was wearing just such a pair. Wasn't she?'

Uncertainty arose among the ladies, even sudden and total loss of memory. Ariana saw that the Lady Zima must have a pair of bracelets exactly matching hers. That meant an unmistakable relationship between the lady at the Villa Brunetta and Prince Galeotto. Her husband.

It was perfectly natural for Galeotto to have amused himself with someone, or several someones, after the death of his wife, and to continue to do so if it would occupy his time; but this was different. This Zima had been given the double of the Prince's wedding present to his bride. She was so important to him that either he had soothed her for his marriage with this gift, or she had demanded and got it. Ariana meant to find out which. This smiling, curtseying creature in front of her meant her to find out too, so it was to her, equally bland, that Ariana gave her order.

27

'Tell the Lady Zima to wait on me today.' She paused, aware of the turbulence in her stomach which was complaining of her burdening it so at the banquet . . . A mistake to see this Zima until she was feeling better, more herself, *prettier*. 'Let her wait on me this evening. I will find time to see her then, and send for her.' She gave a charming smile and swept an arm dismissively; she found she was less pleased with the glittering slide of the bracelets than she had been. She resisted a quite strong impulse to tear them off. The watchers who surrounded her should not have the satisfaction of seeing how she felt. Nor should her husband – yet.

Galeotto never found it hard to be satisfied with himself and he had an extra cause for self-congratulation when he waited on his bride later in the morning, to lead her to yet more entertainments devised by the busy Florentine; his Princess received him with a grateful sweetness that made him preen before her ladies, and he completely missed the glint in her eyes when he remarked on the augmented beauty the bracelets received from her arms. Who said redheads were awkward to handle? This girl was a dream.

The dream planned on becoming a nightmare before the day was out, and she would indeed have her way in a fashion she had not foreseen, but she now floated out to be displayed to the court as a married woman. Ranks of courtiers clapped their applause, bowed, curtseyed, in their bright silks and brocades, flowers before the breeze. The Prince beamed, the Princess modestly smiled. Time to get on with the fun again.

A hunting party had been arranged for the afternoon. The Princess was said to be feeling tired, a fact reported with impassive glances among the senior officials and with sniggers among servants out of earshot. The Prince was graciously pleased to cancel the hunt. It was anyway too hot. Such a consideration had never prevented him before, as some knew to their cost, but he was now naturally solicitous for his bride. The Duchess Violante, a bold huntswoman, was disappointed until she recollected how many opportunities there are for unfortunate accidents during the hunt. Instead, she welcomed the small orchestra of citherns, lutes and harp that the Prince sent to console her when everyone retired to rest after a bountiful cold collation at midday. She wanted to question Sigismondo but he had vanished.

It was odd that such a conspicuous man had not been seen by anyone, but it brought to Violante's mind that he was a specialist, and that another specialist might be the person he was tracking down. The men who had put up the effigy had already been flogged and hanged, and Galeotto was ready to forget the whole thing. She was not.

Sigismondo was tracking nobody. He was enjoying an excellent meal at a cook shop in the town, with Benno. Feasts do not cater for men from nowhere and both of them were hungry. Rabbit stew with cinnamon and onions might perhaps not be recommended on a hot day, but eaten in the shade of a rush-mat awning and washed down with strong red wine, it was good. Biondello sat at their feet gulping gravy-soaked sops of bread. The eating shop's benches were all occupied by men discussing, mostly, the wedding and the boost to trade it would bring. No one evinced concern at the omen of the day before. After all, no one had been killed, had they? The hanging of the incompetents had taken place at midday in the main square. It was muttered that the Carpenters' Guild was not best pleased. Tonight was to be a *fête champêtre*, dancing and fireworks in the Prince's gardens along the lake, a private affair for the court; for the citizens, the main fountain in the abbey square, an opulent convolution of allegorical marble, was to run wine, and everybody, including the pickpockets, was looking forward to a very good time. Benno was sorry to gather that he and Sigismondo were not to be there, but was immediately consoled to learn that they would be at the palace instead.

'The Duchess wants to see you, then?' He knew this question might not be answered, but his master shrugged.

'She may, before the night is out.'

The palace gardens were on two levels. One, a terrace laid out in parterres and shaded by ilex, ended in a balustraded walk with, at one side – reached from the palace either through the terrace garden or along a tunnel arbour – a small decorative pavilion overlooking the stream below and with a view of the lake. Steps led down from this terrace and from the palace itself to the lower gardens which in turn descended in three wide shallow terraces to the lake shore. Given this setting, the Florentine had toyed with the idea of an episode from the Arthurian romances, but he had visions of the one delegated to swim well out into the lake and hoist up Excalibur at the appropriate moment – trumpets would have been blown in the woods, torches placed along the shore – failing to hold it steady. A wavering sword, like a falling effigy, does not inspire confidence.

The Florentine had opted for a dance of Moors with torches. Later, Diana, in an interestingly short tunic of white silk which would glimmer in the moonlight, and with a silver crescent in her hair and a silver bow in hand, was to aim her (invisible) arrow at a deer, now ready in a cage to be let out at a given signal. The deer, the

Florentine well knew, could not be trusted to do anything except scatter the ladies, ruin a parterre or two, and escape into the woods. It would be nice if it could be panicked into swimming the lake but he had small hope of that. Then a fawn, a tame one thank Heaven, garlanded with flowers, was to be led to the Princess while a singer, prudently concealed beyond the cypresses because his voice was the only asset he had, announced that the creature had come to give itself to Beauty in person.

All these would no doubt have gone extremely well. The Princess, however, announced that she must rest first. She would watch the ladies dancing, from the pavilion. A wide bench ran round two sides, honeysuckle and jasmine climbed the trellis. Where was a place more charming for a Princess to rest and watch?

The Lady Leonora, who had so kindly given Ariana information already that day, had also let drop the fact that this pavilion had been specially constructed at the Prince's bidding, not in prospect for his new bride, but for the lady of the bracelets.

It was in this pavilion, ensconced among silk cushions on one of the benches, that Ariana was going to send for the Lady Zima.

When, an hour later, the Princess had still not emerged to grace the festivities, to dance with her husband and receive the fawn, tribute of Diana, the Duchess Violante said to her own ladies that she felt it incumbent on her to remind her stepdaughter of her obligations. The cancellation of the hunt had been enough. They had seen Galeotto enter the pavilion at one time during the evening, perhaps to remonstrate with his too retiring bride for they had heard raised voices despite the music in the garden.

31

'This behaviour will not do. It reflects poorly on Altamura.'

'And on her upbringing.' An older woman, a sardonic Altamuran who had become Violante's friend, went on, 'The brusqueries of a wedding night happen to us all.'

Violante suppressed a smile as their eyes met. 'I'll send our Princess a message.'

The Lady Leonora was the one nearest the steps to the pavilion. She was of sufficient rank to bear a message from a duchess to a princess. Violante beckoned.

When the lady came down from the pavilion she was alone. She came swiftly across the grass past the dancers and her face when she curtseyed before Violante betrayed anxiety.

'Your Grace, her Highness is asleep.'

'Then *wake* her.'

'I tried, your Grace.' There was panic, barely held down, in the woman's voice. 'I *can't* wake her.'

Violante rose, with a great rustle of silks, and beckoned to her friend. The dancers fell back as the two women crossed towards the pavilion. As they climbed the steps, Violante murmured to her companion, 'The girl's capable of any pretence to get out of what she doesn't want to do.'

Yet it did not seem that there was pretence. The girl was so soundly asleep that she did not waken when Violante touched her, spoke in her ear, shook her; she still reclined, turned a little away from them, propped on her cushions against the low trellis behind the bench.

'Can the stupid child have taken a sleeping draught?'

'Perhaps too much wine again.' The Lady Clea indicated the glass goblets on the small table nearby.

Violante put her arms round Ariana to turn her. Both women now caught a full view of her face.

32

'Really, this is no time to be defying her Grace—'

The girl's tongue protruded, as so often, at her stepmother. But this time the eyes protruded too and, as the moonlight fell on the upturned features, dark specks, darker than freckles, showed all over her face. There was no mistaking that the Duchess held a corpse in her arms.

Chapter Six

Fireworks

Screams burst from the pavilion. The music broke into discord that squawked to a stop. The dancers froze for a heartbeat of time. The orchestra, trapped in their little gallery, leant and strained to see, but the dancers ran, hoisting and bundling skirts, the men flying ahead.

What they found in the pavilion was Lady Clea providing the screams, and the Duchess Violante, hands to her head, rigid as if she had seen the Gorgon and staring out at the moonlit dark. Of the Princess there was no sign.

Others leant to look where the Duchess stared. Halfway down the slope to the stream, the Princess lay spreadeagled in her satin skirts, arms and legs askew, hair tumbled free, a discarded doll. Some stayed peering and gasping, some ran down the steps and went over a low wall to clamber along the slope to the Princess. Someone shook the Lady Clea and stopped the screaming.

'Horrible! It was horrible! Her Grace threw . . . dropped her . . . She fell over the edge! Her face!'

It was not supposed at first that the Princess had got more than a fall. Not a few of those who had observed her at last night's feast, and at the noon meal, supposed she might have been drunk.

The Princess had landed face down. There was a

confusion in the effort to lift her without hurting her, and a plethora of advice, contradictions, calls for a mattress, for a litter, warnings that her Highness could have injured her head. In finally raising her among them, the courtiers became aware that they were being assisted, even directed, by a man in black whose shaven scalp gleamed in the moonlight.

As they carried the Princess up the slope, those above held out torches, her face came out of shadow and one of the courtiers yelped. Someone put a kerchief over it. There was a silent revision in some minds of masculine contempt for the Lady Clea's screams. They admitted she had reason.

Prince Galeotto could be heard in full voice in the terrace garden, demanding to know what had happened. The now silent procession reached the low wall, their feet slipping on the rough dry grass so that the body in their arms seemed to be struggling. As one of them slid down the bank and let go, the man in black relieved them all of the burden, and in a few strides bore the Princess to the low wall, stepped over it and was at the foot of the little curving flight up to the pavilion. There, the Prince met them.

By the light of the torches, he looked like an angry baby. Wisps of hair stuck out under his cap, his lip pouted, his chins shook. This was an angry baby told that its toy had been damaged. Only a few people as yet realised that the pretty toy was broken.

'Is she hurt? How did she fall?' Galeotto peered at the face, which was now suddenly illuminated by a torch's movement. It had lost the kerchief. He drew back so fast that he trod on someone's foot. 'God's Bones! She's dead!'

His wife, with lolling head, seemed to nod in

agreement as other men, of rank and position, tried to relieve the stranger of his burden. He could spare a hand to pull back the necklet of pearls Ariana wore. Beneath them was another band, so tight that it had almost disappeared into the skin which had swollen round it, dark in the torchlight.

'Strangled, Highness. The Princess was strangled.' In the silence after Galeotto's cry, this voice was deep, unhurried, offering a fact. The word spread in sibilant whispers. Someone cried out. A woman began the whoops of hysteria.

'*Strangled?* Who could have strangled her?' Galeotto gobbled with astonishment and dismay. He put up his hand to adjust his cap, knocked awry in his haste through the gardens, as if he would adjust his wits; which prompted him to pull his cap off in the Presence that was with them. Still his uppermost thought came out. 'Who would dare kill *my wife*?'

Benno, naturally among the press of servants drawn along with the great ones to this focus of horror, heard the bewildered bellow and thought: Can't see anyone coming forward to claim the honour, right? Poor young lady, she's really had no luck, first the Prince and now this. Seems like that image of her, falling, was a bad omen after all. But then Sigismondo said that wasn't an accident.

At this moment, Galeotto recognised the shaven head and remembered too.

'You warned me! Do you *know* who has done this?'

'Highness, it's possible that I could find out.'

Galeotto grasped at the confidence imparted by the man's voice. 'You'll be rewarded. Gold. Jewels. You can choose.' He made rejecting, pushing gestures towards the body of his one-day's wife, so sickening now to look on.

'Let the women take care of . . . they will do what's . . . Come with me. We will discuss . . .' In the flaring, shifting light of the torches he was glistening with sweat. Perhaps it had just occurred to him that with his wife had died the alliance with Altamura; that he might – would – be held responsible for Ariana's death by her powerful father. When Sigismondo had surrendered Ariana's body to the women to carry to the palace, Galeotto put a fat, white, ringed hand on his arm. 'Come. Must speak in private.'

'Your Highness is a huntsman. You will know that a trail is best followed when it's warm. Will your Highness permit that I report to you later?'

The hand closed on Sigismondo's arm. 'Track them down. *Track them down.*' His glistening face came closer, wine stale on his breath. Sigismondo bowed and, withdrawing, seemed to melt into the crowd.

Benno, in the confusion and shadows flung by both torches and moon, was pushed this way and that by the crowd that ebbed through the gardens. The Prince's guard was vainly trying to stop the whole court and the guests from trampling the careful patterns of lavender and marjoram hedges of the parterres. The deer, waiting to be released from its osier cage for Diana to aim at, burst the willow bars in alarm at the shouts and screaming, and added its own destruction of the lower gardens in its dash for freedom, straight to the shore where it did what the Florentine had not dared to hope for and swam picturesquely to the further shore, noticed by no one.

The swirl of people on the terrace had set towards the palace, to which the Princess had been carried and where news and subsequent gossip could be expected. Benno, by cramming himself into corners, keeping to the darkest parts and finally walking back down the great tunnel arbour that led from the palace to the pavilion, arrived where he guessed his master would be.

There was a light still burning in the pavilion, a lamp encased in a tracery of wrought iron hanging in one of the 'windows', adding its scent of warm olive oil to the air. Sigismondo's shadow was cast huge and wavering on the foliage and the painted tracery of the ceiling. A waft of jasmine came from the plant crushed by the Princess in her fall.

Benno looked round with alert curiosity. He was about to pick up a gold brocade cushion from the tiles when Sigismondo spoke.

'Move nothing. Things will be moved soon enough and we've little time.' He was on one knee now, by a small table close to the couch where, to judge from a crumpled velvet cover and disarranged brocade cushions, the Princess had been lying. Two delicate glass goblets with stems of twisted violet and pink stood on the inlay of the table. One was full and Sigismondo had put his finger in the liquid − not wine but something cloudy and herb-smelling − and now put his finger in his mouth. Suddenly he rose and spat over the edge of the trellis.

'Is it poison?' Benno was alarmed. Even a taste of some poisons was said to be fatal.

'Mm'mm. Whoever drank that would vomit enough to purge any poison.' Sigismondo sniffed the liquid and swirled it in the goblet. 'Yet it has herbs in it for digestion. A contradiction.'

Benno scratched his chest, and regarded the cloudy liquid beginning to settle in the glass. 'If she was meant to drink it, wouldn't she spit it out like you did?'

Sigismondo had the other glass now and was sniffing the dregs in it, apparently wine. 'If she'd asked for a digestive draught, she'd have made a face and got it down. People expect medicine to taste bad, you know that.'

Benno knew that. He'd had quite a few remedies in his time forced down his unwilling throat, such as fried mice. Even princesses would have to suffer if they wanted to feel better. Perhaps remedies made you better because you determined not to need any more of them. 'And she'd have tossed it back fast so's not to taste it anyway. Or mightn't she have wanted to throw up? After last night's eating, like.'

Sigismondo didn't answer. He was tasting the dregs of wine and Benno stepped from between him and the trellis. This time, Sigismondo only shook his head.

'Hey, now a *sleeping* draught. And that, it seems, she drank.'

Benno's eyes widened. 'Sleep, and miss all the fun? Wasn't there going to be all sorts of entertainments, like fireworks and masques? And wouldn't the Prince get a bit cross if she didn't come and join in?'

Sigismondo stood, looking out towards the waters of the lake, its ripples netted in silver under the moon. His forefinger thoughtfully caressed his upper lip.

To Benno's astonishment, he suddenly vaulted the low trellis wall and disappeared from view. Biondello, who had been sniffing at all within his reach as diligently as Sigismondo had sniffed the glasses, gave one of his rare barks and immediately followed, soaring over the little trellis and vanishing below. Benno hurled himself at the trellis but only to peer over.

Sigismondo was working along the slope beneath, looking closely at the ground. Benno thought perhaps some of the Princess's jewels were missing and the Prince wanted them found. You lose your wife, you don't want the family diamonds to go too. As he watched Sigismondo's progress with fascination, and reassured himself that Biondello was unhurt, a heavy hand dropped on his shoulder and he jumped with the shock.

He was dragged from the brink. 'Not so fast, you rascal. What have you been doing here?' The tone made the question a formality. 'Steal' was what the questioner knew Benno would do. The goblets, Venetian and worth a tidy sum of ducats, were just the thing for a thief to make off with and the questioner did not pause to enquire why, in fact, they were still on the table. Benno, hauled back by his collar, was shoved half choking into the arms of a second servant

'Dirty thief! You'll hang for it.' The *maestro di casa* pushed Benno aside with distaste as the second man pinioned him. 'Take him outside.' The *maestro di casa* had come to supervise the removal of silk coverlets, brocade cushions, inlaid table and Venetian glass; he had been delayed by the uproar in the palace, and was now angry with the anger of a man responsible for valuable objects who has been almost too late to retrieve them.

Benno made no attempt to explain or excuse himself. Experience had taught him that his appearance, by itself, prevented belief. He did not mention Sigismondo either, in case Sigismondo did not care to be mentioned. He did not seriously expect to be hanged, for his trust in his master was absolute.

Besides, it was obvious that detaining him was proving a great nuisance to the *maestro di casa*, who needed both servants to transport table and cushions back to the palace while he himself reverently carried the goblets, which he had picked up and now put down again. Benno was very much in the way. How was he to spare one servant to hold him while he helped the other —

41

undignified! And who would carry the goblets? It would take time to send for a palace guard, and the *maestro di casa* was busy with all these untoward events, guests everywhere when they should have been in the garden . . . He looked round and, with some idea of identifying the thief should he escape, seized the lamp and held it high to cast its light on the man's face.

Instantly, the little island, whose wooded silhouette had brooded darkly near the farther shore, burst into an explosion of light and noise. Rockets soared, dazzling coloured flashes appeared with small detonations like a series of dwarf cannon going off.

The men hidden on the island had been rowed there hours before with their equipment and their instructions. They were to provide the brilliant finale for the entertainments that were to charm and amaze their new Princess, and they had at last received the signal for their fireworks to begin.

Chapter Seven

His own victim?

Benno had wheeled in astonishment with the others as the fireworks lit up the sky and turned the pavilion and its inhabitants gold, red, green; but he knew when to seize an opportunity. As the grip on his collar slackened he ducked and snaked past the *maestro*, who fell forward dropping the lamp over the trellis, where it set grass briefly aflame and extinguished itself in a little floating flare on the stream. Benno fled down the stairs into the shadows, and was not surprised to be joined by a larger, darker shadow who thrust a silent quivering little woolly dog against his chest.

Sigismondo was moving into the tunnel arbour, perhaps the only path safe from the erratic glare of the fireworks. Benno, sparing only a glance at what he was forgoing — he dearly loved fireworks — hurried after, stuffing Biondello inside his jerkin.

Behind them, with no lamp to help, goblets, table, satin coverlet and a multitude of cushions had all to be collected and taken back through the terrace gardens in the unreliable scintillations from the island, by servants, one of whom was entranced by the fireworks and walked sideways into every hedge in the place, while the other imagined that someone who strangled princesses would also be concerned with his plebeian throat. The *maestro*

43

was glad to reach the palace with the goblets intact, for there had come into his mind that the person who strangled the Princess might simply be a common thief; suppose the unsavoury creature who escaped them just now had crept in to steal, woken the Princess, strangled her to silence her and now, when the uproar had subsided and everyone had gone, crept back once more to accomplish his theft? There were far too many shadows in the gardens. At any moment the uncouth villain might spring out from behind a cypress and grab the fragile treasures, not even thinking that this might crack or even shatter them. That one glimpse of Benno's features had not convinced the *maestro* that thought was a customary occupation with him.

Unaware of this calumny, trotting fast down the tunnel arbour, lit tantalisingly by glimmers of firework light through the arching thick leaves overhead, Benno arrived at the palace. He was at Sigismondo's heels and well in advance of the *maestro di casa*, the servants and their burdens. The palace guards did not bar their way in, for everyone had seen the Prince lay his hand on the arm of the tall stranger in black and conjure him to find the assassin. It was true that the sight of Benno gave them momentary hope that he had already succeeded, but murderers rarely come to heel of their own accord. He was allowed through after his master with no more than a prod in the chest for looking witless, a prod which earned the guard who gave it an inexplicably bitten forefinger. Biondello had not yet recovered from the fireworks.

Benno got stopped at the door of the Princess's chamber, however. This did not surprise him and he watched as Sigismondo was allowed in. The Prince had come to view his wife now the laying-out had begun. She would be conveyed to the private chapel when all was ready, for the Masses for the dead.

Sigismondo stood, his head slightly bent in respect, while Galeotto, on his knees beside the Princess's great bed, groaned and wept in gusty bursts. Two physicians, identifiable by their caps and gowns, stood at the foot of the bed, looking wise, completely useless. No one has yet discovered a cure for strangling.

Far more to the point at this time was the Abbot, hands pressed together in silent prayer, kneeling opposite the Prince. The Duchess Violante knelt further off in the shadows, her praying hands before her face; the Lady Leonora, elegant in sorrow, and a weeping woman in the embroidered apron and voluminous linen of an upper servant knelt further back still.

There had been no way of radically improving the Princess's appearance. The red hair, unbound as became a bride, had been spread on the satin pillows, the collar of pearls hid the line on her neck, and they had changed the gold-beaded dress with its stains of death for a dark blue velvet with cloth-of-silver bands, but nothing could disguise the purple specks on the white skin. Coins lay on the eyelids to close the bulging eyes, and the tongue had relaxed enough to be pushed back, although in spite of the band tying her jaw, the tongue's tip showed as though she waited for a sweetmeat to be popped on it. There, on her mattress of Cypriot wool, on the bed of cypress wood panelled in walnut and hung with scarlet taffeta with the golden arms of Borgo, lay the girl who had made Borgo's Prince a widower for the second time with such unexpected speed.

No one had tidied up the Prince. His cap lay near his silk gloves on the floor, and his hair stood up on the scalp, showing pink through the ginger, and the fur on his collar stuck together in clumps as though the ermine that donated it had never been well. Even the sleeves of velvet, slashed with cloth of gold and sewn with onyx buttons, seemed, to the observant eye such as Sigismondo's, to be drooping and torn.

'Highness.'

The word, quiet and low though it was, penetrated the wailing of the servant, the prayers of the Abbot, even the muted bellows of the Prince himself. Galeotto turned. He scrambled to his feet, leaning heavily on the bed.

'You've news? He's caught? I'll have him torn apart, flayed alive, burnt to ashes . . .' The programme excited him; he staggered and caught at the hangings. It was apparent that he had already made strenuous efforts to drown his grief. 'My beloved!' He lurched at the Princess, caught his foot on the bed platform and sprawled across his bride whose body bounced in response. Once down, he seized the opportunity and her hands, crossed on her breast, and kissed them fervently. Her velvet sleeves slid back, revealing his wedding gift, the bracelets no one had thought it right to remove. The sight inspired fresh grief in him and his howls brought remonstration from the Abbot: such energy should be directed into prayer; one who died suddenly had much need of prayer.

The women were more sympathetic. The Duchess and the Lady Leonora both tried to get the Prince back on his feet if not, as the Abbot wished, on his knees. As they pulled at him and he floundered on the bed, making the corpse jerk its slippers, the Lady Leonora cried out, 'Oh, your Highness, take care! See where your sleeve is torn!' She picked up the Prince's arm and pointed to the sagging velvet and gold cloth.

Distracted for a moment from his display of grief, for the Prince valued his clothes, he checked his tears and, sniffing, examined the sleeve. He said, 'It is not torn. The buttons are missing.'

The Lady Leonora, rearranging the Princess's hands, putting them back on her breast, sliding the bracelets down to the wrists, paused, holding one inert wrist. 'Why, how strange! Here are the buttons, Highness, trapped in the bracelet.' Certainly, caught in the involved curves of the gold tendrils and wedged so tightly that the Prince and the lady together could hardly prise them out, were two gleaming buttons from the Prince's sleeve. What was also certain, even to the most confused of observers, was that nothing in Galeotto's exertions just now could have fixed those buttons from his sleeve so firmly in the bracelet.

Into the minds of those who watched came, involuntarily, the picture of another struggle, a struggle in which the girl would use her hands to fight the grip of a strangler. Surely, surely the Prince was not mourning his own victim?

Chapter Eight

Lost property

Benno, waiting outside the room, passed his time in gaping amiably at the guards before the door, one of whom was developing a craving to plug Benno's mouth with something large, round and painful, like a mace. They could all hear the distant pop of fireworks. What a waste, Benno thought. He hoped some of the court was managing to get a look at them. It would hardly be well seen if they were to rush out to the shore and clap, with a strangled Princess on the premises, but there must be places in the building where they could watch.

He had formed no theory of his own about the possible murderer, apart from wondering how the Princess could have got across anyone enough in her two days and a night in Borgo to make them want her dead. It wasn't likely to be just someone crazy about hunting, cross at today's hunt being cancelled. No, Sigismondo was the one to work it out and thinking could safely be left to him. Prince Galeotto had done the best thing, putting it all in Sigismondo's hands.

When the doors of the Princess's chamber were suddenly flung open and the Prince came out, Benno, losing himself instantly in the background, thought the Prince looked far from sure he had done the right thing. Puffing, scarlet-faced, beslubbered with tears, pressing a crumpled hat to his chest and glaring straight ahead as he stamped by, the Prince looked as distracted by his wife's death as anyone could possibly demand. Benno was not to know that the Prince had just fallen under suspicion of having caused it.

He was followed by his pages, running to keep up, and by others coming more slowly, talking in low voices, while beyond them Benno could see the Abbot still at prayer. A cluster of women who had been out of sight now came forward to the bed, he supposed to finish preparing the Princess for her lying in state in the chapel.

The man Benno waited for was the last to emerge, at the shoulder of the Duchess Violante. His master, head bent gravely, was listening as she spoke with animation. Coming from Rocca, Benno took a proprietary interest in her beauty. Was she not the daughter of his own Duke? Her blonde hair was plaited up the back of her head with thin jewelled chains, and emerged as a crest on top from a small gold sleeve. Her deep purple dress looked to be embroidered here and there with flowers, then they glinted and you saw they were jewels. Her beauty did not appear in the least dimmed by grief. If anything, she looked stimulated. In the old stories, after all, stepmothers went to impressive trouble to get rid of their stepdaughters, sending them to be lost in woods, to meet monsters, to have their hearts cut out by huntsmen, to eat poisoned apples . . . He'd never heard of any strangling, but it did not seem to him that the Duchess Violante would hesitate on grounds of novelty.

Sigismondo was bowing now as the Duchess gave him her hand to kiss and went on her way down the marble corridor, followed by her ladies in a swarm and saluted by the guards. Now a lady, not one of those superintending the work on the Princess, not an attendant of the Duchess but too richly dressed to be nobody, came to talk to Sigismondo. Benno watched her looking his master up and down in a way that suggested tall men with strong features and shaven heads were just what the physician ordered. Sigismondo's manner, too, was perceptibly different from that which he had used to the Duchess. Courtesy was there, deference was gone; in its place something that made Benno think his master might like to question the lady more closely.

A page in the Prince's colours interrupted them, and the lady at once took her leave of Sigismondo and glided swiftly after the page. Benno envisaged the Prince bawling for consolation, which she looked well able to provide; but there had been little time for Sigismondo to obtain any answers from her. Benno found himself being hurried with a hand at the back of his head, along the corridor between its panels and pilasters of coloured marble.

'Was she any use? Did she see anything funny going on?' Biondello stuck out his head from Benno's jerkin, jolted by his haste, and underlined the enquiry by looking up at Sigismondo.

'Mm. She tells me she found the Princess asleep and could not wake her. The Duchess had sent her to remind the Princess that it was time to appear. The lady was frightened that she couldn't wake her, though at first, she hinted, she'd thought it was a matter of too much wine. Everyone was watching her at last night's banquet.'

'Everyone was drinking a lot at the banquet. Why pick on her?'

Benno received a slight cuff on the side of the head. 'Hey, because *brides* don't drink a lot. Brides don't eat or talk a lot. Brides are good little mice till they're well and truly married; then they can break out a bit. From what I've been hearing, the Princess Ariana broke out a little early.'

'How could she? She din' have time, did she? Only here two days.'

They had arrived at the entrance hall, a huge space of uneven stone-flagged floor, stone walls and lofty roof, originally a courtyard of the old castle, where the swags of bay and myrtle and the hanging banners of Borgo scarlet did not entirely disguise the lowering air of the place or the sense that somewhere beneath their feet lay dungeons to match. Even on a warm summer evening it was cold. Sigismondo had stopped, finger stroking lip, watched uneasily by the guard at the great doors.

'Only two days, Benno, but she'd managed a few quarrels.'

'Had she? Who with?'

'The Lady Leonora tells me: with the Prince. The Duchess tells me: with a lady of Borgo called Zima. We're on our way to see her.'

The house of the Lady Zima Montelucci was a delightful villa not far away, just inside the city walls but nestled in parkland so that it seemed to be in the country. The moon still shone clear when they reached its wrought-iron gate, which stood open, inviting them up to the villa itself and the doors under the pretty classical pediment, white like icing in the moon. The whole place was tiny, like a house to amuse children rather than to live in. This was, in a fashion, explained when, after beating on the door and giving the name of the Prince as their authority, they were ushered by a sleepy servant into the owner's presence.

'His Highness sends for me?'

It was a question asked with a purr, both complacent

and provocative, even so late at night and spoken to a stranger. She reclined on her bed, in a room like the Princess's chamber in miniature, with frescoes – barely visible by candlelight – that opened the small space into a green woodland with lacy trees vanishing into a blue distance. A bed gown of white brocade failed to conceal opulent curves, and had indeed fallen open to show a shapely leg. Benno tried not to stare.

The Lady Zima was doing her share of staring. Like the Lady Leonora, she found Sigismondo worth looking at, and certainly he in no way resembled the usual courtier except for his bow. She herself was worth looking at; Benno, wholly ignorant as to classical ideas of beauty, equated her face with the statues in the palace gardens, though she was pale rather than marble, and not a bit touched with lichen. There was the straight nose, wide eyes and curving mouth all right, but the emptiness of stone eyes, the tranquil pose, weren't there. Benno thought of a statue he'd seen, with one hand modestly across the bosom and the other where a bit of drapery would've come in useful. Lady Zima's hands were in exactly that position, but somehow there was nothing modest about the effect.

'His Highness has not sent for you, my lady. He has sent me to you.'

The Lady Zima looked beautifully baffled and made little swimming gestures with her hands. She seemed perfectly happy to accept an attractive substitute for the Prince, but at a loss for the reason. Lovers don't usually send proxies. 'Why hasn't he come himself?'

Well, thought Benno, that tells you more about Lady Zima than even this pricey little toy of a villa. She thinks it natural the Prince should leave the dead wife he'd married yesterday and come to see her. Either she's very,

very stupid or he's really in her clutches.

Sigismondo had put on a face of exaggerated surprise, and he struck his brow with the flat of his hand. 'Can it be that you've not heard? Were you not at court tonight?'

'Heard? Heard what?' Lady Zima agitated her hands again. Benno, born in a nation of gesticulators, thought he had never seen more meaningless movements. Perhaps she thought she was a butterfly. 'Is the Prince ill?'

'So you were not at court this evening?'

She looked at him vaguely, as if the question had just registered. 'I was ill. The heat. I cannot take the heat.' She put her fingers to her forehead, as though the heat had pressed unwelcome attentions on her; then she caught sight of her own leg and arranged the brocade more decorously. Sigismondo had gone nearer and stood looking down at her.

'You were not at court tonight?' The third repetition was as quiet and uninflected as the first, but it was relentless. It was a question that was going to get an answer.

'Oh . . .' She shrugged and even looked at Benno as if he could be of use in settling this absurdity. 'Only the shortest time I could manage. Everyone was there. I had to be there. I had to come away, though. I missed the fireworks.' She put her head on one side and looked up at Sigismondo, making a moue appealingly. 'Not at all well.'

'Why did you go if you were not at all well?'

She gave a scornful little laugh, as if Sigismondo were being deliberately obtuse. 'Because it was an *occasion*. I had a dress made for it . . . Did the Prince tell you to ask me all these questions? He *knows* I was there.'

'Were you presented to the Princess?'

She flapped the brocade sleeves. 'Of *course* I was presented to the Princess. *All* the court ladies were.'

'Did you see her alone in the pavilion?'

The butterfly was getting upset. 'I don't see why you're asking me all these questions. It's late and I'm not at all well.' She flounced a little among the cushions and the look she gave Sigismondo made clear that she had wholly revised her opinion of him as an attractive interruption to her rest. 'The Prince would not want you to bother me like this. I really think you'd better go away.'

'When you have told me about this.'

Sigismondo held out his hand before her. On it lay a distorted shape of gold, of tendrils and leaves, with flowers in rubies and sapphires, all caked with mud, and with little gaping holes that had held missing jewels. She shrank from it as if it were a snake.

'This was found on the bank where the Princess fell after she was strangled. I believe it's yours.'

Chapter Nine

A bravo for the bride

'*Strangled!*' The word came out like a bat's squeak. Lady Zima sat bolt upright and put her hands to her own neck as if she felt it in danger. 'The Princess?' Her face was now pale as any marble and she looked at the bracelet as though it might jump from Sigismondo's hand and fasten fangs in her throat.

Benno had no clue as to Sigismondo's opinion, but his own was that the lady hadn't the wits to act as surprised as that if she had already known that the Princess was dead. Suppose she had been at the palace, she must have left before the Princess's body was found. She was making horrible little noises now as though her breathing had gone wrong.

'What did the Princess say to you?' Sigismondo had vanished the bracelet and now held one of her hands by the wrist, drawing it away from her throat to which it seemed fatally attracted. 'When she sent for you to the pavilion.'

'I don't know, I never saw her . . .' The breathing had degenerated into panting. The eyes turned up and then closed. She sank limply among the pillows.

Sigismondo let her wrist go and in one swift movement picked up a carved-crystal jug from the bed platform and emptied it over the Lady Zima's head.

The effect was miraculous. In as swift a movement, she sat up, coughing and spluttering. The jug had held wine, which now ran down her face and dripped over the white brocade like blood. Sigismondo stood over her still.

'What did she say to you, in the pavilion?'

'In *my* pavilion! She *hit* me! She dragged them off me and she threw them away.' Lady Zima burst very noisily into tears.

'The bracelets the Prince had given you?'

'He loves me! She's only his *wife*.' The words came out among gasps and sobs. 'He *wanted* to give them to me . . .'

'Who was there when she took the bracelets from you?'

She shook her head, splattering wine all round. The smell of it pervaded the room. 'No one. No one at all.' Her voice indicated that she felt this increased the pathos of her situation. Clearly she did not appreciate the significance of there being no witness to any actions of her own. Would a woman, Benno wondered, kill for a bracelet? Two bracelets? Two bracelets and a pavilion? The lady looked harmless enough, sitting on the bed with wine and tears dripping off her chin, but the bracelets, the pavilion, were tokens of her status. For that, what would she do?

'She said – she said she wouldn't share her bracelets – *her* bracelets – with anyone.'

To Benno, ignorant of the matching pair on the wrists of the Princess, this made no sense, but he was not surprised to see Sigismondo nodding. 'She threw them out of the pavilion?'

'She threw them over her shoulder, as if they were so much rubbish.'

What an awful waste of money, Benno thought,

horrified. He hadn't been so wrong himself in thinking
Sigismondo was looking for diamonds on the slope below
the pavilion. He could quite believe that his master had
expected to find the bracelets.

Sigismondo, humming, picked an embroidered linen
towel from a neat pile on the bed platform, and she
began to pat her face and neck dry.

'Did you see anyone come after you into the pavilion?'

She shook her head, and then stopped, with the towel
over both hands ready to dry her hair, and stared at him
as though what he had been saying was only now getting
through to her after her revived distress over the bracelets.

'She was strangled? Who did it? Was it the Prince?'
Benno envisaged this flattering scenario: Prince, arriving
on scene, finds new wife has insulted beloved mistress
and has torn off her bracelets; so he gives her a necklace
that'll keep her quiet for good. Benno remembered tales
of princes who had accused their wives of adultery and
had them poisoned. Would a prince accused of adultery
strangle his wife? As for all that boo-hooing he'd seen the
Prince doing that night, it could as easily be regret at
losing his temper and, with it, his wife and his alliance
with Duke Ippolyto.

'Did you see the Prince after this?'

If she had inflamed Galeotto against his bride, the idea
of his storming into the pavilion and choking her was not
so farfetched. He might really love this Lady Zima that
much. She, however, was quite vehement on the point.

'I didn't see *anyone*. I just walked out. I mean, she was
a chit of fifteen. I just rushed out of the palace and came
back here. I was *devastated*.'

'Which way did you go through the gardens?'

'I don't know, I don't know! The tunnel arbour, yes. I
didn't want anyone to see me.'

She seemed to have acceded to the Princess's summons without any thought of her anger at the matching bracelets. But the Princess must have known about the bracelets already if she'd sent for her. Perhaps the lady had worn them thinking she could easily challenge 'a chit of fifteen', perhaps so sure of the Prince that she really felt his wife's feelings did not count although she was the daughter of a reigning duke.

All this, of course, if she was telling the truth.

Sigismondo seemed to make up his mind on the spot. Suddenly he was all smiles, bending to raise the lady's hand to his lips while she still held the towel to her hair with the other.

'We'll leave you to your rest, my lady. I've no doubt the Prince will send for you tomorrow.'

As he moved away, she said shrilly, 'The Prince shall hear of the way you treated me!'

Sigismondo turned and bowed to her gravely. They left her staring after them, in stained brocade, her hair beginning to frizz as it dried. After nudging a comatose servant to open the doors, they found themselves outside the villa, under the pretty little pediment in the light of the low-sailing moon. Benno was starting to speak when Sigismondo put a finger to his lips and cocked his head, listening. Alarmed, Benno looked about for shadows in which attackers might lurk, but he could see nothing. He looked up at Sigismondo and found him smiling.

'The nightingale, Benno. I dare swear she means you no harm.'

The notes were like the moonlight itself singing, and Sigismondo made no haste. Benno was wondering, if his master was prepared to interrupt the sleep of all the ladies of the court like this, would they get much rest themselves? He knew already how important it was to follow a scent while it was warm, as Sigismondo had said to Prince Galeotto.

'D'you reckon she will complain to the Prince? You pouring wine all over her, I thought she'd scream or faint or something.'

'She was all set to scream if I hadn't. A risk worth taking. She may complain to the Prince, but he may not hear her. He has enough troubles of his own.'

They were walking through the parkland on an earth path, the nightingale still clear behind them, and they heard, too, the small animals scuttling in the shrubs and undergrowth that the moon silvered as if with frost. Biondello, who had snuggled quietly in Benno's jerkin at the villa, had been decanted and was racing joyfully from one side to the other, in a dream of rabbits. A dog barked sharply from the nearest houses.

'What's he going to tell Duke Ippolyto then? Send another daughter, sorry about this one? Has he got another?'

Sigismondo hummed in appreciation. 'He has another daughter, by Duchess Violante, but she's only a year or so old. If Prince Galeotto turned down Venosta's eight-year-old because he needs heirs soon, he's not going to fall over himself to ask for *that* one's hand. His present problem is to convince Duke Ippolyto that he is in no way responsible for the Princess's death.'

Biondello, alarmed at finding something bigger than himself under bushes at the end of a trail, had come bolting back for protection and Benno picked him up.

'You don't think the Prince did it, then?'

'Mmm. I'm not saying he didn't. The court has been given reason to think he might have, thanks to Lady Leonora seeing those sleeve-buttons in her Highness's bracelet.'

'That the lady he sent for when you was talking to her? Is she his mistress as well as the Lady Zima?'

'The Church tells us we must have but one wife at one time, but I've heard of no rule that limits a man to one mistress.'

It was Benno's opinion that, had Galeotto not been a prince, he would have had inordinate difficulty attracting even one mistress, but having villas and bracelets to hand out did make looking like a pig less disadvantageous.

By now they had left the parkland and were traversing market gardens among scattered houses, the outskirts of the city itself. Benno pulled a radish as they walked and bit into it, considering.

'His mistresses, then. Would they dare kill a princess?'

'Perhaps they wouldn't plot to do it, but no one can predict where rage will carry one.'

Sigismondo's darker tone made Benno glance at him. Had rage once carried his master into something terrible? It was a question he could not ever ask him. He changed the subject.

'We going to talk to this Lady Leonora, then?'

'Another day, Benno. I don't interrupt princes unless I have to.'

They were in the city now, the moonlight not reaching a narrow street nearly all steps which Sigismondo climbed at an easy stride, Benno's shorter legs having to break the rhythm alongside. The darkness made Benno afraid again. The person who killed the Princess could be anywhere, and if people got to know that his master was in search of the killer, what was to stop the killer searching for *him*? Somehow he didn't picture the Lady Zima rushing out of the shadows with a garrotting cord. That was absurd. Yet he felt something more sinister was involved.

It turned out that Sigismondo felt the same. As they reached the square and the steps before the palace, he spoke. 'You've managed not to ask what else I found beside a bracelet on that bank below the pavilion.' He stopped, and turned to look at Benno. 'The grass and earth were disturbed, of course. She'd fallen down it and half a dozen people had crawled all over it trying to get her up. I cast about further down, by the water's edge. Someone had pulled a boat ashore just below the pavilion. There were grooves in the mud of the bank, and stones dislodged. If the music was playing for the dancers in the garden, and they were laughing and talking, it wouldn't have been difficult to get up that slope without the Princess hearing even if she'd been awake. And as it happened she'd taken a sleeping draught.'

Benno had stopped chewing his radish and stood with it still in his open mouth. 'You mean—'

'A professional, Benno. Anybody can hire a bravo.'

Chapter Ten

A sleeping draught

'Is her Grace to be spoken with yet?'

Sigismondo had penetrated to the outer chambers of the apartment in the palace assigned to the Duchess Violante. There had been no hindrance to his progress, for enough rumours had circulated since he was first noticed at the Duchess's stirrup after the effigy fell, then briefly behind her chair at the banquet, to convince everyone that he was in her employ and now, from what had been overheard and freely discussed the previous night, that he was in the service of the Prince as well. The halfwit, whom he unaccountably permitted as a servant, was allowed free passage in his wake, and at the moment Benno was standing vacantly by the door, with Biondello churning restlessly in his jerkin. When they came through the palace, some of the Prince's hunting dogs, enormous creatures with jaws that could tackle wild boar, had been roaming the corridors and sprawled in the way. Biondello had scarcely breathed. In this room he sensed he was unthreatened.

'Her Grace still sleeps, sir, but I will tell you when she rouses.'

Dogs pick up atmosphere quickly, and the comfortable air of the speaker may have contributed to Biondello's relaxing. She sat sewing next to the window, by the early morning light that strengthened every minute, a pleasant middle-aged woman in decent black, with a big white apron and a cap with long lappets that drooped on her shoulders like spaniels' ears. The linen was in drawn-thread work that betokened an upper servant.

In spite of last night's tragedy, which had imparted a gloom to every face in the palace, and in spite of being from Altamura and therefore likely to feel Princess Ariana's death more than most, she had a smile for Sigismondo. The smile gave her dimples which were very fetching, and the eyes that stole a glance from her sewing to size up the stranger were dark and lively. Benno got the impression that this particular servant of the Duchess was not overwhelmed by grief at the death of the Duke's daughter.

'Did you see the Princess last night?'

The dimples vanished. She bent to her sewing as though her life depended on it, taking out a jewelled panel and putting in a plain brocaded ribbon. 'A terrible sight. A terrible sight. God and Our Lady defend us from evil.'

'Amen.' Sigismondo had wandered to the window and leant against the embrasure, looking out. 'I did not mean after her death. Before that, in the pavilion.'

A little cry showed that she had pricked her finger and now she sat sucking it, looking up at him over her hand with eyes suddenly wary.

'The pavilion, sir? At the end of the garden?'

Where else? thought Benno. She's trying to gain a little time. Sigismondo, smiling, picked up a fold of the dress she was working on, heavy dark satin, and murmured, 'Beautiful, beautiful.'

'Is it not? Her Grace must have mourning by the time she rises. If you will excuse . . .' She bent over her work again and the needle started to fly.

'So the Princess sent for you to the pavilion. Did you bring her the draught that was found there? You were nurse to her, were you not?'

He's asking too many questions, thought Benno, who knew what it was to be guilty of that; but Sigismondo was demonstrating that one answer can bring others running after it.

'I was *not* the Lady Ariana's nurse!' The dark eyes sparkled with indignation in the glance she spared from her urgent sewing. 'I am Nurse to the children of her Grace!' She tossed back the lappets of her cap haughtily. 'I am here in her Grace's train.'

'And her Grace's children? They have not been brought?' Sigismondo looked round the room as if seeking a cradle.

'Of course not. Both are too young to travel.' The needle flew with all the energy of her feelings. 'They had to remain at home.'

Sigismondo nodded, and his voice conveyed that he was enlightened. 'You are here for things other than babies.' He bent and fingered a fold of the satin again. 'You are needed to *sew* for her.'

She plucked the satin from him. 'Her Grace has women to sew for her. I can do things no sewing woman can.'

'Such as put together fennel, bridewort and sage of Bethlehem. Or did you use pennyroyal?'

The needle paused. She looked at him.

'Never pennyroyal.' The dimples appeared once more. 'Too risky by far. Suppose she had puked over the Prince—' She half raised the hand with the needle, and her eyes widened; she had remembered that far worse than that had come to the late Princess. Sigismondo bent,

67

one hand on the sill, till his face was close to hers.

'What would you say to herb of grace? Would that have made her puke?'

'Rue!' She shrank back from him. 'I did not put *rue* in it! Of course I did not! Who says I did?'

Sigismondo lounged once more against the wall, smiling pleasantly. 'Why, I tasted it. There was rue, or I can't tell a hawk from a hare.'

The satin crumpled under her hands. 'Didn't she drink it, then? She was sleeping, so I left it for her. The pain she complained of could not have been so bad after all, since she could sleep. And after that gorging the night before, it was no wonder if she did have a pain.'

'The drink you brought was digestive only?'

'I know what I am doing. And neither pennyroyal nor rue. Lady Ariana swore by my draughts. When she could not sleep, I was sent for. If she ate too much, I was sent for. If she had a headache, I must come.'

The Nurse shrugged, and Benno could see that she was more exasperated than flattered by this dependence. 'You must have made a mistake, sir. Not everyone knows herbs. What matter now, since she didn't drink it?'

'What matter now, indeed. What she did drink was a sleeping draught.'

'A *sleeping draught*? Who gave her that? And the evening but just beginning, when she must take part!'

'Was anyone in the pavilion when you came?'

She thought, smoothing at the satin. Princesses were rarely alone; privacy was not for the great any more than for the peasant in his crowded hut.

'No. I remember she had sent her women away; I was told she wanted to enjoy the moonlight without their chattering. A silly enough reason − they would have been silent if she had told them.'

Because her real reason was that she wanted to tear the bracelets off the Lady Zima without all the court knowing that she minded, thought Benno. Biondello had stopped restlessly seething and had his head partly out of Benno's doublet, watching the Nurse as attentively as did Sigismondo.

'You say she was asleep. Did you try to wake her?'

The Nurse laughed, shortly. 'You didn't know the Lady Ariana. Small thanks I'd have got. Best she should settle her stomach with a nap, I thought; and I left the glass I'd brought so she'd know I'd done as she asked.'

'Was there a glass already there?'

She lifted her head from the sewing, and frowned. 'I think there was. There would have been wine. And sweetmeats. Always sweetmeats. She was a child for sweetmeats.'

'And you saw no one as you came away?'

'Nothing but her ladies dancing. I did wonder she could sleep through the music.'

The doors behind Benno opened abruptly, striking him in the back so that he lurched forward and Biondello shot to the floor.

'Dolt! What are *you* doing here?' A waiting-woman with embroidered linen napkins over one arm and a silver-gilt ewer entered. Some of the scented hot water from the ewer had spilt. She caught sight of the Nurse and Sigismondo and stared. The Nurse spoke sharply.

'Take that to her Grace at once. I'll have that spillage seen to.'

Skirting the steaming puddle on the marble, the woman went to the inner doors, rapped, and went in. A yawn came distinctly to their ears. Duchess Violante was waking and would need her mourning dress.

The Nurse snapped off a thread with her teeth, put the

needle for safety through the stuff of her dress above the bosom, and got to her feet, shaking out the folds of heavy dark satin. The jewelled panels lay across the arm of the chair, glittering, discarded. She moved towards the bedroom. Benno, retrieving Biondello who was tentatively lapping the puddle of scented water, thought that an interesting aspect of the Princess Ariana had come to light; but had it helped Sigismondo to untangle any of the mystery? So the Nurse was responsible for the draught left untouched on the table; but she said she had not added an emetic. Benno believed that. You wouldn't get far as a servant to the high and mighty if you caused them to throw up on the landscape without warning. Somebody had, though.

Was the Nurse right? After all, the Princess hadn't drunk from the glass and, sure as eggs, if someone had slipped an emetic into it after the Nurse had gone, it would not be the person who so effectively prevented her from ever drinking it. Shouldn't they be looking for the *strangler*?

Chapter Eleven

Brunelli leaves the palace

'And you tell me she had been *strangled*?' Duke Vincenzo paused and shook his head. 'What a terrible thing. You will convey my deepest sympathy to the Prince Galeotto, together with my hope that the villain responsible is speedily caught and punished. How *wicked* the world is! A child on the brink of life, who might have borne heirs to Borgo . . .'

He let his voice trail into silence.

The envoy from Prince Galeotto knew that he was meant to think about the Duke's eight-year-old Agusta, rejected with all the diplomatic courtesies because the Prince would have had to wait years for an heir. Eight-year-olds have far more potential in the posterity way than have corpses. Obliged as he was to convey the news of his Prince's bereavement to the Duke, the envoy was under no illusion that it would be received with true sympathy, but it would be difficult to judge the Duke's actual feelings from his voice or bearing. Both, whatever he was saying, were apt to convey an impression of deep falsity. At the moment he was regarding the envoy with his head a little to one side with gruesome compassion. Beside him, the Duchess Dorotea, her pale face and dark eyes and hair dramatic, sat very straight in her claret velvet and forbore to alter her perfect features in any way.

'I will inform his Highness of your Grace's sympathy. It will be of comfort to him.'

Duke Vincenzo graciously inclined his head and the bowing envoy withdrew.

'Strangled. A terrible fate. Do you think Galeotto did it himself?'

The Duchess surveyed her rings. She was considered by all to be the perfect wife for the Duke. 'It's possible. He has a temper, we hear.' She glanced at her husband, of whom no one had said that. Vincenzo did not act upon impulse. Someone had remarked that he always plotted his getting up and going to bed. 'Now he must seek a wife again.'

'The negotiations will take him almost as long as if he had accepted Agusta.'

'Might he ask for Agusta's hand now?'

The Duke's fine eyebrows moved infinitesimally upward. 'Not if he can find an older girl somewhere else.' He gave a terrible little smile that deepened the incised lines on his sallow face. 'Fresh negotiations will take a long time,' he said. 'Poor Galeotto.'

'Poor Ippolyto,' his wife responded. 'A dead daughter, and no alliance.'

'Poor Ippolyto,' the Duke agreed, with a trace of satisfaction. 'And that reminds me.' He rose and stepped from the dais, the purple velvet of his cloak dragging after him. Dukes dress to impress, no matter what the weather, but now that the envoy had gone, Vincenzo made a gesture towards the gold clasp on his shoulder – two serpents lovingly entwined – and pages sprang forward, one to release the clasp, the other to take the weight of furred velvet that smelt of camphor wood. The Duke walked out of his cloak and towards his study. The

Duchess, aware that her presence was no longer required, left to follow her own pursuits, in this case the meticulous embroidery of a wall hanging showing the flaying of Marsyas by the god Apollo.

The Duke had just as interesting things to do in his study, although unlike the flaying of Marsyas they did not directly illustrate the dangers of ambition. Ignoring for once his collection of engraved gems, Vincenzo paced over to the great table with its inlaid various marbles and, resting his hands like a pair of tents on the edge, let his eyes range over what was laid out there.

It was a wooden model, constructed in elegant detail, of a fort. The sun shone through the study's long window making the thin pine translucent and casting crenellated shadows from the model onto the moulded humps, painted brown and green, representing the land where the fort was being built. A sinuous river, brightly, improbably blue, curved in a sweep round the fort and provided one edge to the whole model.

Vincenzo watched it quite as if he expected tiny figures to appear behind the battlements and perhaps run up a little flag showing Venosta's knotted serpents.

After a long moment he clapped his hands and a page ducked past the door curtain and came to bow before him.

'Brunelli. Fetch him.'

Vincenzo sat down, turned his face to the sun and passed the time till Brunelli should appear by fancying he could hear a trumpet blowing on the fort's battlements.

'You Grace has sent for me.'

It was not a statement but a complaint, uttered in a growl. Brunelli was a short, thickset man with a jaw that would have come in useful on a boarhound. He regarded the Duke with dark, wild-staring eyes. His tunic of coarse frieze was powdered with, apparently, plaster, as if he had just emerged from a collapsed building. His bow to the Duke was sketchy enough to be all but insulting, but the Duke got up from his chair with a smile easily as benevolent as the one he had given the envoy from Borgo.

'The fort, Brunelli. I want you to think about the fort. Is this model now finished according—'

'Finished?' Brunelli's snort could hardly have been bettered if fire had come from his nostrils. 'What is not finished, nor is likely to be if I am interrupted, is the casting of your statue. I must be back within the half-hour or all will be ruined.'

'Let your assistant see to it.'

The second snort improved on the first. 'Do you expect my assistants to design my models? To paint my frescoes? It was because you wanted the best that could be got that you sent for me.'

Brunelli chose to forget that Vincenzo had not sent for him. He had come to Venosta seeking work, from Borgo where he had, among other things, designed and supervised the building of the pavilion for Prince Galeotto in which his wife had been murdered. The Duke had delighted to secure Brunelli's services; the man was a known genius in design – engineering, painting, sculpture, bronzes. What no one had been there to explain to Vincenzo was that the temperament of genius has various inbuilt drawbacks. Brunelli was a perfectionist for whom his work came first.

'Certainly you are the best.' Vincenzo's teeth showed briefly in what passed for a smile. 'It is because you are the best that I am sending you to the border to supervise the construction of my fort. Today.'

'And the statue?'

The Duke's hand wafted the matter away. 'The statue can await your return.'

Brunelli took a huge breath and cast up his eyes and spoke like a master trying to instruct a maliciously stupid child.

'The metal is heating *now*. If it is not poured at exactly the right *temperature* at exactly the right *speed*, the whole undertaking is ruined.'

'That is all artisan's work, obviously. Let your assistants — surely they are trained men? — get on with it. The fort—'

'*That* is artisan's work.' Brunelli was at the table, pointing, his hand shaking. 'That design is complete. Your engineers aren't stupid, they can build the thing. Whereas the statue—'

'You are to forget the statue. I require your attention at the fort.'

Brunelli was scarlet. His face seemed to have swollen. He raised his arm and brought down his fist on the model with rending force. Glue cracked, slivers of pine splintered, the fort was so much kindling. He seized the plaster base, upended it, and kicked the pieces into the corners.

'*That* for your fort. I am constructing for you a work of art that will convey your likeness to posterity for a thousand years, and you—'

The Duke had rung a handbell on his desk. To the resultant page he gave a cold, swift command. Brunelli's fist was now extended towards the Duke with his thumb protruding between the fingers. 'And that for your fort! A skirmish, a little glorification on the border, when I am providing you with—'

Two burly guards came in as the page rattled the curtain back on its rings. The Duke pointed, and gave an order. Brunelli was seized, and frogmarched towards the door. He continued to compare the Duke's artistic sensibilities to those of a hog, to the latter's benefit. He put out his feet to the sides of the door to halt his exit, only to be swung into reverse and dragged out backward. His voice rose in the lobby and gained in power on the stairhead until one of the guards punched him lightly in the wind. Then there was only the sound of two pairs of boots and one pair of heels descending the staircase past Brunelli's frescoes on the walls, crossing the mezzanine, descending the lower stairs past Brunelli's outlines for frescoes on the walls, and pausing on the expanse of black marble in the hall. Doors ground open. A gruff voice said, 'The feet, mate. Right? And a one. A two. A three . . .'

Brunelli hit the flagstones of the street. The palace doors ground shut.

A scavenging dog, galvanised into flight by Brunelli's sudden arrival, paused, and returned to investigate. Palace garbage had been excellent in the past.

This was not. He got a kick as Brunelli clambered to his feet, rubbing his backside with one hand and fisting the other at a group of urchins overcome with laughter. By now his statue would be spoilt — small comfort that it was of the Duke! Weeks of work wasted. He spat into the Venostan dust. Why were the great such fools? Prince Galeotto had been no better, demanding he paint frescoes round a room in a single night! To surprise his mistress, he'd said. Brunelli flattered himself that what he'd done had given them a surprise all right, even though it meant he'd had to leave Borgo in a hurry.

Now he might have to leave Venosta in a hurry. No matter. All roads were alike to genius and, if all else failed, he would go to Rome where he'd heard the Pope had a chapel to decorate.

In his study, while the work of clearing up the shattered model went on softly round him, Duke Vincenzo had unrolled the plans of the fort from which the model had been constructed. He should have had that fellow Brunelli flogged for his insolence but he was, after all, an artist and did not see the world as others did. Besides, if word got about that Vincenzo of Venosta had had the famous Brunelli beaten, he would be seen as a barbarian and not as the cultivated and tolerant ruler he knew himself to be.

Now he must find a man who really knew what he was doing to organise the building of the fort. Speed was of the essence. He would like to go himself, for no one would slack under his eye; but it was necessary to be here in the city when formal complaint arrived from Duke Ippolyto. Vincenzo smiled. How important it was to take advantage of any misfortune suffered by one's neighbours . . . Ippolyto might think himself in trouble now but it was nothing to what Fate had in store for him.

Chapter Twelve

She'd kill for them

''Course, it's useful knowing he came up the stream, but you can't tell where he came *from* or who he is, can you?' Benno was kicking idly at the mud on the water's edge, dislodging small pebbles that fell into the water and rolled to settle. A bird hovered overhead, waiting for him to do something more constructive, like produce a fish. Sigismondo lounged on the grass bank, long legs stretched out, relaxed in his contemplation of the little island on the lake where the fireworks had made so splendid a display.

'Nor do we know where he was going. He might be many miles away or,' he nodded upstream, 'just round that bend.'

Benno glanced nervously at the overhanging willow where the stream took a turn out of sight. 'Are you sure he was the one that strangled her? Suppose it was someone else in the pavilion before she was found? There's the Lady Zima. Can't have been pleased having her bracelets torn off her and thrown away. Couldn't she have throttled her in a rage?'

'Mmm. As the Abbot says, who can be sure of anything in this world? Have you thought of other ladies who visited the pavilion last night?'

Benno scratched his head, and worked the frayed toe

of his boot round an outsize pebble. 'Other ladies? What ones did, though? I mean, it was Lady Leonora that found her,' he kicked the pebble into the water with a satisfying splash, 'but she hadn't the *time* to do it, did she? They said she came right back and told the Duchess.'

'Hey, how long does it take to strangle a sleeping girl? The same time it would take to try waking her up? And how do we know when she was strangled?'

Benno crouched down almost in the stream, trailing a hand in it and watching his fingers change shape under the water. Biondello left his happy zigzagging among the shrubs and hurried down to see what he was looking at. 'You mean, when the Nurse found her asleep she could have been dead?'

'You heard the Nurse: she didn't try to wake her. In the shadows, with all that hair over her face, and the pearl collar, who would know she had been strangled?' Sigismondo had acquired a sprig of lavender on the way through the gardens and he held it to his nostrils and closed his eyes in the sun, sniffing. 'All we know is that someone put a sleeping draught in the wine she did drink, and someone tightened a scarf round her neck later, when she wasn't likely to struggle. The same person might have done both things.'

Benno stared at the water gliding past on its way to the lake. 'But if it wasn't the same person? If she was killed by someone that came up this bank from here, then he must've known she'd had the sleeping draught, mustn' he? Like, be in league with the one that gave it her?'

Sigismondo hummed his satisfaction. 'You see it, Benno! And ask: how did he know the Princess would be in the pavilion? How did he know when, or whether, she had drunk the wine, gone to sleep, and it was his moment to approach?'

Benno was looking across at the island now, wishing he could have stayed to see the full flowering of the fireworks . . . 'You know when the fireworks all started off? Wasn't it when the lamp was held up and they thought it was the signal, like they said this morning? Couldn't there have been a signal like that to the strangler? Different from the firework signal or they'd have started then; but the lamp was here all along.'

Sigismondo opened his eyes, shielded by thick lashes against the sun. 'Your wits are showing, Benno. Keep looking vacant or someone'll split that skull to see if you have brains.' He crushed the lavender and threw it aside. 'You're right, but who made the signal? Who hired the assassin?'

Benno was dropping twigs into the water and watching them swim away, some getting caught against stones, others swirling boldly on into deeper midstream and vanishing out of sight. Biondello brought him the sprig of lavender and Benno tossed it into the water, where it drifted with a current, spun round once or twice, skimmed over a large stone and got trapped in a small eddy where it stayed, revolving, while other twigs bobbed past. Like us, he thought. We're stuck.

'Well,' he said slowly, 'it's about who wanted her out of the way. I thought, nobody could possibly want her dead, she's only fifteen, she hasn't had time. But the Nurse didn't like her that much, did she? Like she was taking her off the Duchess that she was really Nurse to, her children I mean, and demanding and demanding.'

'A person can arrive at the age of fifteen with quite a few enemies already.' Sigismondo's tone was unexpectedly reminiscent, and Benno glanced round at him. He tried to imagine his master at fifteen, failed, and only noted that there might have been enemies even then.

'Two of her enemies probably wanted her dead, the other just wanted her sick . . .'

Biondello had left the water's edge to bark at a clump of bushes that seemed to excite him. He rarely made any noise that could attract attention to himself, out of natural caution as he regarded most animals and people as beyond his scope of menace, so Benno was surprised. His surprise lessened when Sigismondo called, 'Poggio! Come and meet your old friends,' and the bush parted reluctantly to reveal who had been hiding there.

Benno knew Poggio at once. When first they met, in his native village in Rocca, Poggio had been in fear of his life and anxious to impress Sigismondo favourably. Nothing much seemed different. Biondello had perhaps felt it safe to bark at Poggio because of his size, for Poggio was a dwarf; a jester by profession and inclination. It did not suit his large, clever face, with its sparkling eyes and upturned mouth corners, to look wary. The smile he offered them both as he came forward and flourished a court bow looked much less than happy, however.

'I'd no wish to get in your way, sirs. Thought you might be working at the problem.'

Sigismondo patted the ground beside him. 'So we are, Poggio. Kind of you to come and help us. As you know what we're thinking,' he went on genially, as Poggio came crabwise down the slope to sit at his side, 'you've saved us the trouble of telling you. All you need do is to give us your own opinion.'

'About what?' Poggio looked across the stream, not meeting Sigismondo's eyes. 'My opinion can't be any use. I was nowhere near the pavilion.'

'That's what they *all* say – to start with.' Sigismondo spoke with enormous warmth and clapped Poggio on the back so that he almost lost his balance and went bowling down the slope. Benno, watching, thought Poggio could have crept up the bank from the stream, no problem, without anyone seeing, and as for strangling, he had strong hands. But why would he want to? Sigismondo was going to find out. 'Did the Lady Ariana find you funny?'

This wasn't a question Poggio cared for and it touched him on the raw.

'*Funny?* You mean did she laugh at my jokes or did she laugh at *me*? Oh no, *she* made the jokes. I was a walking gargoyle. One of God's mistakes. I'd come into the room and she'd shriek with laughter. She'd send me out and make me come in again. And again. She'd make me dance for her. Yes, there was a girl with a great sense of humour.' Poggio's face twisted. 'Tell jokes, eh? Give me a chance! Witty remarks, such as her Grace enjoys? She didn't hear them. If she had, she couldn't have understood them. Oh yes, she found me funny.'

'Did it matter? You're here with her Grace's train. You'd only to put up with the Lady Ariana for one week more.'

Poggio contemplated his toes sticking up before him in their red leather pointed shoes. He might be thinking what a very short while he had had to put up with the Lady Ariana. Finally he sighed.

'That was the point. She'd asked her Grace to give me to her. Said she'd die of boredom here without anything to laugh at.' He stole a sudden grinning glance at Sigismondo. 'Though you'd think with her husband . . .' He coughed and assumed a straight face.

'What did her Grace say to that?' Sigismondo was still genial.

'Oh, you know the Duchess. She wasn't pleased. I'm

her property,' said Poggio, complacently, 'and she'd no wish to part with me, not even as a wedding present – of which you may suppose the Princess had plenty. There was quite a scene.'

'They weren't on good terms?'

Poggio rolled his eyes. 'I ask, who *was* on good terms with her? When Duke Ippolyto sent for her from her convent school and got started on the marriage negotiations, everyone at court had to put up with her. The nuns must have said *Gratias Deo* when she left, I can tell you. Her father wasn't the only one glad to see the back of her when we left for here.' He wriggled the red leather toes, instantly riveting Biondello's attention. In the distance came the sound of shears, clipping and pausing and clipping again; the maze of lavender, box and myrtle hedges needed upkeep whether or not princesses died in pavilions.

'You could have got the Nurse into trouble.' Sigismondo's tone was conversational. Like a child, he had split a grass blade and was laying it between his thumbs to make a whistle.

Poggio was startled. 'The Nurse? I don't meddle with the Nurse. What makes you think I would? There's a woman who'd soon clip me round the ear.'

'We're talking about rue. About the rue you put in the drink she left for the Princess to take. She would have got the blame for that.'

Poggio flung his arms wide and would have slipped down the slope if Sigismondo had not grabbed his belt and held on while he regained his balance. He glared round to see if anyone had found this near-accident amusing, but Benno was merely vacant and Sigismondo matter-of-fact.

'I didn't think. I'd just peeped in. It was so quiet I

wondered if she'd got up and gone. I always liked to know where she was so I could be somewhere else. Well, she was asleep,' he slewed round, gripping a tuft of grass, and looked up at the low trellis and the inner dome of the pavilion above, 'lying on that couch there. There were cups on the table and a drink. I stole in − ' Benno could picture Poggio tiptoeing in the shadows − 'and sniffed it and thought, she'd never notice a bit of rue in all that. And,' he gestured at the landscape, 'there's rue all over. I know what it can do. Practical jokes go on at court, and I've puked my guts out after a doctored posset before now.' He grimaced at the memory. 'So it was easy: slip out, pick a bit of rue, shred it and pop it in that smelly draught of hers. If it tasted twice as nasty as usual she'd only have expected it'd do twice the good. She trusted Nursey. Nursey was invaluable.'

Sigismondo blew through the grass blade, a thin noise like a gnat complaining. 'How would the lady manage when Nurse went home with her Grace?'

'Who said she was going home? If the lady got her way, Nurse was going to be another wedding present. Ask and get, that was her way. She got what she wanted by being a hellcat if she didn't get it.' Poggio beat an inquisitive bee away from his face. 'Covetise. That's what the nuns didn't manage to teach her about. Gluttony too. She mostly over-ate − convent food had been terrible, I expect. She certainly let out her belt at court; and she found Nurse could put her stomach to rights for her afterwards. Then she'd get too excited, dancing and playing games and teasing. Nurse would have to produce something for that.' He leant forward, hands on knees, and looked sidelong up at Sigismondo's face. 'I heard she'd had a sleeping draught last night. Did Nurse give her that?'

'She says not.'

'If she was asleep when Nurse came again with the digestive drink . . .' Poggio put his fists together under his chin, pulled them vigorously apart to his ears, and grinned. 'If she left the drink and it *wasn't* taken, who would suspect her?'

'You think she would do that to avoid being left here? Desperate measures, Poggio.'

'*You* might well be desperate if you knew you were going to be at the beck and call of the Lady Ariana for ever. And what about Nursey's darling babies left at Altamura?'

'She has children there?'

'Her children are her Grace's. She dotes on them. They're her nurselings, her darlings, she'd kill for them. I know it.'

'And all you meant to do was to make the lady sick.'

Poggio's mouth was made for laughing. It turned up, irresistibly. 'If she'd puked on the Prince! What a party that would have been!' He slapped his thigh and Biondello, taken off guard, barked. Benno, alarmed, thought: he mustn't make a habit of that. Can't have my shirt barking at people. Get me turned out of places even faster than usual . . . Threatening dwarves is going to that dog's head.

'Master Sigismondo! There you are.' A page in the Prince's livery, out of breath and anxious, stood at the low wall above the slope. 'His Highness wishes to see you at once.'

No guesses why. Benno, following Sigismondo as Poggio scrambled into the undergrowth, wondered what his master was going to say when the Prince asked him if he'd found his wife's murderer yet. Spoilt for choice. If the Princess had lived, and gone on behaving as the nurse and Poggio made out, perhaps the Prince would have got around to hiring an assassin himself.

Of course, he might already have done just that.

Chapter Thirteen

'Would I lie to you?'

Prince Galeotto was in very poor shape.

Losing one's bride would be shock enough for a man, but when that man is a prince and loss of the bride could mean loss of an alliance, the shock is doubled.

The Prince therefore had done what any man might do on such a night of tragedy: he had drowned his sorrows; so that only now did he feel capable of sending for the mysterious man belonging to the Duchess. He received Sigismondo sitting on his bed, with all the appearance of one who would rather be lying supine upon it with curtains drawn against the world. His face was a study in shades of lavender and tallow.

'Have you found him?' The question was as aggressively loud as a very bad headache would permit. He knew perfectly well that the assassin had not been found, for the villain would have been dragged here in chains and flung at his feet. It was necessary all the same to demonstrate his anxiety that his wife's killer be tracked down. This Sigismondo, known and trusted by the Duchess Violante, would undoubtedly report to her all that passed here.

'Highness, I am confident—'

'Do you realise — do you realise that they are saying *I* myself might have killed her?' Indignation deepened the

89

lavender to a mottled purple. 'That I was heard quarrelling with her in the pavilion.'

'And did your Highness do so?'

Galeotto made a noise with his lips like a cork coming out of a bottle. 'Poh! It was nothing. A lovers' tiff. You know what women are.' He glanced at Sigismondo, decided he probably did, and wondered if when his own hair finally wore off his scalp he would look anything as impressive as this man; clearly, shaving it before it got thin was a worthwhile move, but his own hair was still good. 'She was jealous, you see. I'd given some bracelets to the Lady Zima . . .' The man would have heard already. Everything was always known at court.

'So the buttons from your Highness's sleeve were caught then in the Princess's own bracelet.'

The tone was deferential but the question was enraging. Still, Galeotto had known that it would be asked. Ippolyto would get to hear of it, so the explanation would have to be given. 'Oh, those buttons! I told you it was a lovers' quarrel. We made up. Embraced. It must have been then that the buttons caught in her bracelet.' He seemed to review what he had said, and added, 'A *passionate* embrace, you understand. Ah! We had but one night, I and my beloved bride!'

Galeotto's effort to mark the pathos of this caused him to smite his thigh above the knee, and this did actually bring tears to his eyes even though it worsened his headache. He let the tears run down his cheeks. In fact, he was wondering if Ippolyto would demand back some of the dowry.

'Did your Highness happen to observe if the Princess had drunk from the glass on the table?'

Galeotto goggled at the idea of noticing something so trivial. The attention of princes is hardly to be wasted.

'*Wine?* I've no idea. What has that to do with my wife's murder? What have you found out?'

'Your Highness, it appears that the assassin may have approached by the stream below the pavilion. There are signs of a boat having been beached, and footprints—'

'Footprints? *Footprints!* How can the man be found?'

'From a description, Highness. A man was seen poling a boat down from the pavilion. At one moment the moon shone full on his features.'

Galeotto goggled again. He had no ideas about professional assassins and whether they habitually showed their features by moonlight. 'What does he look like? Why haven't you got him?'

'As for his looks, your Highness will understand if I don't tell you,' Sigismondo laid a finger to the side of his nose, 'where walls have ears. Besides, your Highness will, I hope, see the villain by tomorrow. I have other information that will lead to his capture.'

Galeotto almost forgot his headache. The man was a wizard, a sorcerer! The Duchess Violante was right to treasure him. Yet nothing at the moment was of more importance than his alliance with Ippolyto; it must be saved at all costs. He could smile, he found; he extended a hand, which Sigismondo kissed. 'Bring him to me and I'll make you rich! Go without delay. I know the Duchess wants to speak with you.'

Sigismondo was, of course, right about walls having ears. When he left the Duchess's rooms, he found Benno outside astonished at what he had been hearing from the palace servants.

'They're saying you know exactly what the assassin looks like and where he is. Why didn't you tell me?'

'Hey, would I lie to *you*, Benno?'

Chapter Fourteen

The target of desire

'You lied to the Prince?' Benno scarcely breathed it. He knew his master was never unnecessarily generous with truth, but surely misleading princes could get him into danger? Sigismondo smilingly returned bows from passing courtiers, so swift to single out one who was in favour and in fashion.

'Not at all. I told him what *might* have happened; just as I told the Duchess just now what I believe did happen.' Sigismondo's hands spread wide. 'Truth is a fish hard to catch. We must cast a net.'

Benno's vision, mixed with Truth being at the bottom of a well, was of a drowned woman hauled to the surface. Unfortunately his mind's eye gave her the features of the strangled Princess. 'What did you tell the Duchess then?'

Sigismondo took the steps down to the palace courtyard at a breakneck run. Benno gripped Biondello in his bosom before he followed, and nearly stumbled all the same. His master was in unaccountable good spirits. 'I told her Grace that someone at court was in league with the assassin; that someone had given the Princess a sleeping draught to make her an easy victim.'

They arrived at the centre fountain, and Sigismondo laved his face with the falling water glittering in the sun. He dashed the drops off his bare scalp, and then stroked the head of the marble lion from whose mouth the water sprang.

'I told her that someone had signalled to the strangler that the Princess slept and that it was safe to come.'

Biondello suddenly thrust his head from Benno's jerkin and tried to lap from the fountain. Putting him down on the rim, Benno stared at Sigismondo. 'But then won't whoever did that get to hear that you know and if they're in league with the assassin won't they tell him and then won't he come looking for you?' he gabbled in dismay.

Sigismondo sat down on the step and wiped his mouth with the back of his hand. 'How else will I find him? If he's still in the city, word should soon reach him that a meddler wants a grave. He might not come on his own account – why should he? – but the one who provided the draught and gave the signal will need me dead before I find them out.'

Benno was silent. Biondello, who had immersed his nostrils too enthusiastically, sneezed wetly over them both and almost slipped into the basin in his vehemence. Benno, removing him to the ground, sat down slowly. Sigismondo's throat was broad and strong but Benno had heard that stranglers could sneak up with a weighted cord, flick it round and jerk it tight before one knew.

Yet, if this man who might come to kill his master was a professional, so was Sigismondo.

But it was a scaring feeling, that Sigismondo had set himself up as a target. Here in the courtyard of the palace they might be safe for the moment. The only people here were palace servants going to and fro on their errands and preoccupations, with covered dishes, messages, trestles – two labouring with a heavy painted chest. All were too busy to spare more than a glance at the men on the step of the fountain.

A sudden babble of talk and laughter came from a party of ladies on their way to the south wing, released momentarily from the decorous hush supposed to envelope those mourning the Princess who hardly was. They were in black, violet and grey, though with gold nets for the hair and sleeves slashed with silver.

'Master Sigismondo!'

The ladies were not too absorbed to look around them, and the man with the shaven head drew all eyes as he rose and came forward. The one who had said his name was rustling to meet him. It was Lady Leonora, she who had been called away to console Prince Galeotto the night before. Benno watched, impatient to hear; his master listened, bowed and came back to the fountain. He was smiling.

'What she say?'

'She wants me to go tonight, Benno, to her house in the city. She can't talk here. She said it would be too dangerous — for both of us.'

Dangerous! Benno, following Sigismondo through Borgo's streets that night, was torn between wishing the moon were not so bright, providing the blackest shadows where he saw murderers concealed; and wishing for complete dark where at least everyone, including possible assassins, would be equally at a disadvantage. Luckily the lady's house was not far from the palace and from the abbey, where the Abbot still kindly allowed them the hospitality of a cell.

'There's the Botardo arms, and the shop of the silk merchant. Now for the secret.'

As Sigismondo raised his hand to knock, the door rather eerily opened, and a servant stood there with a

95

light. Bent and toothless like a witch, she mumbled
something and motioned to them to follow up the stairs
to the *piano nobile.*

She left Benno to sit on a bench in the dim bare
corridor where the night air came in from an unshuttered
window. Sigismondo she ushered into a room, hardly
better lit, but with scented air, gilded wood and gold-
starred indigo linen curtains, hardly stirring in the soft
breeze, across the entrance from the loggia.

'My lady will be here.'

She shut the door, leaving him to look round the
luxurious little room. Mother-of-pearl inlay gleamed on
the wood of brocade-topped stools, on the chests, on the
base of the bed populated with gold-embroidered
cushions. Customary as it was to receive guests and
callers in the bedroom, here was no ordinary reception
room. Frescoes here were not like the Lady Zima's
peaceful landscapes. Along one wall Venus and Mars
entwined, watched by a flock of putti, some flying, some
at play with Mars's discarded armour. Next to the bed
Leda lay supported on clouds, enfolded by the wings of
her swan, the feathers soft on pearly flesh. Colder than
she, a statue of Venus on a pedestal was shedding marble
drapery.

The bed's curtains, light, rosy summer silk, spread out
from a crown near the ceiling and were looped back, with
somehow an impression of open arms displaying the bed,
welcoming.

A soft sound, and Lady Leonora came in. She turned,
with a swirl of bronze satin, to shut the door, and then
moved towards him. She had taken her hair from its
court headdress and coiled it in a simple knot. The
bronze satin was a loose robe.

She gave her hand to Sigismondo to kiss and, as he

bowed over it, she moved on, her fingers closing on his, drawing him with her in a rich aura of frangipani. There was a chair between the marble Venus and the bed and she ushered him to that and without speaking began to pour wine. The cups and flagon stood on the bedhead shelf, so that she was close to him.

'What had you to tell me, my lady?' Sigismondo had not obeyed her invitation to sit, and she glanced up at him, holding out the winecup. She had a small mouth, the nose a little tilted, lazy eyelids; her smile was self-assured. She sat down on the cushioned bed step, and he took the chair.

'Yes, it is a serious matter.' Her voice regretted the need to treat a serious matter with seriousness. 'But also I wanted to say more; for instance, I cannot believe there is any evil conclusion to be drawn about the sleeve buttons caught in her Highness's bracelet. She had been wearing it all day and there was chance enough . . .' She leant her elbow on the bed, and the bronze satin slid away, exposing her shoulder and as much bosom as any court gown would show. 'No, when I saw them I was surprised, but later it came to me what anyone might think, and because I know the Prince . . .' She drank and put the cup in her other hand. Her voice, here in private, was soft and she spoke without emphasis. 'The Princess was young and very wilful. It is true her behaviour . . .'

Her hand seemed to move independently of what she was saying. She reached out and undid the metal clasp of Sigismondo's cloak and pushed the cloak off his shoulder onto the low chair back. He regarded her, his eyes in shadow, rocking the winecup to and fro beneath his nostrils to inhale the bouquet. She went on.

'Indeed, had she lived, she would have learnt the ways of court, and no doubt . . . but this extraordinary

97

tragedy . . .' Her hand travelled, unhurried, down his chest to the buckle of his belt, where her fingers worked as if of their own accord. 'No one can understand it . . . Obviously the Princess had enemies who pursued her from her former home, for no one here had cause . . . A wife's position is unassailable, she would have come to see that one does not resent any of lower rank whose position depends only on the whim of the Prince . . .' The buckle opened and his sword belt fell aside, the sword lying among the cloak's folds against the chair.

Sigismondo's face was turned towards her attentively but, like hers, with no expression. He seemed to be regarding her lips' movement, their meeting and parting, their lift and fall. She put her hand on his and raised his cup to his lips. He smiled, tilted it deeply, swallowed, and put it aside on Venus's pedestal.

She stood up, slowly, as he wiped his mouth, and put her own cup aside, turned to face him and held out her hands. With no change of tone she said 'I think you and I have better things to do than to discuss unhappy events all night.'

He rose and smiled down into her face. 'Mmm, it's true.' He did not take her offered hands but stepped forward so that either she would be close against him or must retreat. She did not move except to put her face up and look at his mouth; and, as he bent his head, her lips parted.

She slid her arms round him and gave a murmuring sigh. Then she drew away, stepping up on the bed dais, the robe falling apart although its folds still framed her golden nakedness. Somewhere behind him, Sigismondo heard a small sound and he dropped on one knee as if in homage to beauty. An odd whirring noise filled the room like an invisible bird in flight and, suddenly, the head of

Venus snapped off and crashed to the floor.

Sigismondo had sprung aside, the knife from his boot
in his hand, to face the man who lunged from the
shadows. A candle-flame ducked and hissed as
Sigismondo hurled a cushion from the bed, knocking
aside the knife that had arced flashing from the man's
hand. A second later, another glinted there. Sigismondo
was back by the chair, had snatched up his cloak and
wound his left arm into its thick folds. Then there was no
sound but the panting gasp of the woman pressed among
the cushions and the shift of feet on the floor as the two
men circled, watchfully, sizing each other up, seeking a
chance to dart in and bury a blade in throat or heart. A
feint from the stranger was evaded. The face opposite
Sigismondo was calm, intent, a handsome narrow face, a
little weathered, with a mole beside the wide mouth; no
trace of nerves. This was the professional Sigismondo
had been looking for, a man who had tried the bolas —
the flying knot — and a thrown knife. If he was as good
as Sigismondo supposed him to be, he might become
lucky at any moment.

A scuffle, and Sigismondo's arm was bleeding into the
folds of the cloak; the man stumbled from a kick on the
thigh but jinked away from Sigismondo's knife.

'*O loveliest she, the target of desire . . .*'

With a twanging lute, a tuneless voice wailed in the
garden.

'*That kindles yet while she consumes my fire!*'

There was no mistaking the voice. Prince Galeotto was
in the garden. Everyone in the room above had stopped
moving, even for a moment had stopped breathing. Then
the scene dislimned. The stranger backed swiftly, soft-
footed, his gaze never leaving Sigismondo till he
disappeared again into the shadows by the loggia curtain,

which seemed to sigh on the breeze.

Sigismondo did not stop even to glance at Leonora crouched on the bed, but picked up his sword belt and, in another swoop, the knife and bolas the stranger had sent his way. He found the door bolt had been shot, and slid it back, and was out of the room, had collected Benno and was down the stairs.

In the garden, Prince Galeotto reached the second verse.

Chapter Fifteen

Harm about to happen

On his bench outside, Benno had heard nothing. From his knowledge of his master and from what he had seen of the lady, he did not expect the interview to be a short one so he was astonished when his master appeared and, like a whirlwind, bore him down the stairs and into the entrance hall. The crone, dozing beside a candle in an alcove, woke with a mumbled protest as Sigismondo opened the door; he looked out, pushed Benno out, threw a coin to her and was gone.

Sigismondo neither spoke nor gave Benno a chance to. Sooner than disturb the porter at the abbey gate, they scaled the outer wall of the monastery garden, Benno throwing Biondello over to be caught by Sigismondo, and adding only one small tear to his jerkin's assortment as he climbed over to join them. Even by moonlight, without heat to draw out their scent, the herbs perfumed the dimness as they crossed to their cell.

Benno's curiosity had reached a critical level. 'What *happened*?' He was reckless with his questions, though he kept his voice to a whisper, and took hold of Sigismondo's reddened sleeve. 'What did you do? Did she do this?'

Sigismondo, head down, was massaging the back of his neck, as if some tension needed treatment. 'Didn't you hear? We were interrupted by the Prince.'

'The *Prince*? Was she trying to get you hanged? And what about this?' He shook the sleeve.

'Wash it. I've a salve here . . . Yes, it's possible, quite possible that she had something in mind of that sort, considering the wine which I didn't drink.' He laughed suddenly. 'You tell me you didn't hear the Prince in the garden? Singing?'

Benno poured water. 'Singing?' He cast his mind back to the moment before his sudden enforced descent to the street. 'I thought I heard a cat.'

'Cats, too, believe that their noise is a serenade.'

Benno was undoing Sigismondo's sleeve and turning it back. His master leant to hold the arm in the moonlight from the doorway. Benno said, relieved, 'It's not much . . . Serenading? Serenading the Lady Leonora when the Princess was murdered last night?'

'Hey, Benno, princes' ideas on what is correct are strange because what princes do *is* correct. The rules are theirs. You may, however, deduce that Prince Galeotto is not racked by sorrow.' He was undoing his roll of herbs with his free hand. 'As we saw soon after the Princess died, he needs consolation; and at the moment, the Lady Leonora seems to be the one providing it.'

'It wouldn't be good if Duke Ippolyto heard of it. But how did you get *this*?' Benno demanded, applying ointment. 'And what's that about the wine?'

'Mmm, problems. My problem is that the strangler has escaped.'

'*Escaped?* From where?'

'He tried to kill me just now.' Sigismondo shook his cloak out onto the bed, and picking up what fell from it, held his hand into the moonlight. Across the palm lay a knife and a curious cord with a weight knotted into either end.

Benno was confused. Sigismondo sat here, palpably not dead, so the man who had tried to kill him must himself be dead; but he had escaped. That was not like Benno's experience of Sigismondo. The arrival of the Prince had interrupted them, of course; and Benno felt dissatisfaction, even anger, in the air, something unusual with his master. He was preparing to sleep now, wrapping his cloak round him on the pallet bed, laying his sword by his side. The moonlight had reached the crucifix on the wall, showing it looking down at them both.

'I didn't kill him, Benno, because I deserved to lose him. My only good move was to doubt the provenance of the wine, which was probably drugged.'

Benno, who dared ask no more on hearing that tone of voice, lay watching the slow shift and disappearance of the moonlight, hearing the softer, deeper breathing that showed his master slept, and wondering what on earth had gone wrong. His belief in his master's infallibility was unshaken. Perhaps a mistake had been made – then Sigismondo would retrieve it with triumph. Benno banished the thought of the weighted cord, shifted Biondello who had come to lie on his chest, and slept. He did not wake when, shortly after, the abbey bell went for the first service before dawn and the cells on either side of them quietly emptied and the monks crossed the courtyard to the abbey church. Borgo needed their prayers. Today was the day of Princess Ariana's funeral.

It was to have been the day of a magnificent hunting party arranged for the bride, which would have made up for the one cancelled the day after the wedding. The kennelman in charge of the Prince's hunting dogs was despondent; he had hardly hoped that the Prince would so far neglect decorum as to go on with the hunt, but it distressed him that days might have to pass before his Highness could indulge in his second favourite amusement. To cheer himself up, after the hounds were fed he called his best mastiff, Warrior, to him and buckled round its muscular neck the collar it should have worn if all had been well, the deep boiled-leather collar with studs and small spikes of steel against the jaws of its prey. He held up its muzzle, stroked its jowls, and spoke loving words to it in promise of hunts to come. A sudden noise, the boom of the abbey bell that was to sound all day, startled them both. Warrior broke away – it was a nervous as well as an aggressive beast – and galloped wildly off. The hound master was not seriously worried, for the Prince's hounds were accustomed to roam the palace and the grounds. Harm to Warrior was unlikely; few strangers would care to approach him.

Harm, however, was certainly about to happen to someone.

Chapter Sixteen

On the way to the grave

The funeral of the Princess was to be as impressive as could possibly be contrived, as a good account of it positively must be taken back by her stepmother to her father. Duke Ippolyto could not attend, although the journey to Borgo would take only a day and a half. He was not well, so he sent word. It was assumed that he was overcome with grief.

Prince Galeotto's councillors feared that the Duke's indisposition might indicate a belief that his son-in-law was implicated in Ariana's death. Rumour rife in Borgo could have reached Altamura, and rumour was not remiss in suggesting that Galeotto could have lost his temper and his bride simultaneously. The Duke might be waiting only for the safe return of his Duchess to show his anger; even to declare war. It was true he had no condottiere on hire at the moment, but there was always someone on the lookout for a likely little war with a minimum of fighting and the maximum of loot. Prince Galeotto's councillors were nervous. There was a lot of loot in Borgo.

Moreover, the Prince had needed the Altamuran alliance to strengthen his position with another neighbour, Vincenzo of Venosta. There would be certain difficulties about asking Duke Vincenzo for *his* daughter now that the Prince was burying Duke Ippolyto's. It didn't inspire confidence.

The procession had but a short way to go, from the palace chapel where the Princess had been lying in state — surrounded by the splendid frescoes Brunelli had done before he had to leave — to the Abbey, where the Abbot was to conduct the funeral Mass. The route therefore was through two squares only, although it went round three sides of the Abbey square, ostensibly to allow more people to pay their respects and just incidentally to make more of a show. Both squares on this Thursday would be busy with the weekly market and fair, and, because people have to live though others die, there was no attempt to cancel this activity. In fact, what with the peasants bringing in their produce from the surrounding countryside, the Prince thought the increased numbers could be made to appear like a tribute to the Princess.

The stalls were therefore set up in almost all their usual places in both squares and, during the procession and Mass, stallholders would respectfully cover their goods with cloths and overt trading would cease. The Prince's Marshal had inspected the route and made sure there was room for the procession to get round and for the crowds to line the route without being a hindrance. Barriers blocked off the crush at the ends of both streets that debouched into the palace square; and the Marshal's guard and the palace guard, in a mixture of musty old and hastily sewn new black tabards, shared the duty of controlling the crowds. Some country folk who had been too hard at work to come in for the excitement of the wedding found that their routine visit to the market carried the extra bonus of a funeral, with more people to sell to and entertainment for free.

A muffled drum announced the start of the procession

at noon. By that time the route was lined to overflowing, the press of people extending into the streets and alleys leading to both squares. Windows were crammed, stalls decently draped, the guards stood with pikes reversed, men removed their hats and hoods, some women were crying – she had been fifteen, life was before her. Her fate made one think of some of the Abbot's sermons: Death is everywhere and he comes when least expected.

Benno, half crushed behind a barrier, on the slight slope where the palace square narrowed before the abbey square, crowded so close that Biondello had half emerged from his jerkin to place his forepaws on the wooden bar and look intelligently down the route, was far too conscious of this thought. Worse, Death could be *anywhere* and was, quite certainly, looking for his master. Nor was Sigismondo going to be inconspicuous. The Duchess Violante had expressly required him to walk at her shoulder. Sigismondo had not told Benno if she had given a reason but perhaps, remembering the fall of the effigy, Violante felt that processions of any kind had their dangers. Perhaps, Benno thought, she felt as he did that stranglers were likely to be on the lookout for another chance.

Others felt the possibility of risk: Prince Galeotto's councillors and courtiers urged him to wear a breastplate under his doublet and a gorget for his neck. He had rejected this with scorn – what strangler could get close enough to a waking, strong man to hope for success? And did they really imagine an assassin could force a way through his guards and stab him?

In fact, he had in privacy tried on a breastplate, put his doublet of black velvet over it, and decided that it made him look actually fat. He knew himself to be well-built, and conceivably a little fleshy, but . . . He took it off.

Besides, this Sigismondo had warned him of an assassin arriving from nowhere – well, to be precise, from the river – and taking his chance. There would be no 'chance' in a funeral procession. What did trouble him, and cast an appropriate gloom on his face and bearing as he paced to the chapel, was Sigismondo's other suggestion: that someone at court was in league with the assassin. He argued to himself, however, that this unknown person was most likely in Ariana's train. It must be so! Most important, of desperate importance, was that Ippolyto should not think he was in any way involved. With this in mind, Galeotto gave a supporting hand to the Duchess Violante pacing beside him, and squeezing out a tear he also squeezed her fingers and turned his face to her so that she would see.

The Princess was borne down the steps from the palace, to the muffled drumbeats and the tolling of the abbey bell, in an open coffin carried by six monks and flanked by six nobles. These were to have carried it but proved too inept, one being rather short and none of them able to keep step.

The coffin was lined and draped in black velvet sewn in gold with the arms of Borgo and Altamura. The Princess lay in white brocade, a touching emblem of her purity and youth although technically inappropriate to a married woman. There was a good deal of morbid curiosity as the crowd strained to see their strangled Princess, but the open coffin had not been decided upon until skilful cosmetics had bleached out the purple speckles on the face; now that the starting eyes were closed and the swollen tongue relaxed enough to push back, nothing could remind spectators of what had happened.

On either side of the mourners pacing behind the coffin walked men of the household. Galeotto noticed that the Duchess had got Sigismondo close to her. He rather wished the man were closer to *him*. The Duchess's face under her black veil looked perfectly calm. It was easy to see that she had been only a stepmother to Ariana and that the sweet girl had not had time to establish herself in her affections. He was reminded that if anyone ought to show grief it was he, and he managed a sob. Drifting incense smoke mingled with the strong odour of the rosemary sprigs everyone was carrying. Galeotto hoped he would not sneeze.

As the coffin drew level with Benno, the thud of the drum and the solemn pacing filled his eyes with tears. He had to blink them away. Here was another priest with a censer. Here was Prince Galeotto and the Duchess and Sigismondo who did not, like the others, watch the coffin. His gaze swept the crowds and rose above their heads to the house fronts bordering the route.

From a sudden frown of concentration on his face, Benno knew something was about to happen.

No one else expected Sigismondo's sudden attack on the Prince and the Duchess. A violent push sent the Duchess forward almost into the file of monks supporting the coffin. The Prince, struck on the shoulder by his other hand, staggered into the gentlemen of his household pacing on his left. The bell continued to toll, the coffin continued on its way, the drum beat; only in this spot was there confusion. The Duchess's ladies swarmed towards her, shedding their sprigs of rosemary, a couple of guards tried to seize Sigismondo and, a pace or two behind the commotion, a man in the front of the crowd dropped dead.

He had been picking the pocket of the man next to him

but could not have thought judgement from on high would be so speedy.

At the time, hardly anyone saw him fall except Sigismondo who had expected to see someone fall. A second before he struck aside the august principals of the procession his eye had caught movement in the blackness of an upper window, a whirling, a tiny violence in the air that took the sun for an instant.

The guards were making vain efforts to get Sigismondo's arms behind his back. The crowd shouted and screamed, the monks carrying the coffin slowed to a halt. The Duchess, recovering her balance, put her women aside and came to her rescuer. Luckily for him, she had understood at once.

'Where? What was it?'

Sigismondo in reply took her by the arms and placed her behind the shield of the coffin, whose bearers were trying to turn their heads to make out what had happened.

Prince Galeotto, too, would have liked to know. Restored to his feet, examined for damage by the bruised gentlemen of his household, he was more relieved even than they were to find himself with no dagger wound. He had dropped his hat, his face was turnip green and he looked almost as much in need of a coffin as was his bride.

Chapter Seventeen

The bird of death

'Highness, that was slingshot. It came from that window.'

The guard made another attempt at seizing Sigismondo's pointing arm. The Prince turned apprehensively to scan the houses. Galeotto, something of a coward but not a fool, knew, as did the Duchess, that he had been saved.

The master of his guard was beside him. 'Have that house searched,' the Prince ordered. 'Oh, let go of that man, idiot. And go on, go on – let the procession go on.' To Sigismondo he added, very firmly, 'Walk *here*.' His finger designated a point behind both the Duchess and himself.

The crowd was left wondering, with increasing noise, as the procession moved on. The sinister shaven-headed man in black, whose function as the Duchess's shadow was most intriguing, had seemed all at once to lose his wits. Benno heard all sorts of speculation as the pickpocket's body was taken up. No one could tell what had felled him so inexplicably. Could it be that the strange man was a sorcerer who had diverted onto the dead man a fate intended for the Prince?

One pair of ready eyes had noticed more. Biondello, put down as the crowd's pressure eased up, trotted over

111

the dust and gravel of the roadway and brought back to Benno a round pebble. He was used to fetching things that had been thrown and, although he thought it was the pickpocket who had thrown it, he saw no reason why his master should not have the object.

The crowd still buzzed with the attack made on the Prince and Duchess by the man who so resembled an assassin. The royal pair had not condemned the man — even for actually taking hold of the Duchess. What omen had made him thrust the principals out of the way to let the thunderbolt, or evil eye, fall on the pickpocket?

The procession, meanwhile, wound its way through the abbey square; was received by the Abbot, and filed into the nave, dazzling with innumerable candles. The long ceremony began, and the Princess was interred in the family tomb, an agglomeration rich with porphyry, serpentine and chalcedony, next to Galeotto's first wife.

It was when the court had processed back to the palace, where the Prince was to entertain the ambassadors and notables, that Sigismondo was free. The Prince's Marshal had caught his eye as they emerged from the abbey and was waiting for him now. A small man, with a decided limp, he vouchsafed only the information, 'They'd gone, of course.'

Sigismondo shrugged. 'Was the house empty?'

'As a miser's heart.'

'I want to see.'

'I thought so,' said the Marshal. As he was setting off, Sigismondo turned to Benno and asked if he had noted the spot where the pickpocket had been standing. Benno nodded and pointed.

'Stand there,' he was told.

The front door of the house had been battered in by the guard and raw wood scarred the jamb where the lock had hung. A clear view through the house to a door open on a communal yard at the back showed where the assailant had most likely gone. One of the Prince's guard stood up lazily from the floor as they entered.

'Of course no one had been looking out at the back,' the Marshal said as he led the way through. A precipitous flight of stairs was thick with dust, plaster and footprints. Sigismondo bent to look but the Marshal tapped his shoulder and pointed upwards.

The front room, where the open shutter let daylight in on walls shedding plaster and a floor deep in dust, plaster and mouse dirt, had one set of footprints only.

'Kept my men out of here,' said the Marshal.

Sigismondo gave a long, appreciative hum. 'You're a man who knows what's what.' He went down on one knee to look along the tracks and see where the man had stood. Then he went forward to examine the several prints of the shifting feet in the dirt. Finally he stood in the same spot, and looked down at Benno. He crouched a little.

'Yes,' said the Marshal, 'I thought, a small man.' He came forward and, as Sigismondo made way, placed his own feet alongside the prints. 'He couldn't have seen his Highness from here.'

'Small feet so most likely a small man,' Sigismondo summed up, 'but even a taller man couldn't have seen the Prince at this angle. It was the Duchess he was aiming for.'

'Or you,' the Marshal said.

'Mm. It might be. I think not, however. I was further to the side.' His forefinger rubbed his lip. Then he turned to the Marshal with a smile. 'Who knows, after all? Now, was there anything else in the house?'

'Someone, perhaps more than one person, slept in the

loft lately. And it looks to me as if this shutter was opened yesterday or before – see where the dust has blown over the footprints under the window. Today, he waited back from the window.'

'You're a good tracker, sir.'

'I was the Prince's huntsman until a boar met me.' The Marshal rubbed his thigh.

'You going to tell the Prince the man wasn't aiming at him? Be a weight off his mind, won' it?' Benno had bought a piece of sausage from a stall and was dividing it between his own mouth and the one in his jerkin.

'I doubt it. He's had a shock and he's convinced he's the target. His subjects won't be seeing so much of him in future.' Sigismondo accepted a piece of sausage and strolled on past the stalls. The market life had reasserted itself with increased vigour, as if the procession and the tolling bell had made people feel their own life more fully, reminding them that they were not dead, and had things to sell and a need to buy. The covering cloths were folded away, fruit was burnished with a bit of spit and a sleeve, food began to fry succulently, lengths of linen and wool were spread to show their quality, even toys and sweetmeats were displayed to tempt the moneyed children. Those too poor still clustered round the stalls, admiring or waiting for the unlikely chance to steal. Little concession had been made to the thought of funeral, except the addition of black ribbons to the toy birds the stallholder on the corner was selling. The little crude birds had each a whistle carved into its body, and he demonstrated their desirability by whirling one round his head. The ends of black ribbon fluttered and a reedy piping sounded as though the bird sang on the end of its string. The seller was a tall man, his height disguised by a slight stoop, and no one could see, under the convincing beard, the mole at the corner of his mouth. All anyone had eyes for were the coloured birds on their strings. He was making good sales, and had his head down, counting out change into a child's palm, as Sigismondo and Benno passed near enough for him to see their boots.

Sigismondo was going up the steps to the palace and Benno, following a few paces after, heard a strange sound like an invisible bird's whirring wings.

Sigismondo stopped, as though halted by something no one could see and, hands to his throat, he stumbled and fell.

Chapter Eighteen

Two necklaces

Benno saw his master go down. He had no idea what could have happened. He had not been in Leonora's room when the bolas took Venus' head off and he did not know the sound. He scrambled to his master's side. In the square, the toy vendor had shut up shop and was gone.

Benno knew slingshot could kill. He thought only of that. Not the Prince, not the Duchess they'd wanted dead, but his master all along. He pulled at Sigismondo's shoulder with shaking hands, trying to turn him.

'Where . . . Did you see . . .' Sigismondo got to all fours and rose. 'He may still be . . .' He could hardly speak but, uncoiling the cord from round his neck, was down the steps and into the crowd before Benno even stood up. It was easy to follow his head, however, and a relieved Benno forged through to find himself at the street corner, where children had undone a straw poke of toy birds and were helping themselves, laughing at the man who tried to stop them.

' . . . asked me to keep an eye,' the man was saying to Sigismondo. 'Now I ask you! What? *Where* did he . . . ? Down that alley.'

Sigismondo set off down the alley, Benno still after him. A pair of scavenging geese hung out their wings and hissed, and Benno, feeling Biondello's nose pushed against his ribs in terror, hoped the geese had gone for the strangler. Ahead of him, Sigismondo cleared three shallow steps at a stride and turned the corner. Benno thought he heard hoofbeats, then nothing. The long dark narrow street with overhanging house fronts had not a soul in sight.

Sigismondo said something under his breath, and then aloud, 'Too late.' His voice had lost its hoarseness and was angry. 'I'm too late. Again.'

He leant on the wall. He was coiling the bolas round his hand. Benno, seeing his face, didn't remind him that he hadn't been too late to save the Duchess or the Prince a couple of hours ago. Sigismondo's collar was pulled awry, and showed another collar, high round his neck, with studs of metal. Benno saw why his master had made friends with the stray mastiff that morning, at the sacrifice of a battered heel of bacon from Benno's shirt cargo – to the resentment, silent but intense, of the hidden Biondello.

He put Biondello to the ground, and he scouted about while Sigismondo brooded.

Sigismondo suddenly looked round as though taking his bearings and set off fast the way they had come. Benno whistled up Biondello and ran after, in time to follow his master down an unexpected side alley so narrow a cat could have jumped across from house to house. He knew Sigismondo's sense of direction could take him to the right places in cities where he was all but a stranger. He could hardly be picking up the assassin's scent from the air.

Benno thought he recognised the house they shortly came to after many twists and turns, although he had last seen it at night. When the same crone opened the door –

118

without the candle − he knew he was right. Of course, Sigismondo had seen the assassin at the Lady Leonora's, but why should she know anything about him? Did the man live here? Did Sigismondo expect the man to follow him here a second time?

'The Prince has sent me with a message to your mistress.'

That's changed her mind, thought Benno, as the crone backed of a sudden to let them enter. We'd be shut out of a lot of places if my master didn't lie so beautifully. There was some mumble about the lady being in the garden, but Sigismondo did not wait to be announced. He ran for the back of the house too fast for the old woman. Benno, following, supposed other servants were still taking their siesta; or that the crone by herself could be counted on to keep out those the lady didn't want to see. Would she want to see Sigismondo?

As it happened, she couldn't.

Sigismondo found the door beyond the staircase that led to the garden − a more spacious one than might have been expected. First a parterre spread, with lavender hedges no higher than their shins, through which a path of gravel led to a fountain, all dolphins and Nereids, at the far end. Tall white-plastered walls gave it privacy. In the late afternoon sunlight, with the bees searching the lavender, a drowsy undercurrent to the plash of the fountain, it was a place of peace where a lady might go to recover from a shock.

There was no sign of the lady.

Sigismondo turned, scanning the garden and the high walls almost as if he expected the lady to have vaulted over one to escape his questioning. Biondello sniffed the air with enjoyment and then went trotting to the fountain for a drink.

119

His single, sharp bark brought Sigismondo instantly.

Beyond the spouting, flowing statuary in the centre, hidden from them until now, was the Lady Leonora.

She lay face down, half in and half out of the water over the low edge of the basin. A cupid poised above her with stone flowers in his hands looked at them with an arch smile as they came.

When Sigismondo dragged her out of the water she lay dripping on his arm, her hair like waterweed across her face and her head at a curious angle. She was wearing two necklaces, one of gold. The other had twisted three times round her throat and dangled a stone on either end.

Chapter Nineteen

Even the dead can kill

'*Strangled?*'

Prince Galeotto was not taking the news of his mistress' death at all well. To lose one's wife by strangulation is a cruel blow of fate. To lose a mistress by the same means begins to look like persecution.

He had been eating grapes when Sigismondo was shown in, grapes offered in a silver-gilt dish by a page on one knee, and the bunch he had been browsing from dropped to the floor while juice ran down his chin.

'Not by a scarf, Highness. By one of these.' He showed the weighted cord that had brought him down on the palace steps. The Prince glanced and, not reassured by the distinction, shuddered. He wiped his face with his napkin, leaving grape pips from the linen on his cheek.

'Did you see who had done it?'

Sigismondo shrugged expressively. 'Such men don't wait to have a portrait taken, Highness.'

'But how . . .' Galeotto gestured widely with the napkin and the page flinched. 'Why? He could not even have known the Lady Leonora.'

If Sigismondo had any theories about this, he was silent on the subject. 'I believe he had a horse, Highness. There were traces under the east wall of the garden where a horse had been standing. Perhaps he stood on the saddle to climb over, but the wall is covered with a vine and he had not climbed over it. He would have seen the lady in the garden and thrown the bolas from there.'

Galeotto made an effort to spring from the elaborate gilded day bed. Courtiers standing at a distance against the tapestries had been in some pain, unable to catch a word of Sigismondo's deep murmur, hardly enlightened but bitterly tantalised by their Prince's cry of *Strangled?* Eyes hastily checked to see who was missing. Lady Zima, naturally delighted at the indisposition which had kept Leonora from the funeral, now found her hopes rise. Everyone leant forward, ears astrain.

Galeotto had floundered to his feet, crying, 'It is a conspiracy!' with surprising energy. 'Who is it who is killing those I love? My wife, sweet Ariana, and now Leonora.' Stating the fact seemed to bring it home to him and he stood, feet splayed, and bawled, tears running past the grape pips on his cheek. The courtiers stared at one another, and produced a general murmur of sympathy, Zima managing to convert the noise she made into a sob.

This interesting scene was interrupted by the arrival of the Duchess Violante, changed out of one mourning garment of dull splendour into a simple unadorned gown of twelve yards of purple velvet. She had come to lend her presence to the ceremony of receiving the condolences of envoys and ambassadors which she had supposed her host to be engaged in. He had in fact postponed this necessary business until he should have recovered somewhat from the acuteness of his grief. The envoys and ambassadors had therefore retired to their various lodgings to write accounts of the funeral and their theories about this disaster that had overtaken Borgo, to their various masters who would rearrange their foreign policies accordingly.

The Duchess was confronted with whispering courtiers – interrupting their gossip distractedly to make her their obeisances – and a loudly weeping Prince. Both were no novelties to her since she had come to Borgo. Seeing Sigismondo, she beckoned to him, demanded to know what had happened, and listened with a furious frown and lips pressed together as he told her.

'So what is happening?'

'Your Grace.' Sigismondo bent his head and dropped his voice so that only she could hear. 'I think it wise you should leave for Altamura. At once.'

The vivid blue eyes, startling among so many dark ones, opened wide. 'There's danger here still? And for me? For me in particular?'

'Your Grace may be a target for this assassin. You would be safer out of Borgo. How soon can your Grace leave?'

She looked at Galeotto, now being comforted by a number of courtiers and allowing Zima to hold a cup of wine to his lips. 'The Prince has asked me to stay another week.'

Sigismondo shook his head. 'Can your Grace find a reason to go which will satisfy his Highness? Best to leave with no delay; and to tell his Highness nothing of what I have said.'

Duchesses and their trains and escorts are less easily moved across country than armies are. An army has most usually a degree of discipline – except among the gentlemen of the cavalry; and the Duchess's train was the equivalent of that. Another comparison might be with a menagerie.

The Duchess Violante's decision was firm, in spite of noisy pleading from her host. There had fortunately been a messenger from Altamura and she could inform the Prince that her husband was ill, suffering from the shocking death of his daughter, that he wished for her company and her duty was to him. This set in motion the whole customary hubbub of hasty packing, cording of chests, discovery of things omitted, readying litters, preparation of food and feed, harnessing and saddling, among commands, counter-commands, and curses. From this, order emerged and the Duchess was ready to go.

Galeotto, forced to comply, begged for a report from Altamura of her safe return and her husband's health, and he reiterated that for his own part he considered the alliance with Altamura to be as strong as if his beloved Ariana were still living. She was to bear back with her the assurance to Duke Ippolyto that the villainous murderer would be tracked down and punished as hideously as the Prince's torturers could devise. All this was stated in the letter he also gave her, and he said it again as he rode with her to the city gates. What was not mentioned at any point were the bride chests of Ariana's dowry. Galeotto had told his conscience that, although it might be honourable, to suggest the return of any part of them might somehow imply dissatisfaction with his part of the bargain.

He excused himself over and over for not riding with the Duchess to the border. Grief had debilitated him. He embraced her at the city gates with more tears. It was an awkward embrace for more reasons than one, as he wore a breastplate under his doublet. It made him look as fat as he had feared but he explained to the Duchess, as she put her hands on its unyielding bulk, that consideration for his subjects forced him to preserve their ruler. The Duchess must tell Duke Ippolyto — here a trace of *ennui* overcame the Duchess's schooling but was gone at once – must tell the Duke that he, Galeotto, was the target of enemies who had delivered the cruellest possible blow in depriving him of his adored young bride.

'Didn' want *you* to go either, did he?' Benno had edged his horse up beside Sigismondo's great black, a little way behind the Duchess, from where Sigismondo could command a comprehensive view all round.

'Perhaps he wanted me to stay for the same reason he wanted her Grace to stay.' Sigismondo smiled, unexpectedly genial at being questioned.

Benno thought hard. The same reason . . . ? But the Prince wanted the Duchess to stay so that she could be impressed with his desolation at losing his bride, which she was to report to her husband. All that was politics. His desolation would hardly impress Sigismondo.

'Oh, he wanted you to protect him, didn' he? And find the strangler.'

'Or for the strangler to find me.'

Benno considered this with mouth open. 'He wanted you *dead*? And the Duchess too? But why?'

Sigismondo hummed, riding at ease, still watching the landscape. 'Hey, there are possibilities of all sorts, Benno. It may be we should look beyond Galeotto himself. Any principality is surrounded by others who may have covetous eyes; Duke Francisco of Castelnuovo, for one, is known for his need for land and he is not known for scruples in ways of reaching out for it. But as regards the Prince, you've not talked to the servants about Princess Beatrice of Borgo?'

'The one that was married to Duke Ippolyto's father? That died and they said he'd poisoned her? But that's years and years ago even if it was true. You don't mean

Prince Galeotto's avenging *that*?' Benno was familiar
with the saying that 'revenge is a dish best eaten cold' but
this sounded not just cold but carrion into the bargain.

'I mean stranger things have happened than that.
Princess Beatrice was aunt to Galeotto, his blood kin. It
all happened before anyone alive now was even born, but
things are not forgotten.'

'But if Galeotto's father didn't do anything *then*, if he
thought his sister'd been poisoned . . . You'd expect he'd
go to war with Altamura. Why didn't he?'

'Perhaps he hadn't the money to hire an army.
Perhaps he wanted something more subtle. He died a few
years ago, but he had already put out feelers for the
marriage of Ariana to his son. Even dead men can kill –
Galeotto may have been acting on his father's secret
commands.'

Chapter Twenty

Sigismondo spits

Here Sigismondo said, 'Stay,' and swung his horse out of the procession and set it up the hillside. He made his way to a rocky spur from which he could survey the road ahead and the country round. Seeing him there, dark against the blue and so exposed, made Benno fearful; and glad that his master had not restored the mastiff's collar. There might be little chance that the strangler would emerge from the landscape and try the bolas again, with so many people on horseback who could hunt him down, but Benno had started to believe that the man could not be caught. After all, Sigismondo himself had so far failed to catch him.

The idea of Prince Galeotto being behind the murder of his bride, in family revenge, was distracting and, if it was fact, the Duchess might be at risk all the way to the border and perhaps beyond. Any moment there might be some sort of attack, which was of course why his master was sitting his horse up there on the hillside watching out.

Benno as he rode also looked all round. There was plenty to see. The Duchess's train straggled back into the distance, brought up by sumpter mules loaded with chests and bales holding the dresses of the Duchess and her ladies. Their essential portable furniture, necessary to camp overnight and to enjoy alfresco meals along the way, had gone ahead, but the mules had their own pace and were definitely not prepared to mend it. Most of the servants had congregated there, ostensibly seeing to the luggage but in fact enjoying an almighty gossip. Their stay in Borgo having reinforced their conviction of the superiority of Altamura, they were returning with the certainty of an eager audience for all they could tell. The Duke's daughter had not achieved universal popularity but the gruesome details of her death would certainly do so.

Ahead rode the escort of soldiers, the guard, and then, also guarded, the Duchess and her companions. Though in deepest mourning, the Duchess was not so overcome by grief as to be blind to the possibilities of sport and there she was, gorgeous in black silk and pearls, her blonde hair plaited with silver under a plumed hat, with a hawk on her pearl-sewn gauntlet. She had been cheated of the hunting parties planned; now at least there was a chance of flying her little merlin at anything that offered itself along the way. Her falconer strode a short way behind. She was not leaving Borgo without extracting some amusement there.

As she was busy finding her own amusement, those responsible for providing it officially could do as they pleased. Benno was startled to hear a voice issuing from the spine of a servant who rode up alongside, and it relieved his mind to see Poggio duck into view round the servant's arm. He seemed in need of conversation and, in a minute, had got himself helped across and settled quite comfortably, pillion on the pack behind Benno, his arm hooked in Benno's belt, while the servant rode off.

'You never been to Altamura, have you? Like it there, you will. Those Borgese are a mean lot, don't know how to laugh at jokes, don't know what a joke is. Duke

Ippolyto now, he can laugh and he's generous with money too. You'll like him.'

Benno was silent, wondering how ready the Duke would be for jokes. with his daughter dead. He thought that Poggio might have to wait a while for gratuities. Still, that didn't seem to bother him and he rambled on about the pleasures in store in Altamura.

'Oh, and won't it be nice without the Lady Ariana making mischief. Shouldn't speak ill of the dead though *she* spoke ill enough all round when she was alive. Poor Lord Tebaldo won't find it easy to mourn, you bet.'

'Lord Tebaldo? I know him. Our Duke of Rocca's own nephew, the crippled one. Ever so nice to me he was, when I wanted to bury a dog once.' He checked that Biondello was still trotting and not yet plodding, along the roadside. 'He got them to find me a rosebush in the gardens. He came with the Duchess to Altamura when she married, right?'

'We was both exiled, in a manner of speaking.' Poggio sighed reminiscently, a puff on Benno's arm. 'Poor Lord Tebaldo never had much luck, what with being so ill, and his father and that; but isn't it like the Duchess to look after him? She's as kind as she is beautiful.'

'Why will Lord Tebaldo be glad the Princess is dead?'

'He was glad she was leaving to get married and he wouldn't have to see her no more. You wouldn't think perhaps but he fell in love last year, with one of her ladies. We all have feelings, you know, whatever we look like. And everyone at court was wondering if he'd actually marry. She did seem she might, when it was all broke off. On account of the Lady Ariana.'

Benno twisted round. 'What'd she do?'

'Do? Just ruined everything. She told the girl what a fool she was to let a cripple woo her; told her if she married him she'd give birth to little monsters, all twisted like him; said he was even worse with his clothes off, she'd die of horror on her wedding night.'

'How come you heard all this?'

Poggio snorted into Benno's shoulder. 'Don't get to think she said all this in private. She wasn't ashamed of saying it – nothing to be ashamed of, not like Lord Tebaldo. Oh, he'll have been glad to hear she's dead. If he could have got away with it he'd have choked her to death himself before she left.'

Benno shook his head. The Princess had collected enemies busily, those who could either have killed her themselves or hired to have it done, without looking for others who'd get rid of her not for what she'd done herself but on account of politics or a family feud. Still, Sigismondo would want to hear this; Benno did hope it wasn't the Lord Tebaldo who'd hired the strangler, but it sounded as though he'd certainly had cause.

Sigismondo wheeled his horse and sent it picking its way down among the boulders and loose scree to join them on the road. He saluted in return to Poggio's greeting when he came past, but evidently was not in the mood for conversation as Benno had hoped. He rode on without stopping, towards where the Duchess chatted with her ladies.

They were approaching the border, the River Larno where it flowed between the crags of Borgo and the flatter lands of Altamura that spread richly before they rose to the precipitous mountains among which the city itself perched. Already, in spite of the noise of their passage, they could hear the sound of the river and now see its glitter through the dust. Spirits rose and the pace increased – not far, and they would be out of alien territory and home and safe. Few people thought that the nearer you are to safety the closer you are to danger, but it was one of Sigismondo's maxims.

Men of the advance guard were deploying across the water downstream of the ford, in case any of the party got into difficulties in crossing, and the ladies had grouped on the shore. The Duchess, like Sigismondo, had been keeping keen eyes open and now she laughed aloud and tossed her hawk up into the air. It beat its wings strongly, rising and rising until it should be above the hapless bird the Duchess had sighted, that now flew urgently downriver. All heads save one were tilted to watch, the black plume in the Duchess's hat sweeping her shoulder.

'Isn't he fine, Sigismondo? A ducat that he brings it down.'

Strangely, there was no reply. Unused to such treatment, she glanced at him, to see him spit into his hand. While she still wondered, the pebble he had been carrying in his mouth was whirling in the sling, round his head and then spinning violently away towards the crags. In the same moment she heard a cry, shrill and agonised, sound among the rocks and she herself was struck from her horse.

Chapter Twenty-one

A blow in the face

Sigismondo was down in a moment and kneeling by the Duchess; she sat on the ground, feet wide apart among her black silk skirts, her hands supporting her. Her hat was missing, her hair had come unwound so that it fell in a blonde cascade to the ground behind her.

Her blue eyes were brilliant with rage.

'Did you kill him?'

There was no need to explain to her. The Duchess directed her glare towards the hillside. Sigismondo and Lady Clea helped her to her feet while a page caught and gentled the outraged horse; the guard clattered back across the ford in fountains of spray and men from the party were clambering, shouting, up the rocks from whence both the slingshot and the scream had come. A body lay spreadeagled, head down, dark against the grass; the foremost climber had nearly reached it. Two more figures, scrambling higher, were for a moment silhouetted against the skyline. Sigismondo had another pebble in the sling already and sent it hurtling towards them. Amid the neighing of startled horses, the cries of the ladies as they surrounded the Duchess — now restored to her palfrey and demanding her hat — nothing could be heard from the hill, the only testimony to Sigismondo's aim being the abrupt disappearance of the figures on the skyline as one plunged from sight and the other followed.

Ants disturbed by the lifting of a stone run about with apparent aimlessness but in fact protect what is most precious to them. In spite of the noise, confusion and crowding up of the baggage train, the returning guard had circled the Duchess, swords drawn and facing outward. The Altamuran captain, once assured that the Duchess was unharmed, had instantly gone to direct the hunt up the hillside. Some were returning now, dragging the body of the man Sigismondo had hit; others had gained the top of the rise and were out of sight.

'I know that man!'

Two of the guard, obeying the Duchess's imperious gesture, had brought the body, and the Duchess looked at it with no squeamish flinching; though many of her ladies turned away or, if they looked, did so through their fingers, which in Benno's opinion was more a matter of not wanting to be seen looking.

The man's skull had been fractured and blood still drained stickily from his scalp, though his features were not obscured. The nose was hawklike, the mouth open in the black beard showed teeth that were not good, and the dark eyes no one had thought to close stared out accusingly towards the Duchess as if his spirit challenged still.

'Your Grace, it is Raimondo Malgardo. Your Grace will remember how the Duke exiled him and his brothers three years ago for making mischief in the city.' It was the captain of the guard, who had ridden up to see the body. The Duchess nodded, still regarding the man who had tried to kill her.

'I remember. He cursed us; and his Grace would have changed exile to hanging if I had not pleaded for his life.'

She raised her eyes at last and said to Sigismondo, who stood gravely by, 'So he repays me.' She turned towards the captain. 'And the others?'

Her question was answered by the tumbling descent of another body flung from the crest by the hunters. The captain, riding over and examining what was left of his features, confirmed that this was – had been – brother to Raimondo, as spiteful and ill-starred as he. Expert with the slingshot they might have been, but their fate was to encounter a man whose aim was better. Raimondo's shot had hit the great coil of the Duchess's hair at the back of her head, had swung her sideways and carried her from her horse.

A shout from the rest of those on the hill drew people's eyes. They had a man slung head down over somebody's back, his arms lifelessly dangling. If Sigismondo had hoped to question any Malgardo, he did not show disappointment. It was the Duchess who said, 'Fools! He could have told us how they killed the Princess. We could have taken him back to suffer his Grace's justice. No matter. Bring them. Their heads shall be put on the city gates, for all to see what comes to men who threaten the lives of those set over them to rule them.' She paused, and added generously, 'One head shall be sent to Prince Galeotto to display in Borgo.'

With that settled, she took her hat, which had been found by one of the pages setting out on its own voyage of discovery down the river. Dashing water from its brim vigorously enough to scatter her ladies, the Duchess clapped it on her head. Her hair still rippled free down her back, and on the hat's black velvet a huge pearl brooch wept tears from the river. Duchess Violante was ready to enter her husband's country.

The exhilaration felt by all the company at the death of

these mysterious villains was expressed in the energy with which horses were spurred into the river; in the loud talk and banter, the laughter at the clouds of spray as the water was churned up. Their Duchess was freed from a threat. Not only were they coming home, but – the purport of their dark clothes notwithstanding – they were coming home triumphant.

Benno sounded out his master on this. Poggio had shrieked like a parrot when the successive Malgardi were brought down by Sigismondo's sling, and his ears were still ringing, but Sigismondo rode in silence.

'You got him, then?' Benno offered. 'The one that killed the Princess?'

'No.' A calm, firm monosyllable – but not repressive, and Benno went on.

'You knew him, though? The man that tried to strangle you?' Benno could feel Poggio, avid with curiosity, all but slip off the crupper as he craned to hear.

'As far as I know that man is alive still.'

'But the Duchess . . .' Benno fell silent as he balanced the probability of his master being right against the possibility of the Duchess not knowing what had really happened. '*Wasn't* the Princess killed by the Malgardi, then? Getting their own back on the Duke for exiling them? And they tried to get the Duchess before she left Borgo?' For of course exiles, under pain of death if they returned, would think twice before crossing the border into Altamura.

Sigismondo guided his horse across the stones of the ford, the rush of water almost drowning the deep voice as he answered. 'It might be that the Malgardi hired the man who killed the Princess. I don't think so.'

'You mean – you mean they could have done it themselves with slingshot any time.' They plashed up

through the pocked mud of the bank. Some of the escort
were circling and shouting in celebration. Sigismondo
rode through them and prompted his horse on to catch
up with the Duchess. She rode with some of the guard
and some of her ladies, talking, their sombre clothes
belied by their tones.

'Poor Princess,' said Benno, spurring after. 'No one
cares much, do they?'

'Not easy to mourn her.' Poggio was jolted as he
spoke.

The best part of a mile further on, with the party
spread out to avoid the dust of those ahead, the track
began to climb into the beginnings of the hills. They
could expect to halt soon, for the sun was high; riders
and horses sweated. Benno had been made uneasy, after
a brief respite when he had thought danger was over, by
Sigismondo's saying the murderer still lived.

After their halt for a short meal, and their siesta, the
Duchess set quite a pace. She led the van of the party up
the slope of a ridge that crossed their road, and halted at
the top to look round — at the train spread out behind, at
the steep hillsides of Borgo already receding, and then
upriver.

Her whole body tensed. The blue of her eyes was quite
frightening, Benno thought as he came up with the
group. The Duchess, staring upriver as if she had the eyes
of a basilisk and could kill what she looked at, said,
'*God's Bones!*'

From here they could see what a long slope of Borgan
hill had concealed. A great sweep of valley lay beyond,
thick with olive groves. The river curved to this side of it,
glinting cheerfully. On an eminence among the olive
trees, tall poles of scaffolding rose up; earthworks and a
sizeable footing of wall stood among them and above,

lazily spreading, folding and unfurling in the wind, was a banner whose colours and arms were new to Benno.

'Venosta,' someone said. They had all gone silent and the Duchess was white to the lips.

Poggio rumbled with curses. The escort crowded to the top of the rise to look where the Duchess stared, and now vituperation broke out all round. Benno looked to Sigismondo for enlightenment, but his master was surveying the landscape keenly and in silence.

Finally the Duchess pulled her horse's head round and set off on the road. Slowly the others left the sight and fell in behind her. The silence spread as she made no answer to their eager, furious questions and comments; as they rode on, the shadows were lengthening in more ways than one.

They came to the spot where camp had been pitched for them, a luxurious camp in a little hanging valley where a stream ran through, and pavilions had been set up.

By this time Benno had heard the story: two years ago, Poggio said, the Larno had changed course in the spring floods, veering to the Altamura side of the valley and carving itself a path under the western hills. Duke Vincenzo had at once claimed that, as the natural boundary agreed between their states since time immemorial had altered, so it was the will of God that the valley should become his. Until now the matter had been a diplomatic question. Vincenzo's fort was a blow on the face for Ippolyto.

The Duchess sent for Sigismondo as dark drew in, and he came back to Benno by firelight. Benno and Poggio had made a little bivouac with saddles, packs and a useful boulder, and had collected the allotment of meat, bread and wine.

The deep voice spoke in a murmur as Sigismondo took his place, settling his back to the big rock, firelight gilding his profile.

'Don't make yourself too comfortable, Benno. We're not staying.'

Chapter Twenty-two

The luck of the hunt

Duke Vincenzo of Venosta was supposed, by quite a considerable number of his subjects, to become a werewolf at night, when the fancy seized him to stalk about churchyards and, in general, indulge in deeds people rather shrank from imagining. Venostans who did not credit this would still sooner not meet him after curfew. The men employed in building his fort on the alluvial gravel of the River Larno were sorry to see him even by daylight.

They had been getting on well under the supervision of the architect Mario Marietti, who himself enjoyed the wonderful freedom from the exigent demands of that perfectionist Brunelli. When Brunelli left the palace, cursing its unfinished frescoes and the unfinished statue − which had, as he prophesied, been spoilt in the casting by an inexperienced guess at the temperature of the molten bronze when pouring − Marietti had instantly been despatched to the border; his remit, to make the fort as impregnable as possible, as soon as possible.

Brunelli was not, though, the only person to distrust those who worked for him. Vincenzo, not letting much time elapse, took horse himself to pay his latest military toy a surprise visit. As he arrived by daylight there was no chance whatever of his being mistaken for a werewolf, but he was quite as welcome.

Men who had been transporting stones in wicker baskets, on shoulders or on padded caps, were impelled to speed up under their Duke's eye. They lost the safe rhythm of their work. One man, climbing nimbly up a ladder with a laden basket, came face to face with his Duke on the scaffolding above and lost nearly all his burden onto workmates beneath. Luckily no bones were broken.

Vincenzo did not abuse or threaten, his grating voice was hardly even raised; yet Marietti wished the Duke would realise that in actual fact the fort was going up more slowly. Mistakes and stumbles happened and some tried to avoid the Duke's gaze by hurrying away where they could not be called.

In fact Marietti had moments of wishing for Brunelli instead.

Everyone understood perfectly why the Duke wanted the fort raised with such haste. Marietti had been warned that he should look out for scouts from Altamura, although the Duke did not really expect any just yet — Duke Ippolyto was supposed to have his attention occupied, mourning his daughter; so Duke Vincenzo was seizing the moment. Even when, eventually, the Altamurans woke up to events, there would be diplomatic protest first; envoys would ride to Venosta with letters of complaint, and back with letters of justification. The proper moves would be made in the power game the Dukes were accustomed to playing. This instant fort on the land the river had relinquished to Venosta was merely the boldest of Vincenzo's moves so far. When Ippolyto had recovered from his bereavement, or when news of this military mushroom was reported to him, then the fireworks would begin.

Duke Vincenzo, riding back to his city and his palace, satisfied that he had incited everyone to work at the pace he wanted, could have no idea how soon the fireworks would begin.

Work was finished for the day not until day itself had ended. The Duke's insistence on haste had instilled in everyone that the fort had best be ready for use by the time he showed up again.

This idea had been reinforced by the second visit Mario Marietti had received that day, not long after Duke Vincenzo left them.

A stranger, riding unattended and fast, had arrived from the direction of Venosta city. He was a man of powerful presence and a commanding manner, whom Marietti at first mistook for a general from the Duke's small standing army coming to assess the military potential of the fort. He was less important than that: an engineer summoned by the Duke to make a report on the structure. Marietti was surprised that he had not met the returning Duke, but it seemed he had been summoned not from the city but from a small farm further west, and so had missed the ducal party. It did not in the least surprise Marietti that the Duke had not been content even with a visit in person but wanted a professional opinion as well.

To Marietti's pleased surprise, the engineer was inclined to praise rather than criticise, to listen than to hold forth. Marietti found himself warming to his disquisition, received with grave approval. The man had eyes for everything and knew the subject, asked about all that was planned – the walls that must bear the vibrating shock of a gun's recoil, that were as yet hollow and being filled, about the platform on the tower top – and he showed agility in shinning up ladders to see every part of the construction under way. He was interested particularly in the cannon which the Duke had sent, dragged by labouring mule train. The afterglow of the sun shone on his shaven scalp as he bent to examine the touch hole and run his hand caressingly over the crouching metal bulk. Marietti wondered that a head so naked could look so little vulnerable. He looked more a fighter than an engineer.

'And the gunpowder for this spitfire? The Duke wants assurance that no risks are taken with its storage. Where do the men eat and sleep?'

Marietti did not immediately make the connection between the men's quarters and the safety of powder, but then hastened to point out the camp some way off, clear of the mound dominated by the fort, where the men cooked, ate and slept. He showed the engineer the kegs of powder, under tarpaulin, and was gratified that their site was approved. Although perhaps the gun's purpose was cosmetic or political rather than warlike, as its firing could constitute an overt act of war against a still friendly neighbour, yet it had to be capable of being fired. The Duke liked his toys to work.

By the time the engineer left, dusk had fallen. Marietti felt confident, so far as he could judge from the man's bearing and remarks, that his report to the Duke would not fault the arrangements made; he also felt sure it would be clear and precise.

Certainly Benno and Poggio, sitting in the scrubland some way below the fort, found it so on Sigismondo's return. Neither of them had been idle in his absence, and Sigismondo, with a grunt of satisfaction, took the results of the hard work and wound it round his waist, under his doublet, several times. 'Hey, a way to get fat without eating.' They could not see his expression but his voice smiled. Then he sat down with them and they waited.

It did not take long for Marietti and his gang to fall asleep. The local wine was good and they had been thirsty as well as tired. Their sleep was sound. The cooking fires died down. Wrapped in cloaks or a blanket, in the open or under their makeshift tents, they slept as those do that work hard for a living. They had no cause to be wakeful and they were not military enough, or suspicious enough of anything, to set a watch.

Marietti dreamt that the impressive engineer was reading aloud a report that praised him by name, to someone seated in a chair of state, unpleasantly resembling a wolf with a man's head. He woke from this nightmare, thankfully blessing the saints that it was a dream.

It was no dream what was going on inside the fort.

Between the inward-sloping outer shell of the fort and the perpendicular inner tower was a hollow, still for the most part awaiting its infill of rubble. Inside the open-topped tower, three men were busy, watched by a safely tethered little dog. The kegs of gunpowder had been manhandled by the most powerful of the trio to the side furthest from the camp and nearest to the river. Ropes from the pulleys were untied and employed. A cloud covered the moon as the smallest of the three was lowered into the greater darkness between the walls, holding grimly to the rope that held him as it was paid out inch by careful inch by the two above. Even before this, the outer wall on this side had been searched for a place spotted by the 'engineer' earlier still, and a small gap had been enlarged by the point of a dagger and then by a sharpened pole.

Kegs of gunpowder, secured carefully and lowered into the cavity, were disposed by the little man, working by

145

feel. Had anyone been outside a while later, he might have been alarmed to see in the shifting moonlight a snake, hesitating and then emerging by fits and starts, slithering down the fort's outer wall, down the slope until it was grasped quite fearlessly by a small, bearded man and bathed, as if it were a pagan deity or at least the creature of some prophesying god, in an offering of oil.

Scaffolding poles and wicker baskets were stacked where they might do good, and the three, after work with flint and steel and tinder at the snake's head, made for the river and hurried downstream along its bank as they had come.

When the fort blew up, the explosion made the earth shudder even where they were, and flung them all down, even the crouching Sigismondo. Biondello, clutched tight, quivered too and gave dismayed yelps no one could hear in the thunderous roar. The hurtling stones fell, thanks to Sigismondo's calculations, towards the river and nowhere near the workmen's camp, but the explosion brought a vivid white light momentarily over everything and then a red glow; scaffolding fell in flames down the sky, a display which the stunned workmen, sitting abruptly up or crawling from tents, were unable to enjoy. Rocks rolled, scree scattered, and finally the waiting gun gave a convulsive lurch and trundled head first down the wreckage of the wall, down the glacis and into the river, churning up the new bed and making the basis for a fast-forming dam. Birds for miles around were jolted awake. In burrows and dens animals shook and wondered as the earth moved around them.

Luckily for Duke Vincenzo's peace of mind, the hills between the border and his capital hid the unmannerly eruption from the eyes of anyone awake there, although many citizens were aware of a distant thunderstorm.

Mario Marietti stood, hands clasping his head, and all that he knew was that his future had just been blown apart.

Sigismondo and Benno picked themselves up at once and found Poggio, curled up, complaining of his ears. Biondello, who had only one to complain of, shook it vigorously and then seemed ready to leave a scene whose stability could not be relied upon. Dust, descending through the dark, settled palely on their clothes and bleached their hair, Benno's beard, their eyelashes.

As the sound's reverberations died in the hills and their ears unblocked, Sigismondo spoke.

'I think there should be no need to tell her Grace that we succeeded.'

The Duchess and her retinue had spent the night in camp in a fold of the hills that protected them from the night breezes. The next morning's ride would take them into the city, and there was no point in making the baggage train and, in particular, the ladies, travel by night. There was music to accompany dinner, and in the pavilions every comfort of life was provided. The summer dawn came early and, even before the pavilions were taken down, the party was ready to move off, the Duchess impatient both to see her husband and to get in a little hawking along the way.

Everyone had been woken during the night by the distant noise of the fort, and the Duchess had started up to laugh and clap her hands. The news she brought home would not be all bad; though perhaps Duke Ippolyto might be concerned in case such an overt act of hostility could be traced to his wife's orders, she considered the existence of the fort at all showed the initial hostility to be Duke Vincenzo's.

Sigismondo and his party, arriving where the Duchess's party had encamped, found only trampled turf, scars of the cooking fires, a ribbon from a lute, no more. They had, they knew, only to catch up with the party which had been riding towards Altamura since dawn. What they did not know, as they urged their horses on, was that the Duchess was not of that party, having taken only her estringer and his hawks, a servant or two and a page, to follow a direct path across the hills and enjoy her favourite sport before riding down to meet the rest.

Poggio knew this direct path and recommended it as a quicker way to join the cavalcade. It was Sigismondo, some way along it, who reined in his horse abruptly, put up a hand to halt the others, and cocked his head to listen. Up in the gloriously brightening sky a lark sang, piercingly joyful. Benno remembered the nightingales at Lady Zima's villa and marvelled at his master's interest in birdsong. Then he too heard it.

More of a gasp than a groan, it came from a small ravine to the left of the road. Sigismondo had dismounted and, sure-footed as a cat, was negotiating the boulders at the ravine's edge. Benno swung from his horse, helped Poggio down, and they clambered among the boulders to peer at what he had found.

A boy of about fourteen lay in the gulley, limbs asprawl, supported on Sigismondo's arm. The right side of his face was covered in blood. So were his clothes, yet it was possible to distinguish the livery of the Duchess Violante.

Chapter Twenty-three

The eyrie

If Violante had ever known the name of Rodrigo Salazzo, a thorn in Altamura's side in days she had only heard of, she had forgotten. By the time she saw him she needed no telling that he was dangerous; his actions had already told her.

She first heard the hoofbeats on the turf as she was looking up under her hand watching her merlin's stoop, and the dazzle was still in her eyes when she heard cries and grunts and the clash of swords, and felt the bridle pulled as her horse was dragged round. The next moment someone had vaulted up behind her and clasped her, hard, crushing her arms to her body so that she could hardly struggle and scarcely breathe. Her horse was urged forward into a gallop and her yell was jerked from her throat and lost.

Not until later did she see his face. They had ridden hard, even with the horse bearing a double burden, for as long as the path was practicable at speed; and had then wound up a precipitous and devious way among rocks and clinging trees, and she was exhausted with attempts to struggle, with fear and with anger by the time they reached where they were going. By then, help was far to seek — those who crowded to watch them riding in were there to jeer and applaud, not to help her.

Earlier on, she had thought that if only her captor had tried to muffle her shouts she would certainly have bitten his fingers to the bone. She doubted this when she saw him, and not just because he was pulling off gold-stitched gauntlets.

The eyes were dark under hooded lids, with as much compassion or human understanding in them as her hawk's. Their glance ranged over her now as though looking for flaws in her beauty. She stood, doing her utmost not to seem shaken by her ride, by her situation, by her presence in this room into which she had been pushed with no ceremony. She tried to believe his glance assessed only the value of her clothes and jewels.

It was a handsome, brooding face, proud, somehow self-absorbed and discontented. When he turned to throw his cap on the chest she saw the broken nose, the strong chin. His hair, like Galeotto's, was growing thin and, without his velvet cap, showed a high forehead and streaks of grey in the dark locks. The hands were broad, short-fingered and curiously coarse. She could still feel their brutal grip. The doublet he wore open, on an embroidered shirt not quite clean, was almost absurdly brilliant, a coat of many colours, of rainbow jewels and gold brocade, too showy even for a prince.

'Do you know who I am?' She was relieved that her voice did not tremble, but her anger grew as he did not at once reply, taking his time, plucking absently at the gloves and staring at her under level brows.

'What if I do?' The words were offhand, almost indistinct as though he could not be troubled to articulate. 'What can you do about it, your Grace?'

'What you can do is to remember that my husband will reward you if you escort me back to him unharmed. And punish you if you do not.' As she ended, she wished she had not added the last few words; they made him smile.

'*Punish* me . . .' One short-fingered hand turned and moved on the air as if in search of adequate words. 'Punish Rodrigo Salazzo?' He glanced round at the bare walls, at the leather curtain drawn across the loggia, and went to tug back the curtain with a screech of rings. 'See out there, your Grace?' He leant one forearm on the wall and stared out, as if in unwilling admiration. She did not move to look. 'My mountain. My people.' He swung to her in quite serious enquiry. 'Who is going to come and *punish* me?'

She remembered the crossing of the river and the steep ascent. She was not even in Altamura. From the direction they had taken, this might not even be Borgo but Venostan territory. That meant Ippolyto, once he had found out where she was – and how would he do that? – would have to protest first to Vincenzo. Suppose Vincenzo came to know it was she who had caused his fort to be blown up?

'Let me go at once.'

Thank Heaven it had come out as a command, not a plea. She held her back straight and looked at him with all her fierce fury, gripping her skirt with both hands as though ready to turn and leave on the spot. He made no move from his negligent pose, one hand on the wall, but looked at her thoughtfully, almost as if considering compliance.

'At once?' The muted, slow voice brought out the words in a parody that showed how feeble they were. 'Before we have drunk wine together? Celebrated our meeting?' He shook his head as though disappointed in her, and thrust away from the wall with a suddenness and a shout that sent her an involuntary step back. '*Wine!*'

The door opened at once. A man hurried in, flagon in

one hand, cups in the other. A second man came after, with a silver-gilt dish. She did not look at them, but could smell sweetmeats. These were all set out on a painted chest that stood at the foot of the bed. This, with its closed green curtains, dominated the room.

The men, bowing to Rodrigo, staring at her, retreated and shut the door.

'Come, your Grace.' He filled the two gilt cups and held one out. 'Let's drink to our better acquaintance.'

Looking at him, smiling, his glittering doublet gaudy-bright against the curtains' dark green, Violante thought of how safe she had felt, in her own duchy and almost at home; and she wished with all the intensity of her being that Sigismondo could discover where she was.

It was too late for any of Sigismondo's salves. The boy spent what remained of his life in words almost too faint to be heard even to Sigismondo's ear close to his lips. Benno and Poggio, crouched on the rim of the gulley above, could only watch. Even Biondello forbore exploration of the stream to come and sit, quietly, head on one side, as though he tried to fathom human tragedy.

The boy ceased to murmur. Sigismondo stayed for a moment, still listening, then moved his head to the boy's chest to listen there. He sat back on one heel, put a hand to the neck under the bloodstained curls, and sighed. Benno and Poggio took off their caps and crossed themselves while Sigismondo, bowed head shining in the sun, said a Latin prayer.

It occurred to Benno that whoever killed the poor boy might still be about, but no: if they'd carried off the Duchess, they wouldn't wait. Sigismondo, after the 'Amen', and after covering the body with the boy's own cloak, stood back and looked all round.

'There'll be more dead. There's no time to see to them. It must be done later.'

'Mayn't they be still alive?' Poggio had none of Benno's instilled caution about questioning Sigismondo, who shook his head and came climbing swiftly out of the gulley. As he made for his horse he said over his shoulder, 'We've no time to lose. Let's not waste the lives they gave.'

Benno tucked Biondello into his jerkin and helped Poggio up to the pillion. His quick survey showed him no other bodies. What had become of the Duchess's people? Why hadn't they protected her? What had that poor boy told Sigismondo?

'What did he say to you?' Thank God for Poggio. Sigismondo was leaning from the saddle and casting about to study the ground, but he answered.

'He knew hardly more than you do.' He set off up the hill among young trees and Benno wheeled to follow. They were riding away from Altamura city.

Sigismondo pointed into the sky. A hawk hovered on the wing, observing. 'That too will die when its jesses catch on some branch. We're looking for something like it, in human form and wild, that preys on travellers.'

'Robbers?'

Sigismondo rode, still looking down, and did not at once answer. Not until they came to a shoulder of the hill and could look up through a river valley did he stop and, peering ahead, indicate a distant crag dark against the brilliant sky.

'That's where we'll try. That's the eyrie. Roccanera.'

Benno, bent over his horse's neck as they set off along a high ledge, was not wholly delighted at the thought of meeting human birds of prey. For a moment he saw an eagle face, man-size.

Now they were going down towards the river, and going fast. He hoped Poggio had a good hold. If robbers had got the Duchess, what use were the three of them going to be?

It was hours later when this was explained to him, when dusk dimmed everything around, when they had left their weary horses by a stream below and had climbed to a little hollow among boulders at the foot of Roccanera itself. His stomach rumbled, his clothes were still damp from fording the river and he longed for a chance to sleep; but from what Sigismondo was saying, sleep must wait some time. At least Sigismondo had produced a flask of wine, some bread and cheese from his saddlebag. Benno had burrowed inside his shirt and contributed some radishes he had stocked up with. They ate, and Poggio rubbed his legs.

Biondello had caught something, even smaller than he was and evidently not expecting him, and was chewing industriously at Benno's feet.

Then they climbed again.

They heard Roccanera before they saw it. Not every day did a duchess come into their hands and a huge carousal had got under way. Benno, peering between the roots of a pine and a boulder soft with moss, could see the light of a bonfire. A few more yards of climb and Sigismondo, breathing 'Lie here,' left them for a while. When he called them up, he was crouched over an inert man in a hollow among the rocks. The moon had risen and there was a slight red glow from the bonfire. Sigismondo held up a flask, but the smell of wine was enough to say why the sentinel had not been ready; Benno thought it wouldn't have made a great deal of difference had he been alert as a watchdog, against Sigismondo.

'Now. Look carefully.'

Benno and Poggio surveyed the eyrie. The bonfire glow showed a sort of village – huts of daub, of brushwood, little huts of log, a range of thatched stables along one side, and above the square a long, higher building with a tiled roof, a balcony across the front, and steps slanting up its rocky base to the door. Sigismondo, pointing, gave his orders.

The populace was round the fire, some dancing, most sitting or lurching about, with a pipe or two producing music at odds with the voices.

Benno and Poggio began to make their way down the hillside behind the stables. Sigismondo took a circuitous route above.

He came upon no more sentries. It might be wondered there were any on a night of such festival, and no doubt the man Sigismondo had found would wonder, when he woke, at the power of the wine. Sigismondo went softly down the slope among useful tree roots that gripped the earth among the rocks, and stepped onto the tiles of the main building's roof. With care he slowly worked his way to the ridge, among houseleeks and lichen tufts, and lay there and looked over.

Horses were stepping, hesitantly and with tossing heads, out of the stables. As he watched, some came out in a rush, driven no doubt by Benno's urging hand. Fire flowered behind them, tentative for a second in the thatch then flaring in a great burst high in the air, crackling, snapping the rafters. The horses screamed and scattered. Revelry broke apart in dismay, in terror, as the horses trampled through the crowd and drunken men blundered in the lurid smoke trying to make sense of a world gone demented.

Sigismondo went cat-footed down the front slope of

the roof and crouched there. He had not long to wait. A figure in a doublet that echoed the flames came out on the balcony below and, leaning, shouted at the throng. Sigismondo dropped.

Rodrigo, alerted by God knows what sense, half turned and his knife came into his hand as he was felled. They grappled, and rolled under the leather curtain, a shifting conundrum of wrestling holds, Rodrigo trying to wrench Sigismondo's hand from his throat. They rolled on the floorboards, the uproar from outside almost drowning their sounds of struggle. The knife fell bloodied from Rodrigo's hand. He was uppermost but on his back, Sigismondo's arm round his neck.

The Duchess Violante, dishevelled, her dress torn, her hair streaming loose, pounced on the knife; her lips tight and her eyes wide, she stabbed Rodrigo, two-handed, in the chest. He went lax in Sigismondo's grip. She could not get the knife out or she would have stabbed him again, but it stuck in the grimy folds of his shirt as Sigismondo rolled him over. There were deep scorings of nail marks on his cheek and on his neck, and his lip was cut.

Sigismondo was hauling the showy doublet off Rodrigo's back. Violante, staring in fury still at the body, breathed harshly and did not move. Then, as Sigismondo put on the doublet, she glanced at him and, as if to ready herself for the next action, began to gather her hair and coil it.

'Leave it, your Grace. We have to get out through that,' he gestured at the tumult outside. 'He is going to carry you out.'

He did not wait for her reply. There were shouts beyond the inner door, and someone hammered on it. Sigismondo had picked up Rodrigo's cap and pulled it on; now he heaved up Rodrigo's body and flung it onto the bed, tossing the lamp on top of it. There was a flare of burning oil and black smoke rose, the green curtains caught; it became a pyre. Sigismondo swept the Duchess into his arms and put her across his shoulder, draping a handful of her hair over his head and face. He unbarred the door and plunged down the staircase past a frantic servant, who followed them; he found the main door open and came out on the platform at the head of the steps outside.

Horses still wheeled and screamed in the great courtyard among the huts and hovels; gledes from the stables drifted down, smoke eddied and flowed, and men and women stumbled, howled and fought. A strong voice from the top of the steps came in a roar.

'Out of here! Downhill, downhill! Go!'

They looked up and saw above the smoke the figure in the bright doublet carrying their chief prize. His voice, his gesture gave them ability to move. They began to swarm away down the hill as he descended the steps, wreathed in his captive's hair, and was lost to sight.

157

Chapter Twenty-four

The woman at the ford

Mario Marietti had known that the Duke would come himself to inspect the fort's damage. Had there been a priest to hand, Marietti would have made his final Confession first. In the time it took for the messenger whom he sent to reach Venosta with news of the explosion, and the time it took for the Duke to reach the border in response — which was sooner than they hoped — Marietti endeavoured to find out what had caused the disaster. The destruction, however, had been thorough and he was left with his first theory: accident. By some unforeseen freak of nature, the night breeze must have carried a spark from the men's fires which had somehow, against all likelihood, found its way to the powder store. It was flat impossible to suggest to the Duke that a bolt of lightning had descended to fry the fort. That would seem to imply God's judgement on the Duke's venture, an idea that in its turn would lead rapidly to experiencing the Duke's judgement in its worst form. Marietti had thought of flight but, a conscientious man and perhaps a little unworldly, he did not see that he had done anything for which he could be blamed.

'Your engineer approved everything yesterday. He looked at the powder kegs very carefully and said the site was the best that could be arranged.'

'My engineer?' The Duke's eyes were enough to make a man's skin crawl: black and burning. He had not raised his voice or berated anyone since his arrival, but Marietti was under no illusion. He was searingly angry. They stood now on the gravel bank watching as the men tried to lever up the cannon that was making its own minor alteration to the river's flow, having dug its snout into the riverbed in a spew of gravel. '*My* engineer?'

'Your Grace? The man you sent to inspect the work after you left yesterday. The tall man with the shaven head. He was going to Venosta to report to you.'

The Duke's riding whip flickered by his side, making a small dry noise for a moment like a snake. 'And he shall. Before he dies he shall tell me everything.' This he said as though to himself; and then he turned to Marietti once more. 'He showed you my seal, this engineer? To warrant his inspection?'

Marietti had the chill impression that his future, which had blown up with the fort, was now coming down around his ears.

At about the hour when the Duke of Venosta was contemplating the remains of his fort, the Duke of Altamura was faced with far worse news. The captain of the guard escorting the Duchess had almost reached the city when it was borne in on him that the Duchess ought to have joined them by now. He thought it best to halt and send men back to remind her Grace with all possible tact that the Duke would be meeting them at the city gates, or if he were still unable, through illness and grief, there would be his representatives and the notables and loyal crowds of Altamurans. It did not cross the captain's mind that any ill could come to the Duchess in her husband's own domains.

160

It was only when his men took so long to return that he became anxious. Had her Grace been thrown from her horse? But her people would have sent word. Still some premonition made him half expect what happened – his men riding back without the Duchess and with bodies across their saddlebows. She had been snatched – by brigands, it must be – and those few who had been with her were all dead. How was he to tell the Duke?

In fact, Ippolyto had made the effort to leave his sickbed and come to the gates to greet his wife; he was waiting, still patient, by the time the captain arrived with the appalling news. He had lost a difficult and hardly known daughter, and was sorry. Now came this news of a passionately loved wife. Ippolyto ignored his fever and fatigue and the protests of his physician and organised search parties to scour the countryside. As night fell, a band headed by the Duke, with torches and heavily armed, set out across country. At about this time Sigismondo, Benno and Poggio were crouched in undergrowth below Roccanera, preparing also to rescue the Duchess but with the advantage of knowing where she was. Rodrigo Salazzo was still alive, and spending his last hours as probably he would have wished.

Duke Ippolyto, although in pain with furious impatience, had summoned his huntsmen to join him. They were not, like the Duchess's estringer, for sport, but for tracking from the scene of the attack. Forced to camp and attempt to rest during the dark of the night, as soon as there was light before sunrise the Duke's huntsmen were casting about over the trampled ground above the ravine. One came to say that the trail led towards the river, upstream, towards Venosta.

Until then, strangely enough, Ippolyto had not thought of Salazzo. Never had the brigand invaded

Altamura. From the wilds of the Venostan mountains he had contented himself with preying on a trade route to the north. Ippolyto had despised Vincenzo for suffering this ulcer on his flank, though storming the crag would have been hard. Now he cursed him. To enter Venosta with an armed band, even to rescue his wife, could be called an act of war if Vincenzo chose. How many men were there at Roccanera? How well was it fortified? And most dreadful of all, would Salazzo kill Violante if he was attacked?

He sat his horse, leaning stiff-armed on the pommel and beginning to feel the sweat and trembling cold of his fever come over him again. He heard the subdued voices of his men and the sound of the river idling past in the shallows. Then he heard a hail, and raised his head, to stare.

Two horses were fording the river at this shallow stretch with two riders on each. The Duke's eyes skimmed over one, burdened with a small man and a dwarf, and fixed on the other, where a tall man rode with a woman before him.

The woman was waving.

Chapter Twenty-five

A love song

Misfortunes are definitely easier to bear if someone can be blamed for them. The citizens of Altamura were in a quandary because they did not know whom to blame. The misfortunes that had befallen their Duke and therefore themselves were various, and the naturally disaffected were inclined to blame the Duke in spite of all logic. Among these were the young men who attended the classes in rhetoric and philosophy given by Polidoro Tedesco, said to have tutored the Duke before his succession but scarcely needing such a recommendation; among Humanists his name was respected not only here but as far away as Rome. His pupils contended that those who wield authority attract evil, since authority itself is evil; therefore the Duke had brought on himself the loss of his daughter and now, it seemed, of his wife. A tyrant must be prepared to suffer more than should an ordinary subject. Flaws in this conclusion were not pointed out by their teacher; by definition a teacher might be unwilling to examine how much respect was due to authority.

Most Altamurans who had seen the Duke, pale, ill and distraught, ride out by torchlight on the search, were fiercely concerned for him. Duke Ippolyto, handsome, generous and not known to possess any vices that could distress his subjects, was popular. His second marriage, to the widowed Violante, daughter of the Duke of Rocca, was particularly approved as it had resulted in an heir, still in his cradle but reported to be in lusty health. The Duchess, beautiful and spirited, was an object of Altamuran pride and her abduction was deeply resented. Robbers might be to blame, but the Altamurans also muttered darkly about Galeotto of Borgo or Vincenzo of Venosta. Of course Galeotto could have seized her in Borgo, but might there not be subtlety in waiting until she'd left it? As for Vincenzo, that impertinent fort-building was bad enough and the accident that punished it was hilariously just, but such impertinence might have been taken further by such a man, and possession of a neighbour's wife might give a certain edge in the rivalry between the two states. Of course, when the stories about Vincenzo's wife were considered, he might not care to bring another woman into the palace even as prisoner.

In Ippolyto's palace, Violante's capture desolated many. One was the Nurse, who arrived home with the train and their dreadful news and hurried at once to the nursery where she alarmed her small charges, little Lady Camilla and Lord Andrea in his cradle, by weeping over them as if they were already motherless. She was at least able to relieve her feelings by scolding the nursemaids for not doing precisely what she would have done when the little girl suffered colic; and the scolding redoubled when she found the child had been allowed to eat plums.

Someone who had no such outlet for his feelings, and could only turn his distress inward, was the Lord Tebaldo, cousin to Violante. He lived here because she had befriended him on his father's death. Crippled from birth and in almost permanent pain, he took hardly any part in court life but spent most of his time in Ippolyto's splendid library, reading and cataloguing the manuscripts the Duke already possessed and those bought by his agents in their searches abroad. Propped with cushions in his chair-couch, and examining the detail of an illuminated manuscript or deciphering an ancient Greek or Roman holograph, he could forget the slights and inconveniences of daily life and even his own pain. He descended to the library on his chair hoist as usual that morning, but he left his couch to limp up and down the long room until he was exhausted and had to sink down again, tormented by fear for the only person he knew to care for him.

There was, therefore, a frenzy of rejoicing when Ippolyto returned in triumph, bearing Violante with him. Citizens rushed into the streets and to their windows and balconies, shouting, banging pans, some singing a ragged *Te Deum*, the yell of *Viva!* above all, so that Tebaldo staggered from the library to a loggia to look down into the street, and rejoiced to be deafened by palace trumpeters giving a fanfare of welcome. Nurse screamed with joy and hugged the little girl. Even the baby beat the air and crowed, and Tebaldo went back to the library and wept.

The palace was alive with chatter and with preparations for wholesale rejoicing. The *maestro di casa* ordered a banquet to be set in train, confident that one would be called for. Orders were sent to the gardens for green branches to make garlands; a page carrying the front handle of a wicker basket full of ornamental shields slipped on the stairs and rode the basket down the stairs and across the hallway among courtiers assembled for an audience of formal greeting to their Duke and Duchess.

Various stories were already in circulation about the event itself, the favourite being that the Duke had engaged in mortal combat with a bandit chief and snatched the Duchess from his vile grasp. Everyone was agog to know the real details and there was an undertow of indiscreet speculation about what precisely the Duchess might have suffered before her rescue, but it was the Duchess's bearing which gave the lie to those who would have liked to believe the worst; a woman to whom the worst had happened would inevitably look beaten, humiliated. No suffering was evident in the Duchess's face or carriage. She looked radiantly undamaged as she paced through the palace with her hand on her husband's. The Duke had obviously recovered miraculously from his fever and regarded his restored wife as if he could not see enough of her. A man paced behind the Duchess, one whose presence baffled many, a man wearing what was universally recognised as the chain of gold birds and emerald leaves which the Duke had been wearing when he left, a chain worth at least a house in town and a villa, with lands, in the country. This man, tall, well-built, with shaven head and in scuffed and dusty black, was quickly whispered about by the Duchess's ladies and others who had been to Borgo. He had saved the Duchess's life there already from attacks by the Malgardo family. Was it for this he had been rewarded? The Duchess's attendants had not seen him, his deplorable servant or Poggio the dwarf since the night after the Duchess had caught sight of Vincenzo's obnoxious fort. By the time they reached the private apartments, Sigismondo had been declared to be a renegade priest, a condottiere, in love with the Duchess, a son of the Pope, master of a Levantine fleet, a Venetian, and a Muscovite. Here was Poggio, strutting and throwing kisses to right and left, and the servant, his clothes sooty and more crumpled and frayed than ever, clasping a bright-eyed grey woolly dog. Poggio was about to find himself in great demand as a source of satisfactory information.

The Duke was discovered to have no wish for a public celebration as yet. He and the Duchess paused at the chapel for a brief thanksgiving, but he was now aware of the fatigue of the journey, the strain of his fears, and the weakness from his late illness. He dismissed the crowd, all except his chief counsellor Bonifaccio Valori, and Sigismondo, and he shut himself in the small audience chamber, a room opalescent with pale marble, veined and clouded, its windows open upon the sunlit distance, the sound of the river just audible from below as it washed the foot of the castle walls.

Ippolyto, in his great carved chair, held Violante's hand as she sat beside him. He was silent, collecting himself for a moment or two while Bonifaccio Valori regarded Sigismondo. How could a man who looked like a bravo − those strong muscles of the neck, that head like a wrestler's − how could the face of such a man also hold subtlety enough for an ambassador? He did look like one who could well have helped the Duchess's father to find out the murderer of his wife, as Bonifaccio was aware he had done. Could he help Duke Ippolyto to find the murderer of his daughter?

The Duke, too, was studying Sigismondo as he spoke. 'What you have done for her Grace puts us for ever in your debt.'

Sigismondo bowed acknowledgement but did not speak. Bonifaccio thought: Yes, a diplomat; it would be mistaken modesty to disclaim the importance of such an action.

'So we ask more of you, as is the way of princes,' said Ippolyto. 'As to Prince Galeotto, do you think him free of blame? Could he have killed my daughter? In a fit of rage? Her Grace,' his hand caressed the one beneath his, 'told me as we came of his mistresses; of the bracelets he gave to my daughter and also to one of them.' A curl of his mouth showed what he thought of this, and Bonifaccio made a faint gesture of distaste. 'Might her death have occurred in a quarrel, a struggle?'

Sigismondo did not reply at once, but looked downward, considering. Bonifaccio thought that he must well know what an affirmative must lead to. Duke Ippolyto would call the Prince to account for his daughter's death; war must follow if Sigismondo nodded his head. But he shook it.

'Your Grace, I do not think his Highness personally was to blame. He did quarrel with her. It was heard. But, unless he had an assassin ready to hand to murder his bride,' the lift of Sigismondo's shoulder and the tone of his voice indicated what he thought of this, 'she did not die because of anything he did.'

'By your Grace's leave.' Bonifaccio Valori felt that a question was being begged here and must be put. 'Could not one of the ladies concerned have hired the assassin, if assassin there was? What makes you, sir, confident that it *was* an assassin?'

'Because, my lord, he tried to kill me when it was known that I was, as his Highness commanded me, looking for the murderer.'

Valori inclined his head a little to one side and smiled. A bear is an animal notorious for giving no clue of its mood in an apparently amiable appearance, and Valori was a rotund man with very sharp eyes. 'You'll understand me, sir, if I say that a man might have personal reasons for trying to kill you. Can you be positive that this attempt upon your life was because of your investigations into her Highness's death?'

Sigismondo smiled broadly. 'It is true, my lord, that there are some who would be relieved at my absence from this world but,' he became serious, 'although I can't swear to it, I believe the man who tried to kill me — twice — was the one who killed the Princess. Also I believe the lady whom he killed just before we left Borgo was his accomplice.'

'His accomplice?' The Duke leant forward, his hand closing hard on Violante's so that she glanced at him. 'What lady?'

'One of the Prince's mistresses, your Grace.'

'Leonora or Zima?' The Duchess had listened to her ladies' talk. She turned to her husband. 'Zima had the bracelets, but Leonora saw your daughter last in the pavilion. It was she who came to say she couldn't wake her, so I went—' She grimaced suddenly and snatched her hand free, putting the back of it to her mouth. She seemed to live again the spasm of horror that had made her cast her strangled stepdaughter down the slope below the pavilion. Sigismondo spoke.

'The Lady Leonora, your Grace. It may be that she administered a sleeping draught; I found the smell of it in the Princess's winecup. It made her an unconscious victim for the man whose tracks were below the pavilion.'

The Duke frowned. He regarded Sigismondo while his hand reached again for Violante's, and she gave it him. 'Unconscious. Thanks be to God.' He crossed himself. 'If this Leonora was his accomplice, what made him kill her afterwards?'

Valori held up his hand to forestall Sigismondo's reply, and offered, 'Your Grace, I see what is meant.' His slight smile and his tone made it clear that for him the puzzle of the Princess's death was a game of the mind alone, without involvement of emotion. 'Take it that the Lady Leonora fell under suspicion, and were questioned, she would without doubt have betrayed the name of the one who employed both her and the assassin. Once the assassin had failed to kill the questioner,' he bent his head towards Sigismondo, 'he must eliminate the one who might be questioned. Am I not right?'

'It is precisely what I concluded, my lord.'

Valori was pleased, and gave again his slight lopsided smile.

The Duke said, 'But this does not tell us whom she might have betrayed.'

'No, your Grace. He was successful in preventing that.'

Ippolyto, a little impatiently, tapped a scroll on the table at his side. 'This letter from Prince Galeotto: he tells me that he is sure the Princess's death was part of some revenge on him and on his; that at her funeral there was an attempt on his life, which you foiled; and even before that, at the moment of his meeting my daughter an attempt of some kind was made, by . . . *slingshot*?' His voice suggested that such a method added vulgarity to outrage. Poison or the knife might be the death of sovereigns, but to be brought down like Goliath was offensively plebeian.

'Your Grace, that first attack was, to my mind, aimed more at her Grace or the Princess than at his Highness. Also, the shot at the funeral was from such an angle, I discovered later, that it must have been meant for her Grace. The Prince could not be seen from where the man had stood.'

Ippolyto raised Violante's hand and pressed his lips to it. 'I have not recompensed you enough, I find.' He paused. 'But the man who slung the stone, whom you

170

killed by the river, my captain tells me – Raimondo Malgardo, whose body hangs with his brothers' by the heel at the city gate – surely he could have been the one who killed my daughter. He cursed us root and branch, and swore revenge, when I exiled them. He might have seized his chance in Borgo to make me suffer from afar.'

'I don't deny, your Grace, that Malgardo may have tried to kill the Princess as she was entering the city; the fall of the effigy was caused by his weapon; but Malgardo was not the man who tried to kill me.'

Bonifaccio Valori stirred. 'Where were you, sir, when this man attacked you?'

The dark eyes turned coolly to him. 'In the house of the Lady Leonora.'

'Were you alone with her?'

'I was.'

'At night?'

'At night, and she received me in her bedchamber, my lord. But no, I do not think jealousy was his motive.'

Valori shrugged, spread his hands and directed a significant glance at the Duke.

'What are your grounds for thinking so?' The Duke did not discount Valori's idea but he was impressed once again, as he had been at Rocca three years or more ago, by the man before him. Not difficult to imagine a lover wanting to rid himself of such a rival – much harder to suppose it would be a simple task. If this Sigismondo had not killed the man, that man must be strong and skilful indeed.

'Partly, your Grace, because of the means he used. Malgardo was an expert at slingshot—'

'No more than you when you killed him!' The Duchess seemed exhilarated by the memory and her husband glanced at her fondly before he turned once more to Sigismondo.

'You mean, Malgardo would have used a slingshot to kill – to kill her Highness. Might she have been in a position he could not reach? A man who uses slingshot for preference still has hands to strangle. Did the man who attacked you try to strangle you?' He looked speculatively at Sigismondo's neck, that wrestler's neck his counsellor had already noted.

'After a fashion, your Grace, but from some distance.' Sigismondo searched the pouch at his belt and brought out the bolas he had taken from his own neck. 'With this.'

Bonifaccio came forward to take the weapon from Sigismondo and, examining it as he came, brought it to the Duke. 'I've heard of this, your Grace. It is called the bolas. But her Highness was not killed by such means.'

'As with slingshot, the method was not suitable.'

'So, indeed,' Bonifaccio pressed the point with satisfaction in his reasoning, 'this man you saw was no more likely than Malgardo to have killed her Highness.'

'Nothing is certain in this world, my lord.'

There was a note of constraint and weariness in the deep voice and the Duke heard it. He was reminded of what this man and the woman at his side had undergone so recently. As Valori took up the argument, Ippolyto interrupted.

'My lord, we must be brief. Her Grace needs rest. Sigismondo too, I am sure.' As the man bowed, he went on, 'One thing only. The one you believe to be the murderer of my daughter is still at large. If it is not possible to tell who could have hired him, may he not be a present danger to us?' He drew Violante's arm through his as he waited for Sigismondo's reply.

'Your Grace, it may be so.' Sigismondo's face was sombre; and unexpectedly, Violante pulled her hand from her husband's and covered her face. She took a sobbing, shuddering breath and Ippolyto put his hands on her shoulders, looking at her in horrified remorse. It measured what she had endured, that this woman of courage and spirit should so give way. He would protect her. Here in this palace in his own city no harm should come to her. He would hire Sigismondo to be her special bodyguard when she went in the city — a man who seemed invulnerable. All would be well.

Unseen, Sigismondo lightly curled the fingers of his left hand, cupping the palm so that the slow trickle of blood inside his sleeve should not drip to the marble floor.

Away on the borders of Altamura, a man with a handsome, weatherbeaten face, and a mole at the corner of his mouth, urged his horse forward but without haste. There was plenty of time. He had completed one mission and been well rewarded for it. The next task might not be easy but he was confident of achieving it. As he rode, lounging in the saddle, he sang in his light, pleasant tenor. It was a love song.

Chapter Twenty-six

A knock at the door

Sigismondo had concealed the extent of his wound. Benno had to conceal his shock at the sight of it. He had waited outside the audience room, regarded with distaste and frustration by a strew of palace servants longing to hear more of the Duchess's rescue from someone so qualified to know as the rescuer's servant. They had initially plied him with questions, but Benno had turned on them a face of such vacancy that they quite soon gave up. When Sigismondo emerged, they fell back. This was not a man of whom one asked questions.

The *maestro di casa*, alerted by one of them, hurried from the next room to bow before the Duke's guest and do him the honour of himself showing him to the room found for him.

It was not a large room, but airy and modern, with panelling in light wood up to the coffered ceiling whose beams were painted and patterned in gold. Two servants were still busy clearing the painted chest at the bed foot; a courtier less high in the Duke's favour had been demoted. The *maestro di casa*'s gold-tipped wand indicated the door and they all but dropped their armfuls of clothes in their haste to obey. When the *maestro di casa* had ascertained that food and wine would be welcome, he bowed himself out and Sigismondo sat down quite abruptly on the bed. He took a cloth from his scrip and wiped his hand, holding it so that no drop touched the bed's pale linen cover or curtains. Benno had frozen.

'Water, Benno.'

Looking round, Benno saw in a corner a majolica cistern above a basin in a tripod stand with a pail beneath it. He filled the basin and brought it carefully to set it on the chest, where Sigismondo had unrolled his scrip of herbs. Benno smelt woodruff, like new-mown hay, saw leaves of plantain and hyssop, thyme, a clove of garlic. He had learned that all these were specific against a wound's becoming putrid, but some needed hot water to make a poultice.

'I'll go—'

A knock on the door, and it opened to admit two servants, one with a can of hot water which he set down by the majolica pail, the other with a large dish crowded with two cold chickens, a bowl of apricots and a loaf of bread. A child followed with wine. The *maestro di casa* knew how to treat the Duke's guests.

When the servants had gone, with covert glances at the forbidding figure in black with the Duke's chain round his shoulders and the scrip of herbs mysteriously displayed beside him, Benno sat about the tricky business of removing the black jerkin and blood-soaked shirt without causing his master too much pain. In this he took unnecessary care, and Sigismondo was more brusque.

Rodrigo Salazzo had made a mistake, understandable at the time, over the location of Sigismondo's heart. He had lightly scored the ribs but cut more deeply into the arm, and the torn strip of cloth Sigismondo had applied soon after was soaked through. Benno, cleaning the angry wound, thought of the ride back to Altamura; and as he wrung out the cloth he glanced at the gold links of the chain, with their emerald leaves, strewn across the bed. Did such a reward make up for endurance without a sign? For taking risks that brought one far too near a grave?

He sniffed the herbs in the hot water. 'He nearly got you then,' he remarked as he made up the poultice.

Sigismondo hissed as the hot cloth met the wound. Then he smiled. *'Nearly* is not what counts, Benno. Hey, who gets *buried* is what counts.'

'Buried isn't what he got, was it?'

'A funeral pyre like that of the ancients. His men think him still alive. It's going to puzzle them when he never appears and news reaches them the Duchess is home in Altamura.'

'If they caught a good look at her when he was taking her to Roccanera, I bet they'll think she killed him. I'd say the Duchess could be handy with a dagger.' Benno was busy unrolling a strip of clean linen round the arm. Sigismondo's face was noncommittal. Following his own train of thought, Benno remembered, 'I meant to tell you. When Poggio and I was listening to see was the stables empty, so we could nip in and turn the horses out and start that fire, two of them was talking.' He fell silent, involved in the intricacy of knot-tying.

'I never thought they were dumb.'

Benno glanced up and grinned, and set to work on the lesser wound. 'They were gabbing all right. A lot of it was boasting about Rodrigo and how he could do anything he liked and no one could stop him and now he'd got a duchess for his whore − I had to hang onto Poggio then, I can tell you, or he'd have been at them premature − and they said what a bit of luck he'd been tipped off she was on her way.'

177

Benno stepped back to admire his handiwork and nearly put his foot in the basin. Sigismondo rolled up his scrip of herbs thoughtfully, fending off Biondello who had jumped on the bed excited by the smell of chicken and willing to investigate everything for edibility.

'Mm-mm. Perhaps Malgardo and his brothers had more men with them who got away.' He scooped Biondello from the dish and gave him to Benno. 'The captain of the guard assured the Duchess his men saw no one running off beyond the hill except the one they speared, yet . . . It's possible to stay still and not be seen if men expect someone to be running away.'

Benno supposed Sigismondo knew this from experience.

'You think this man did get away and went to Roccanera to get Rodrigo Whatsisname to carry off the Duchess? How was he to know she'd go hawking and just have a few people with her?'

'She was flying a hawk when they attacked with slingshot. She may have said as we came up to the ford that she'd go alone, once across the river − voices carry and they were uphill from us.' Sigismondo said no more until he emerged from the opening of his shirt, fine cambric selected by Benno for court wear. As he manoeuvred his bandaged arm into the sleeve, he added, 'Your wits are showing again, Benno. Either Rodrigo knew, or he must have watched and waited in hiding, in case a chance should present itself.'

Benno was by now attending to the contents of the dish. It was some time since he had eaten and the cold chicken was delicious, stuffed with spiced wheat. The wine was a happy surprise, a quality he didn't often get to drink, a wine to savour. Sigismondo ate sparingly, as if the wound had deprived him of appetite. He seemed to

put more in Biondello's mouth than in his own. As
Benno chewed, and licked his fingers that tasted of thyme
and garlic from the poultice as well as of chicken, he
considered the situation.

Several people who'd wanted the Duchess dead were
dead themselves, thanks mostly to his master; but the
man who'd tried to kill Sigismondo was still alive.
Perhaps that man had really been hired only to kill the
Princess and wouldn't bother them any more. Benno was
just starting to say this when a knock on the door
heralded an imposing figure.

Chapter Twenty-seven

Violent intentions?

You noticed the eyes: a sallow, hollow-cheeked face was dominated by the dark, clever eyes under thick eyebrows, the mouth sardonic, the hair showing grey under the wine-red cap that covered the ears. The gown was of fine red cloth and furred despite the summer heat. To leave off fur that showed status would be as crazy as for an animal to shed its distinctive skin. A boy, obsequious in his shadow, carried a wooden case he set down on the chest next to the dish, and was then dismissed. It was obvious from all this that here was a physician, and one of the grandest sort. Benno had scrambled to his feet, dropping a piece of chicken skin Biondello took care of.

'Sir Sigismondo? I am Master Valentino, physician to his Grace. Her Grace directed me to enquire after your wound and to see if I could be of assistance in its treatment.' He sniffed the air as he advanced, and Benno could bet he diagnosed instantly all the ingredients of the poultice. Sigismondo had risen in spite of the physician's admonitory gesture, and was smiling.

'I am grateful to her Grace; but I am accustomed, as a soldier, to look after the hurts I get. I cannot hope for such knowledge as yours to aid me on the field—'

'Nevertheless, as it's now offered to you free, Sir Sigismondo, you'd do well to avail yourself of it.' Master

Valentino indicated Sigismondo's shirt and made a peremptory lifting motion. 'Do you think *I* can afford to return to her Grace without a report upon your wound or an account of what I have done to alleviate the hurt you have suffered?' He folded his hands together and looked forbidding, but the crease by his mouth deepened.

Benno took the shirt Sigismondo had just put on as he took it off, and watched rather sadly as his carefully tied knots were undone so that the physician could view both the cuts. That beak of a nose came into operation again as Master Valentino sniffed the wounds as well as the poultice and laid the back of his hand against Sigismondo's skin to test for inflammation.

'Very laudable. I approve your poultice.' He summoned Benno with a wave of a ringed hand. 'Put back the bandages, fellow – clean the grease from your hands – just as they were. Now, as to the degree of fever . . .' He pushed Sigismondo down on the bed and, sitting beside him, took his wrist. After a few minutes, during which Sigismondo breathed calmly and Benno stood with the loops of bandage in his hands, Master Valentino gave his opinion. 'Excellent. You might be asleep.' He gave Sigismondo his wrist back and turned impatiently to Benno. 'Well, fellow? Don't let the air get to the wound. Do you know nothing?' His eyes focused on Benno's face and the sardonic look came back; he gave a slight shrug.

'How does her Grace?'

The black eyes turned to Sigismondo. 'She has had an ordeal, sir, the extent of which she will not speak about but at which I can guess. I have given camomile to soothe, and peony root to hang at her throat against evil dreams, as I fear her rest will be disturbed by what she has suffered.'

'Purslane to scatter on the bed?'

Sigismondo was given a very sharp look. 'Possibly, sir. And now, I shall prescribe for the inflammation.' He stood up and opened the box on the chest, surveying its contents which Benno was unable to see. Biondello had not his diffidence and ran along the bed to peer round the box's lid. 'Let me see. Perhaps agrimony. And *trigonella foenum graecum*, that will cool the blood. By your leave, Minimisse,' he tapped Biondello on the nose, and he withdrew a pace or two. Measuring drops from glass phials, which stood each clamped in its own little wooden cell, he murmured to himself, and then held out a small cup to Sigismondo. 'Take it in the hour ruled by Mercury and say two Hail Marys before and one after.'

When Sigismondo had accepted the cup and put it on the small shelf by the pillows, Master Valentino seemed in no hurry to depart. Instead, he strolled to the window whose shutters stood open on the sweet summer air. From below came voices chanting a song, and the plash of oars. A bird cut swiftly across the sky and the hum of the city sounded distantly. The palace of Altamura had once been a fortified castle, and here they were in the old part, washed at its foot by the river that divided the city. Master Valentino leant on the stone sill, sniffing the air. Benno thought that a physician's nose, trained to detect disease and obliged to spend time close to gangrene and pisspots, might particularly appreciate a holiday. The sweet air, however, seemed to remind Master Valentino of someone no longer there to enjoy it.

'The Lady Ariana – the Princess – you were there when she was found dead?'

'Shortly after.'

Master Valentino waved away a bee that was mistaking his cap for an exotic flower. 'A bad business, a bad business. It shook everyone here. Indeed his Grace has not recovered yet.' He sighed, and turned to face them, folding his hands before him again. 'The injuries of the mind and spirit can be heavier afflictions than those of the body.' He paused, then added in a casual tone, 'You have no idea, sir, who could have done a thing so dreadful?'

Sigismondo forbore to shrug, keeping his bandaged arm still. 'If I knew, the Duke would be quick to punish.'

'When she left here, she was all excitement. Volatile, sir, a temperament of fire. I had to prescribe sedatives, though I fear she poured them away and took the concoctions of that nurse of her Grace's. Who could have known to what fate she was going? Yet Tristano Valori was mourning for her from the moment the marriage was announced, as though he knew it would be her death.'

'Tristano Valori, sir? Kin to the Duke's counsellor?'

'His son. You may have heard of his father's great service to the Duke? He saved the state when the Duke's father died and there was an uprising. A mob attacked the palace. Tristano believed that his father's services merited a great reward: the hand of the Duke's daughter for Bonifaccio's son.'

'The Duke did not think so?'

'Even Bonifaccio did not think so. The alliance with Borgo was more important by far than pleasing his son. The young man had been a childhood playmate of the Princess, before she went to the convent for her education, and he said they were trothplight; although I never heard the Lady Ariana refer to it. Bonifaccio said his son would soon forget such a fancy. We were all young once! Violent in feeling, headstrong in action.' He glanced at Sigismondo as though inviting reminiscences of a past that would corroborate this. As none came, he went on, 'Love drives the most sensible of men to distraction. How then can we blame the young?'

Sigismondo hummed, which Master Valentino took for acquiescence.

'Yet the Duke was angry, and Bonifaccio even angrier, when young Tristano stabbed himself before all the court.'

Sigismondo blew softly between parted lips. 'When was that?'

'The day the Lady Ariana left. One must suppose it was intended to show he could not live without her. However, the wound, although it bled profusely, was superficial. Luckily I was there . . . I hope that if ever he is engaged in battle, young Valori will have acquired a better idea of where the heart is. You had a much narrower escape than he.'

Master Valentino inclined his head to Sigismondo, crossed the room to his box of medications, shut it and rapped on the door for his assistant to come and carry it away. 'I shall tell her Grace that you are a man blessed with luck, Sir Sigismondo. May you continue to be so.' He bowed and left the room, escorted politely as far as the door by Biondello.

Benno shut the door. He saw his master was pulling the linen bedspread back, and he came to take off Sigismondo's boots.

'D'you suppose that young man went into mourning because he *meant* something to happen to the Princess? Though you'd think he'd rather it happened before she got really married. And could he have hired an assassin?'

Sigismondo lay back, circumspectly on account of his wound. His eyes closed. He murmured, 'A son of Valori would have the money, Benno.'

Benno went to close the shutters, so that light fell only through the panes of glass above them into the shadowed room, and the sound of birds quarrelling outside was cut off. 'Anyway, why should he have her killed if he was going to kill himself? Would it be a sort of meet-me-beyond-the-grave thing?'

Sigismondo did not reply. Tiptoeing nearer, Benno decided it was not because his master thought the question superfluous but because he slept. Biondello, a dog who understood siesta, made himself comfortable by his feet.

All speculation as to the violent intentions of Tristano Valori would have to wait.

Chapter Twenty-eight

A building sight

Nuto Baccardi was not wholly pleased with the new lodger. He offered good money, it was true, and his clothes, though dark and not such as you would notice or remember, were of a quality that said he could pay. It was not the money which troubled Nuto, it was the face. It wasn't a young face or a kind face, but it had regular features if you ignored the mole above the mouth's corner; and Nuto's wife was young and giddy. He saw her look at the stranger and knew he must keep an eye on them both.

The man was a foreigner, anyway. Said he came from Rocca where the Duchess was born, but he didn't vouchsafe more than that and Nuto did not, somehow, feel able to enquire what his business was in Altamura. The money he was paying entitled him to some privacy, after all.

Nuto's wife thought that the stranger had a secret. She knew it from his face, before her husband admitted he knew so little about him. She determined she would discover his secret before he had been long in the house. No matter if he didn't respond to her glances or seem to notice when she rolled her hips walking in front of him to the door. Just give her time. She'd find out everything about him! Think of lying in his arms and caressing that mole by his mouth as he talked, of making him smile . . . It was some girl that had made him so closed up, so indifferent, had hurt him in a way that she alone could heal . . . As for Nuto, she knew that look on his face but it didn't worry her. She could lead him by the nose, that ugly, warty nose of his so unlike the stranger's thin, aquiline one. He'd never know the moment when she planted the horns on his head.

Disappointingly, the lodger would not eat with them that night. He said he had relations in the city whom he had come to see, and he would eat with them. After he had left, Nuto asked himself why, if this Lorenzo Corsini were visiting relatives, he wasn't putting up at their house. However poor a man was, he would find room for family. Nuto would make enquiries, next day, about any Corsini in Altamura. He could not say why he felt suspicious, or what he thought, but in his bones he felt that Lorenzo Corsini was bad news.

He was good news to the armourer who sold him a fine bow later that day, of properly seasoned yew, and arrows he examined with the quick skill of an expert. He looked a man who was incomplete without a weapon of some sort. Still, Nuto would have been surprised at the next transaction he engaged in. The owner of a narrow house that seemed to peer dangerously down into the river generally found difficulty in letting a room to anyone not desperate for accommodation − the fishermen gutted their catch on the rocks below and in summer the smell was apparently offensive to those less used to it than he was. He did not feel hopeful when the well-dressed stranger with the bow over his shoulder asked to see a room, but he was delighted when the man went straight to the window, looked all round at the view − impressive, as the palace across the river took up most of it − looked down at the rocks with what the cats had left of fishy entrails, and still took the room. He beat him down on the price but Stefano Cipolla had expected nothing else and assured the man it was certainly, since he asked, safe to leave his bow there along with his pack or anything else he chose to leave. Stefano had no wife, young or old, nor was he troubled that the stranger might mean mischief. Anyone who could ignore a smell that people had sworn would awaken the dead must be a good sort.

Stefano would have been in sympathy with another man having trouble with smells, although in a different city. Bono Ristoni was a rich merchant with a house in Venosta, which for two reasons he was anxious to improve. He desired to give his neighbours and friends, and more particularly his enemies, an idea of the wealth his trading in silk had brought him, for one thing. For the other, his house was unfortunately in a street within wind − an unlucky but not infrequent wind − of a tannery. He had seen his guests exchange glances when the herbs on the brazier weren't enough. He could afford a new house although land was dear, but his aged mother had announced that she was not going to move from a place she had lived in all her married life. Ristoni had to resign himself to the smell, which after all was not constant, and plan improvements that would change the look on his guests' faces and make them exclaim in wonder rather than cough surreptitiously.

To this end he was pleased to be able to employ an architect who had recently worked for the Duke himself. True, there had been some disagreement. Master Brunelli was reported to have left the palace in mid-air rather than on his feet, but then the Duke was notoriously difficult to please. Ristoni looked forward to boasting that he had employed a man who worked for princes — for Galeotto of Borgo as well — confident that his guests would conclude he had paid what only princes and dukes could afford. In fact he was having to trim his daughters' dowries a little to meet the cost, but the finished house would establish his position in Venosta and bring the suitors crowding.

The day he brought Brunelli to look over the work that had so far been done, with simply a builder to supervise, Ristoni did not know that among those working was a man already known to Brunelli. A young artist, of a temperament almost as inflammatory as Brunelli's own, had worked for him at the ducal palace and been fired by Brunelli for demanding to be set to other work than laying plaster for someone else's frescoes. He was now engaged in supervising a team taking a wall down to make an impressive double room where at last his own frescoes would flower everywhere. He, like the other men, had a damp cloth round his face against the dust, but he could still smell the tannery, and he had dust in his hair and his ears and down his neck, and the men were so preternaturally stupid that he suspected they were doing it on purpose. His temper was already at critical level when he heard that Brunelli was to be in charge of all that he did from now on. He knew, immediately, who would do those frescoes now.

Also in the house was an extraneous person who had been well instructed in quite a different role. He had arrived as soon as Brunelli arrived that morning, and he had followed him through the house as Ristoni explained the requirements. A scrawny, dark man of inconspicuous appearance, he kept behind Brunelli in every room, at his heels inspecting the tiled floor in the entrance hall, and held one end of the ferrule as Brunelli measured an arch.

He crouched to observe a piece of carving and came close as Brunelli leant from a window to assess the height of the porch below, but politely drew back as Ristoni came to look too. Ristoni supposed him to be an assistant to Brunelli; Brunelli, who hardly ever noticed people unless he was drawing them, vaguely assumed he was some hanger-on of Ristoni, invited along to give an opinion, inevitably uninformed, which he had no intention of regarding.

There was a point when Ristoni, watching the man following Brunelli as he negotiated a beam with the aplomb of a tightrope walker, thought that the drab assistant, close behind him and having trouble keeping his balance, was in some danger. He did not know that his own gaze, like a talisman, averted the danger from Brunelli himself. Duke Vincenzo had been specific, and his agent understood more than he had been told: that the Duke did not choose Brunelli should work for anyone again; and that it must appear to be an accident.

When Ristoni was called away to appease his mother in her mezzanine apartment, and Brunelli went on by himself, his shadow came closer. They had reached the stairhead. The stairs had been denuded of their confining central wall, opened up and rebuilt, and were awaiting the new modern ironwork balustrade being constructed for them. The steep height of the stairwell echoed to the hammering and trampling and, suddenly, to the overwhelming voice of Brunelli bellowing at the men stacking the peacock-tail roof tiles in the entrance hall fifty feet below. They were to keep in mind that they would pay for any single one cracked.

His ex-assistant, sweating in the cloud of dust, heard the voice and knew it. At once in his mind was the occasion when Brunelli, painting an exquisite pastoral of bathing nymphs before an admiring audience, had caught up with an uneven patch on the damp plaster and, seizing a chisel, had hacked it from the wall, berating him like an apprentice or a negligent child.

He tore the cloth from his face and rushed from the room in the direction of the hectoring voice. Bursting out at the stairhead, he saw a figure in silhouette, its arms raised as though cursing the heavens. He gave a violent push.

As it wheeled in falling with a scream that tore the ears he saw it was not Brunelli. Shaken, shaking, he executed an involuntary little dance on the rim of the landing and plunged after the man he had pushed. He caught up with him on the stacked tiles and finished what chance he had of surviving the fall. In every room men, putting down or dropping their tools or still holding them, ran to see. Ristoni sent up a prayer that it might be some expendable soul and not Brunelli who had met with an accident, and scurried out too.

He was relieved to see Brunelli peering down from the height. The stack of tiles had tipped sideways and, quite slowly in fact, cascaded to ruin. Brunelli's eyesight was excellent and he recognised one of the upturned faces as belonging to his late assistant. He made a long, derogatory noise between his lips.

'*Always* useless! My God, with so much to be done!'

Benno had never been to a philosophy lecture before, and in his experience knowledge was like money: you had to have quite a bit to start with to gain more. He would have been very pleased to gain knowledge, but as he listened to the lecture he found that, while he could make out quite a bit of sense in the words, the main drift of it was all muddled up with stuff he could not understand, some in foreign languages and some resonant of church and therefore most likely Latin.

Blocked from taking in very much by ear, he concentrated on what he could learn though his eyes. The lecturer, for a start, wasn't what you expected a scholar to be, something pale and shrivelled out of a library. This one certainly had white hair, but it framed a strong brown face, lined as though by wind and sun. He wore no spectacles such as were often clamped on the noses of scholars. Instead, his eyes were dark and piercing in the brown face, and seemed perfectly able to read from the books piled up on his desk with slips of paper marking their references, and to glare at anyone who made a noise, as when Benno at the back dropped the folder of papers he was carrying for his master. Benno scrambled to push the papers back into the folder before any helpful soul should pick them up and discover the pages blank. He could see how useful it was to look studious; quite a few of those listening had papers or books, and some were taking notes as Polidoro Tedesco spoke. Sigismondo, who might have looked out of place with his black leather jerkin and shaven head like a wrestler, seemed to belong at once when he got out a small book and took notes. Although he wrote now and then, he was as keen an observer of the lecturer's pupils as Benno was. From their seats at the back of the side of the horseshoe auditorium, there was a good view of everyone except those immediately to their front.

It relieved Benno's mind to see that they didn't all appear spectacularly intelligent. None looked as vacant as Benno was able to, but quite a few plainly found it almost as hard to follow as he did. One young man, with thick crisply wavy blond hair in the fashionable bob, sat in the front row and every so often his head would tilt slowly forward; it took a sharp nudge from his neighbours either side to wake him, and then he would gaze at the lecturer keenly and nod several times as if in agreement before drifting off again. Benno wondered why he was there; but then, if you belonged to some grand family, getting educated was part of what you were supposed to do with your time, apart from hunting and drinking and all the enjoyable bits. He'd bet the young man didn't fall asleep out hunting.

His two friends, who good-naturedly shared the duty of waking him up, looked far more as if they had the right to be there. Both were dark, one was pale with rat-like features, handsome enough but too sharp-faced for Benno, who'd had kicks and no tips from young men with faces like that. The other, curly-haired, had an olive complexion; like his friend, he kept his eyes on the lecturer and their faces had something of the same expression. Benno was reminded of people who followed a preacher from city to city, hearing the same sermons devoutly as though the very act of listening improved their souls. Perhaps these young men thought their minds were getting better all the time. Perhaps they did understand more.

'And you ask, what of religion? How does it comfort us in these troubled times?'

Benno hadn't heard anyone asking but he looked round, as the lecturer did, in case he could see who it was. No one owned up, but the lecturer continued with a grim smile, 'No comfort, my friends, for those in the Church are occupied in supplying comforts to one another. We look to the Church for guidance and what do we find? They guide each other, these monks and nuns you see so holy in their robes, so pure as they accept your offerings. They guide each other on the road to Hell.'

Polidoro Tedesco seemed more pleased than shocked by this, and gazed round with a smile which showed unexpectedly small, regular teeth like a lizard's. His audience, too, exchanged smiles, as though recognising a familiar passage and anticipating still better things. The lecturer picked up a scroll from his desk and tapped with it to emphasise his points. 'Monks and nuns, bishops and abbesses and cardinals, all human and all hypocrites. We, here, talk about the good life and discuss in what it consists. I tell you, *they lead it!* We confess our sins to them, they commit their own! Do we speak in shame of adultery and fornication and beg to be absolved? Who then absolves them when these good nuns pray with those good monks and stifle the results of their prayers? I tell you, nunneries are as full of little bones as Bethlehem in the time of Herod.'

Benno, who had heard such things said as a joke in taverns, shifted in discomfort at hearing them in a public lecture by a learned man. All round him the listeners were grinning and exchanging glances. His friends had woken up the blond young man in time for him to catch the drift and snicker obediently. If this was philosophy, thought Benno, why did Sigismondo bother to come and hear it? There must be more reasons, and they might become clear later, or they might not. Here sat Sigismondo, impenetrably grave, watching Polidoro Tedesco tap his scroll on the desk and invite admiration for his anti-clerical pronouncements. Benno knew his master to be devout, if unorthodox in his attitudes, and supposed that what they were hearing now was hardly news to him. One could never be sure of anything about Sigismondo except that he knew what he was doing.

Polidoro was speculating now on what could be done for the Church. 'These monks, these nuns,' he said, now marking his sentences with the scroll on the desk, 'what will bring them to their senses? Best for them would be if God were to abolish Purgatory. Then no one would be under their thumbs any more, paying for their prayers; they'd be forced to take up their spades again and do some honest work. Perhaps you ask: will they go back to their books again and put us poor philosophers out of business?' He paused, with his predatory grin. 'Why, no. A monk dare not overstrain his mind with study, for he fears knowledge will bring the pride of Lucifer and lead to his damnation.'

The blond was woken up again to laugh at this, and he and his friends also moved along to make way for a newcomer to sit beside them. He had ducked his head in apology to Polidoro, who merely acknowledged with a smile; Benno reckoned that this young man was the sort who could get away with things. His looks would account for a lot, but Benno had seen enough of the world to suppose that he had birth and money on his side as well. He could see the fawn-like brown eyes, the chestnut curls, the sensitive face, but also the extremely thick chain of fine gold round his throat, and the pearl and cameo brooch on his hat, worth a string of horses. No wonder his friends were reaching to pat his shoulders so lovingly, no wonder Polidoro addressed his peroration to him.

'Are we, then, to consider knowledge as leading to evil? Are we to believe with the Church that God wished to keep knowledge from us, that this very knowledge is the Devil's temptation? Is not that a device to keep us from thought, to keep us passive, agreeing to all the oppression, spiritual and temporal, that is laid upon us? Is not that what they all want? I tell you, we must listen to what the ancients teach us. Did not Virgil say: *Audaces fortuna iuvat, timidosque repellit*? If we are to be timid, we shall never grasp what should be dearer to a man than any other thing: Liberty!'

Polidoro looked round almost fiercely as his pupils beat their books and stamped. Benno had heard a few good preachers in his day, like the saintly Ambrogio of Viverra, and he reflected what a shame it was this man was so against the Church when he could have had a very good career in it. Still, he wasn't doing at all badly in his own line; many of the men, young and old, were crowding round him as he stacked his books; but he shook his head to further questions, brusquely gestured to a large Moor who gathered up his belongings, and strode away. A good actor doesn't muff his exit.

Sigismondo remained seated while the audience broke up into groups either anxious to discuss the lecture or anxious to repair to taverns or return home. As the four young men, the sleepy blond coming last with a good-natured smile, climbed the steps towards them, Sigismondo rose and, when the latecomer with the chestnut curls drew level, his friends' arms round his shoulders, the deep voice interrupted their talk.

'By your leave, Tristano Valori. A word with you.'

Chapter Twenty-nine

Still a child

'Who are you?'

If Tristano Valori did not add 'my good man', it might be because he hesitated over the adjective. Benno, deeply prejudiced in his master's favour, still knew that Sigismondo was as daunting an object as anyone was likely to run against. Tristano's friends had bunched up close to him in defence.

'Sigismondo, at your service, sir. An agent of his Grace's.'

Curiously, this did not appear to be a recommendation to the group. The tall blond gaped and glanced nervously at the others. Tristano put his chin up.

'If his Grace needs me, he can send for me. What have *you* to say to me?'

Sigismondo hummed, deprecating the tone. 'I have but just returned with her Grace's train from Borgo. I thought that as the Princess Ariana's friend you would wish to have a favour from her funeral,' the broad hand produced a ribbon of black silk, sewn with the arms of Borgo in silver, 'and to hear an account of what happened.'

What happened now was dramatic enough. Tristano Valori turned the colour of candlewax and sank downwards, fielded by the blond with unexpected speed.

He supported him with ease as he recovered but the other two rounded on Sigismondo.

'How dare you speak to him of the Lady Ariana?' Ratface had features not improved by anger. 'Have you no idea how ill he has been on her account?'

Young Valori certainly looked ill. Benno recalled the doctor's mentioning how much blood the young man had lost in his romantic effort to kill himself. He looked now as if he hadn't a lot left, and his black clothes made it worse. Sigismondo's tone was compassionate. 'Indeed, I thought he would wish to hear all he could.'

The corpse opened its eyes and found the energy to push out of the friend's helpful embrace. He looked at Sigismondo with trembling intensity.

'I wish to hear everything. *Everything*. But not here. Come to my house.'

Sigismondo bowed. As they all set off, Tristano's friends evidently understood the invitation to include them, but the young man was surprisingly firm: he would talk to Sigismondo alone. They represented to him that he was still weak from loss of blood. He pointed out that he had managed to reach the lecture safely and that the Duke's agent could certainly provide support if he should need any. This they could not deny, and they turned away towards a tavern, Ratface scowling and kicking a child in the gutter out of his way. Benno thought philosophers seemed to get thirsty and cross just like anybody.

The Valori house was worthy of the Duke's chief counsellor. Faced with large blocks of rusticated stone in the latest fashion, it also boasted a doorway flanked by Corinthian columns and surmounted by a pediment with a carved Medusa head on it, the snakes of her hair writhing gleefully above the petrifying horror of her face.

200

Benno surreptitiously made the sign against the Evil Eye as he picked up Biondello and followed across the threshold. With that thing watching you go in and out, you might easily get funny ideas about killing those you love and couldn't have.

Tristano, once in his house and away from his friends, became affable. Though very pale, he no longer looked on the point of collapse, and himself took the flagon of wine brought by a servant, filled two silver-gilt cups and handed one to Sigismondo. Benno had contrived, by exerting his genius at being nobody, to be standing by the door rather than getting relegated to a marble bench in the entrance hall. There, he concentrated on looking useful and deaf, while Tristano dismissed the servant and offered Sigismondo a velvet chair, giving a shy smile that went with the fawn-like eyes. Could this young man hire an assassin?

'Forgive my friends, sir. They've been anxious for me.' As Sigismondo made no reply but simply inclined his head, Tristano hesitated as if he would say more, but instead drank his wine. The silence lengthened and he suddenly burst out, 'You saw her? Is it known who killed her?'

A silly question, considering. If it was known, the person responsible would be hanging upside down on some city wall with important bits missing, thought Benno, but perhaps he's used to court intrigue and thinks the Duke or Prince Galeotto are biding their time, or that someone's in prison being questioned. Sigismondo gave no indication that he thought the question superfluous. He said genially, 'It is not known, sir.'

Tristano was alert enough to catch the faint inflection of 'known'. 'There are suspicions, then. Why did Prince Galcotto – ' the name was uttered with disdain, even disgust — 'not arrest anyone? How could such a thing be done and no one know who has done it?'

Sigismondo shook his head. 'Anyone can hire a bravo.'

'But no one would! No one would!' Tristano began to stride about the room and had snatched off his cap the better to fasten distraught hands in his curls. 'So young! So fair! Who could be her enemy? Oh, would she had stayed at home!'

'You think nothing would have happened to her in Altamura?'

Tristano came to a halt in front of Sigismondo, to stare at him.

'Among her friends? Those who loved her? Oh, never. She would have lived a life of joy if she had listened to me! I would have protected her from all harm. But she quarrelled with her fate and went to her death. I warned her!' The young man's voice had risen almost to a shriek and Benno thought, as Tristano turned to stride away, that he looked more than a little mad. She'd have done well to take him seriously, perhaps. At the moment he looked capable not only of hiring an assassin to kill the lady, but of going after her and doing it in person. 'O Ariana, Ariana, why did you not heed me?'

He flung himself onto the velvet cushions of the seat in the window embrasure and, hiding his face in his hands, sobbed. Sigismondo remained silent, hands on knees, and after a little asked in what Benno thought was a kind voice, 'Why did you think the Princess was going to her death in Borgo?'

Tristano, surprisingly, could reply, checking his sobs and pushing himself up straight-armed, showing a face not more marred by tears than is a flower by dew.

'She had betrayed me! The Queen of Love does not permit traitors to live!'

Sigismondo had no time to reply to this remarkable statement, as the door opened and Bonifaccio Valori stood there, his plump hands on his stomach, taking in the scene with disapproval.

'I heard, my son, that you had been out. Was that wise? Sir Sigismondo, you honour our house. To what may we attribute your visit?'

He had both of them on their feet, Sigismondo bowing, Tristano dashing the tears from his cheeks and coming to be embraced. Benno flattened himself against the wall as Bonifaccio came forward and, as usual, no one saw him. Over Tristano's shoulder, as he was clasped to his father, Bonifaccio eyed Sigismondo.

'I came at your son's request, my lord, to tell him about the Princess of Borgo.'

'Indeed.' Bonifaccio held his son away from him by the arms and spoke with gentle severity. 'Did I not say you mustn't seek to increase your grief? The doctor prescribed rest, music, distraction, not this continued dwelling on what cannot be changed. You cannot bring back the past—'

'I can! I can *live* in the past! It is where I choose to be, for the present is not to be endured!'

Tristano, flinging back his curls, ran from the room, hitting Benno with the door curtain as he dragged it aside. His father stood spreading his hands apologetically.

'The disappointments of youth, sir. They pass, as we know, though it is hard to believe at the time.'

'Perhaps the young do not want to believe it.'

Bonifaccio wagged his head in agreement. 'My son is impetuous, but he means no harm.'

Now why should he bother to say that? thought Benno. Bonifaccio had advanced to look out of the window, where his son had lain sobbing. He stood with pudgy hands clasped behind his back, a most solid figure in contrast to the slight Tristano, his very solidity imparting to him a dignity of presence, an impression of weighty counsel, of gravity, that must have its power with the Duke. All the same, Benno could see his eye was rolled sideways as if to calculate the effect of his presence and this silence on Sigismondo.

'Who could possibly wish the lady harm?' Sigismondo, in smoothly echoing Tristano's cry, might not have expected to obtain a list of names from Bonifaccio, but possibly even he was surprised by the reaction he did get. Bonifaccio wheeled to face him, jowls and all quivering with just that intensity which his son had shown.

'Who, sir? Many, sir, many! Because of what she was.' He came uncomfortably close and, looking into Sigismondo's attentive face, gripped him hard by the arm, fortunately not the wounded one. Before he spoke, he glanced automatically round the room as if checking for inquisitive hearers, and Benno instantly drew on his reserves of idiocy, unfocusing his eyes and dropping his jaw. Bonifaccio did not see the bright gaze of Biondello from Benno's dishevelled jerkin, but he was satisfied and went on in a low voice, 'If you told the Duke I have said so he would not believe you, but the girl was evil. Had my son married her she would have been his death.'

Sigismondo hummed interrogatively, and Bonifaccio shook the arm in his grip for emphasis as he continued, 'I warned him. I *told* him but he would not listen. I have indulged him too often, I know; what he has wished for, he has too often been given. But to wish for her was to wish for disaster.'

'Yet you advised his Grace to marry her to Prince Galeotto?' The question was posed with a hint of irony.

Bonifaccio's intensity slowly gave way to an appraising and sly smile. He let go of Sigismondo's arm.

'A princess has greater constraints on her behaviour than has the wife of an ordinary man. And what is trouble to princes? They are born to trouble. Her evil would not have its scope in a prince's court.'

Sigismondo's eyebrows rose, and he blew lightly between parted lips. '*Evil* is your word? A girl of fifteen brought up in a convent?'

Bonifaccio's smile broadened. 'Ask at court and you will find I am not alone in saying so. Ask the Lord Tebaldo. Ask her Grace's self.'

'Always with the proviso,' Sigismondo answered the smile, 'that I do not say you told me.'

Bonifaccio was beaming, his eyes hardly to be seen but regarding Sigismondo. 'Oh, no one would believe you. You will find all the court was glad when the lady left for Borgo, and you'll find few sorry to have heard she's left this world. Except her father, of course.'

'And your son.'

'He thinks she was punished for breaking troth with him. Troth! They were children playing in the garden, innocents in Eden. Tristano is still a child, alas.'

'You don't fear he will seek to take his own life again?'

The smile vanished from the large face. 'I hope all this foolishness will be forgotten.' His voice changed, acquiring a monitory tone. 'I particularly wish that he shall not be reminded of anything painful.' He clapped his hands resoundingly and the door was opened by a bowing servant. 'Nor do I want to hear that you have spoken to him again.'

The smile was back in place as he ushered his guest out, but the level voice conveyed a threat as unmistakable as any weapon.

Chapter Thirty

Prayers for an aunt

Duke Vincenzo was not accustomed to being unsuccessful in his games of intrigue, and the ruin of his fort had struck hard. Now the news reached him not only that Brunelli was alive but also that the man sent to kill him was dead: the body of an unknown man, presumed to be one of the thieves who hang about building sites for what they can pick up, had been buried at the city's expense. The Duke was not pleased. The Duke was not in the mood to be gracious to the envoy from Altamura. If Duke Ippolyto felt he had a grievance in that the attack on his Duchess – from whom harm had so *very* fortunately been averted – had its origins in Venosta, then he himself had a grievance in that his fort had been destroyed by a secret agent acting on instructions from that very Duchess.

The envoy, with infinite politeness, intimated that the fort had no business there in the first place. It was undoubtedly on Altamuran territory. And what reason had the Duke to believe the Duchess Violante was in any way concerned?

The Duke, in his voice that put one in mind of oil over broken glass, begged the envoy to consider that what he referred to as Altamuran territory had by an Act of God been transformed by the flow of the River Larno into Venostan territory.

The envoy delicately put forward that this fort, built in such haste before the sovereignty of the territory had been properly debated, might have been destroyed in what could in similar fashion be called an Act of God. Talk of secret agents might be seeking to put blame where none could possibly be substantiated; whereas there was, alas, no doubt in the world that the Duchess had been snatched away, with loss of Altamuran lives, from Altamuran territory, by a brigand who had been permitted to establish his lair in Venosta.

There was more broken glass under the oil as the Duke replied: one Sigismondo, who was travelling with the Duchess on her return from Borgo, had been reported by the architect of his fort to have visited the fort under false pretences, posing as the Duke of Venosta's engineer, and had ascertained the storage place of that powder which so mysteriously exploded when no one was near. And who, the Duke enquired, had the authority to command such an act? Should one not — and here the Duke reached for and took his own Duchess's hand as she sat severely upright beside him — should one not assume that as man and wife are one flesh, so their will is also as one? If the Duchess Violante ordered the destruction of the fort, it must be because she knew her husband would have ordered it. The man Sigismondo was in her retinue; she must have commanded him. Otherwise what could it profit the man so to offend against a sovereign state?

Here the Altamuran envoy, in elegant circuitous terms, begged to remind the Duke that while this same Sigismondo had been said to inspect the fort, this was only the report of an architect who would otherwise be held responsible himself for the fort's destruction. There was no evidence whatever that the man was concerned. Moreover this same Sigismondo, a man of the greatest ability and one in whom trust could confidently be placed – one who had rendered services to the Dukes of Rocca and Nemora, to the Prince of Viverra, to doubtless many others unknown – this man had been the saviour of the Duchess Violante from the clutches of the vile brigand permitted to make his den in Venosta.

This brigand! The Duke's voice was like vipers gliding under silk. Had his Grace of Altamura any conception of the difficulty of ejecting a robber chief and his band who had set up their eyrie in mountain crags where they could challenge attack with impunity?

His Duchess's hand became rigid under his; and she was right in thinking this was a question the Duke would have done better not to pose, for the envoy asked in his turn, could it be that his Grace had not been informed that Duke Ippolyto's father had succeeded in banishing this same robber chief, that it had been possible, with determination, to rid Altamura of such a creature, who had then sought, and obtained, refuge in Venosta? Also there must be some doubt as to the impregnability of this retreat of theirs as Sir Sigismondo had rescued the Duchess from it.

The Duke was silent a minute, and then called for wine. The envoy recognised this as a pause for refreshment halfway through the game. He drank with pleasure. Despite rumour about Duke Vincenzo's use of poisons against those who disagreed with him, the envoy was confident he would be preserved to convey the Duke's complaints to his master; and Venostan wine was excellent.

It was the Duchess Dorotea's turn to speak, giving her husband yet more breathing time before the next manoeuvre. She wished to express her personal condolences, first to the Duke Ippolyto on the loss of his daughter in so dreadful a manner, and then to the Duchess Violante on her terrible ordeal at the hands of Rodrigo Salazzo. As though she had been serenely blind to the various moves in the game of chess that had been going on, she expressed what might be called the woman's view, extending sympathy to the bereaved father and – it was so delicately hinted that Vincenzo must have been proud of her – the ravished wife.

The Duke, relinquishing his cup to a page, chimed in with his consort. How cruel a fate! How mysterious! 'What does Prince Galeotto have to say of *his* wife's tragedy?'

The implication was there in the Duke's tone. The mystery could, if Prince Galeotto chose to speak, be solved.

The envoy allowed the merest trace of surprise, of question, into his tone. 'The Prince is as distressed as is my master, naturally.'

'Such tragedies,' mused Duke Vincenzo, 'would seem to be a curse of Duke Ippolyto's family. Was not his sister murdered? And did not his father's first wife, Beatrice of Borgo, die suddenly too?'

This was a move of genius, and it was the envoy's turn to sip wine as if considering the taste rather than his own answer, which, when it came, seemed to ignore the question but went to the heart of the matter.

'The treaty of alliance between Borgo and Altamura is to be ratified this week. Both sovereigns have set their seal to it and these documents are being exchanged.'

The Duke considered this without losing the expression of false grief he had put on for the Princess Beatrice. 'I am glad indeed that there is no harsh feeling between the Prince and his Grace your master. What misfortune should any suspicion cloud their alliance.' He leant forward in gentle enquiry. 'Is it known who employed the strangler?'

'At his Grace's desire, Sir Sigismondo is engaged in finding this out. I have no doubt he will prove himself as capable in this as in his other services.'

Duke Vincenzo appeared equally confident. His reply intimated that a man who could blow up his fort would be capable of anything.

When the envoy finally departed for Altamura, with the various messages for Duke Ippolyto, a case of the finest Venosta wine for himself, and several lengths of beautiful black brocade for the Duchess Violante from the Duchess Dorotea – as if by now her stock of mourning must be running low – both envoy and Duke were satisfied with the way negotiations had gone. Neither side had conceded anything, each had established a case of serious grievance. The move was now Duke Ippolyto's.

Meanwhile, Prince Galeotto, unaware that in Venosta aspersions were being thrown on his integrity, was sitting gloomily in the palace chapel at Borgo, hearing yet another Mass for the soul of his late bride. *His* envoy to Altamura had been instructed to report this assiduous attention to the memory of Princess Ariana, and the need to preserve appearances had seriously curtailed Galeotto's customary entertainments. Hunting was out of the question, and his hounds were suffering from the lack of any but formal exercise. Warrior, whose spiked collar was still missing, had grown savage enough to bite the kennel master who, being less important than Warrior, had no redress. The hawks moped and bated. Other sources of amusement had also been taken from the Prince: the death of Lady Leonora at, it was understood with fear and horror, the hands of the same strangler who had killed the Princess, seemed to the courtiers proof that the Prince's close companions were, like himself, the target of malign enmity. As a result of their representations, he rarely ventured from the palace and wore, even in the heat of summer, chainmail under his doublet, adding a physical weight to the mental one apparent to all. Deprived of Leonora, he had regarded Zima in the nature of a spare. To his dismay, the prevailing theory that the strangler was working his way slowly through the Prince's near and dear towards the Prince himself had inspired the lady with an alarm so poignant that she had shut up her exquisite little villa and removed herself to the safety of a convent lodging where she was currently driving the nuns distracted with her demands for better accommodation and a luxury diet. Other ladies of the court, for whom all princes are handsome, were showing inexplicable devotion to their husbands. Galeotto had little hope of anyone in his bed until someone, and it hardly mattered who, could be publicly accused of being the strangler and spectacularly punished. The only talismans Zima would accept for her safety were the hands of the strangler or, thought Galeotto, at least a likely-looking pair of hands, nailed above the gates of Borgo.

Galeotto, as the Mass drew to an end, shifted miserably in his chainmail and decided to have a strangler discovered soon. In front of him was the porphyry tablet to the last Princess of Borgo, princess for hardly more than a day; but his eyes rested on the plaque of polished marble set in the wall above, memorial to a Princess of Borgo who had died as Duchess of Altamura. He must have special prayers said for Aunt Beatrice; he was sure she was watching him from Purgatory.

Chapter Thirty-one

An arrow struck

The library at the palace of Altamura had been converted from two floors of court apartments by Duke Ippolyto's father, with bookshelves of cedarwood made by the finest craftsmen from Milan, but now that Ippolyto was developing his collection of manuscripts, he had for some time been considering both an extension and an improvement. Something more in the classical line was called for and the man he had in mind for the job was Pietro Brunelli, at present, so he heard, working in Venosta. Of course all plans had been put aside when the news came of Ariana's death, and during his own subsequent illness, but now his health and his Duchess had been restored to him, an exceptional opportunity was presented in the shape of Brunelli himself.

It was the same story. Brunelli had been vigorously beautifying Ristoni's town house in Venosta, undaunted by careless accidents such as the one that lost him his assistant and caused the simultaneous death of an unknown thief. There had been whispers of the Evil Eye among his workforce. However, he had met a physical obstacle: his employer's mother. Brunelli intended, when he had finished the classical rendering of the outside of the house, and of its entrance, to make the interior harmoniously correspond in symmetry. The rooms on the *piano nobile* should be equal in number and size on either side.

This would involve demolishing a wall between two chambers where Madonna Ristoni lived, and she flatly refused to countenance it.

In vain her son expatiated on the improved space the alteration would provide for her, on the greater dignity than could be provided by her cramped quarters now. The old woman had lived in these rooms since her marriage. She had given birth to him and all his siblings in one of them and was determined to die there snugly. Brunelli, inadvisedly brought in to persuade her, had ended up in a passionate slanging match with the dowager and had stamped out after ripping the plans to shreds. He left Venosta just before Duke Vincenzo got around to hiring a more efficient eliminator to remove him.

Duke Ippolyto did hesitate to engage Brunelli but not because of the architect's reputation for quarrelling violently with his employers, for each man flatters himself that he knows the way to treat the artistic temperament better than his neighbour does. He hesitated because any work on the library would of necessity disturb his wife's cousin, who spent his days there and whose refuge it was against the world. Lord Tebaldo, since his rejection by his cousin's lady-in-waiting a few months ago, had scarcely been seen in court and was rumoured to spend his nights as well as his days in the library.

Ippolyto was never at ease with him. Poggio could make fun of being a dwarf and had turned an apparent disability into a triumph. One could enjoy his company. Tebaldo, however, was, as Ippolyto knew, usually in pain and although the young man had been a cripple from birth, Ippolyto somehow felt guilty about it, irked that he could not help.

For this reason he did not visit Tebaldo much except when Tebaldo's agents – for he was tireless in his efforts by proxy to improve the library – brought some new manuscript, or news of one for which his approval must be given for purchase. He was very reluctant to break news of his plans to Tebaldo for the library was to become a place of intense activity if he let Brunelli go ahead, a place where there would be noise, dust and a quantity of people – something like one of the circles of Hell for poor Tebaldo. On the other hand, Tebaldo's labours in improving the Duke's collection should be matched by a library fit to receive it.

This was not a problem he wanted to consult Violante about, as the physician had ordered rest and freedom from care after her ordeal with Rodrigo Salazzo, the details of which Ippolyto never intended to enquire into; Violante had not related them and he was sure she never would. The man was dead, Sigismondo had assured him, so he could never boast of his villainy, and if his own men had witnessed anything, Ippolyto was powerless to silence them as long as they stayed in Venosta. Any member of Salazzo's gang who strayed into Altamura would lose tongue and eyes before going to feed the crows on a gibbet. If only Sigismondo could discover the murderer of poor Ariana and remove the threat to Violante and himself!

All this went through Ippolyto's mind as Brunelli stood before him, square, disagreeable and enthusiastic. The idea of improving the library appealed to him. He wanted to start at once. Brunelli, in so often depriving himself of the chance to finish any project, had great reserves of latent energy. He liked Altamura already.

Duke Ippolyto appealed to his aesthetic sense by being a great deal younger and better-looking than Galeotto or Vincenzo. He looked forward also to seeing the famous beauty Duchess Violante. He might even be asked to paint her portrait. He knew Leone Leconti had painted her, and if that insipid idiot had deceived them with his flash technique they would get true quality if they employed him. He scowled at Ippolyto quite pleasantly.

It had its effect. Brunelli was engaged, and stamped off to prepare his plans, leaving Ippolyto to prepare his own for breaking the news to his wife's cousin. Ippolyto consoled himself: the work could not begin until the plans were drawn and approved, which would give Tebaldo time to become used to the idea – and his approval of the plans must be asked, which might help to reconcile him. Besides, he could always take refuge in his little study, off the library, where he already spent much of his time poring over manuscripts and even, so Violante had confided, writing some scholarly thesis or other, on philosophy. Scholars were notoriously able to shut out the world.

In another room in the palace, while the Duke was coming to this decision, Benno was letting the world in by opening the shutters in Sigismondo's room. His master had woken Benno from a nap of his own with the sound of water as he washed in the basin in the corner; Benno, yawning and stretching, folded the shutters back and latched them. Biondello's opinion on how long a siesta should last had not been consulted and he made this plain by firmly sleeping on, nose tucked into tail.

Sigismondo was, Benno had noted, resting more than usual, giving his wound time to knit and himself time to recover. After all, he had had no rest between heaving all those kegs of powder and the journey to Roccanera.

Thinking of all this made Benno wonder what more could be in store. A mild summer breeze brought in river smells and even a faint hint of decaying fish, but did not account for the cold feeling at the back of his neck as he recalled that the assassin who had tried to kill Sigismondo was still alive. Benno hoped he was still in Borgo and had given up.

Sigismondo, carrying his shirt, strolled past him to the window. He stood there pulling his shirt over his head while Biondello, alerted perhaps by the smell of old fish, or thoroughly woken by Benno's emptying the wash water, plunged off the bed and scampered to see what Sigismondo was surveying. The sill was low and he made it in two perilous bounds to the seat and the sill. Benno turned to see Sigismondo swiftly lean to extend a hand between the little dog and the river below.

There was a flicker, a crack as an arrow struck vibrating in the shutter and Sigismondo dropped to the floor.

Chapter Thirty-two

'I must have time to think'

Biondello had been swept from the sill as Sigismondo dropped, and, with the advantage of owning four feet, was the first up. Sigismondo was a close second, raising an arm to swing the shutter closed. By the time Benno reached him he was standing behind it, his forearm pressed to his scalp. After a glance at the arrow and its angle, he put the other shutter almost to, and sighted between them downwards and to the left.

'Is it him?' Benno had picked up Biondello and was clasping him as if he had to express his relief somehow. Once again, Sigismondo was not dead. The sound of the arrow had been shocking, the first Benno had heard so near.

'Him? Give me that napkin.'

Benno snatched the napkin that had come with the hot water. 'The man from Borgo. He must be here and still after you.' He watched as Sigismondo took away the arm's pressure on his head and substituted the napkin. Blood had already coursed down his neck. Benno knew scalp wounds always did bleed a lot but he felt his master had been made to lose far too much lately. As to what would have happened if Sigismondo had not bent to save Biondello from the river, he shied from the thought. Perhaps he should look out the mastiff's collar

219

for his master to wear again. The Duke's physician had said Sigismondo was blessed with luck; thank God it was true.

Something struck him. 'How did he know you were in this room? He had to've been watching the window. Did you see where the arrow came from?'

In the dim light, Sigismondo looked pale and angry. Escaping death by an inch can be invigorating, or infuriating if you think death is hanging about waiting for the next chance.

'*Two* questions, Benno. *Two questions.*' He took the napkin from his head and looked at it – already half soaked – and smiled grimly. 'Easier to deal with your questions than some things, though, so: last item first, no, I can't tell for certain where it came from, somewhere from a house across the river, downstream, is the best that I can do. As for how he knew which room to watch, anyone in the palace could have told him. Whom did we see standing in full view in this window this morning?'

'The *doctor*? You don't think—'

'Who can be sure between the innocent and the guilty? Only God. The doctor has access to all manner of secrets and could be the most valuable of spies. Someone was willing to pay the Lady Leonora to spy in Borgo. Someone would be very pleased to get the Duke's doctor to spy for him here.'

'But a doctor on the same side as an assassin? He could do *anything*, like poison the Duke and the Duchess.'

'Certainly he could, and in that case why have an assassin as well?'

'To kill *you*.' Benno thought back. 'You took the doctor's potion. He could've poisoned you then.'

Sigismondo hummed. 'It should have worked by now – and I believe I would have tasted something. And it may be any servant in the palace who stood here to mark this window for the assassin while we were out, or who told him where we lodge. Still, we must find out more about this doctor. Lend me a hand here.' Sigismondo had picked up his doublet.

'Don't you want your scrip for something to put on your head? Suppose that arrow was poisoned?' Benno's mind, still in shock, seethed with unpleasant ideas. Sigismondo, engaged in the difficulty of working his bandaged arm into its sleeve while stemming the blood from his scalp, laughed.

'That arrow wasn't meant to poison. It was meant to go through my eye. And never mind my scrip, I mean to see a professional about this.'

Benno, trotting after Sigismondo with Biondello under his arm, wondered who on earth his master meant to see. Surely not the doctor. And yet that was just what Sigismondo was likely to do: saunter into the lion's den and ask to look at its teeth.

It turned out that Sigismondo was going to consult the Nurse. She was in a little closet by the nursery, folding linen.

'You told me that not everyone knows about herbs, but I know that you do. Could I come to a better person?' Sigismondo, with a warm smile into the Nurse's eyes, removed the napkin to show her.

Benno, who did not yet know that to let people see they are being flattered is in itself flattering, hoped the Nurse was in a good mood. She hadn't exactly seen eye to eye with Sigismondo last time they'd talked, back in Borgo when she'd been asked about the draught she'd left for the Princess.

'Dear Mother of God! You're bleeding like a pig, sir. How did you come by that?' She was examining the arrow's graze with careful fingers, holding the napkin to it with her other hand.

'The wound I had at Roccanera,' Sigismondo looked down at his arm with a sweep of lashes that would have done credit to a flirtatious girl, 'it makes me clumsy, I miscalculate. A graze from a shutter, no more, but since it broke the skin – I was sure you could advise me.' His voice was a soft purr, and Benno half expected that Nurse would deal him a clip on the ear to add to his injuries; but this coaxing approach, as Benno might have known, was one she understood and appreciated. She tutted, dimpled, put the napkin back in Sigismondo's hand and applied his hand to his scalp again, then bustled smiling to a corner of the closet and groped under a shelf. She came back triumphant.

'Here, sir. Cobwebs will stem that bleeding.' As he moved the napkin and again bent before her, she spread the grey web over the angry red; and she chuckled. 'You men! You don't know what remedies are under your noses. Go to the Duke's doctor and he'd have let you stand there dripping on the floor while he cast your chart to find when it was safe for you to take one of his mucky jollops. Now look, it's stemmed already.'

Benno, craning to see, was not surprised that the wound, exposed to air and held by the sticky webs, had dried. He always used cobwebs himself. What was surprising was that his master had come here to get this treatment.

Nurse was now rummaging in a box for something. A musty smell permeated the closet as she poked among the contents, while Sigismondo asked casually about the doctor. Clearly she thought nothing of his many qualifications.

'Knows more about how to treat books than people. It

222

doesn't make a man learned, being able to read. He's studied in Padua, Salerno, and foreign places no one's ever heard of, but his patients die like anyone else's.'

'Where was he before he came to his Grace, then? In one of these foreign parts?'

The Nurse was muttering something over a piece of paper, which she carried into the nursery. This was a big room where the wet-nurse sat by the window feeding Lord Andrea. A child's voice from the loggia showed where Lady Camilla was playing. The Nurse poured a cup of wine, and held the paper to the light burning under the image of the Virgin in the alcove, with the cup under the burning paper to catch the ashes.

'He's been everywhere, like I said – Castelnuovo, Borgo, Venosta. What I ask is why he doesn't *stay* anywhere. I suppose,' she held out the cup to Sigismondo, the acrid smell of burnt paper in the air, 'he kills his quota and moves on.' She chuckled again, and Benno thought how much her spirits had improved now that she was home, ruling over her beloved nursery. But what concerned him was that the doctor might be the spy, if there was one, in league with the assassin, just as the Lady Leonora had been in Borgo. If the doctor knew what had happened to *her* he might think twice.

Sigismondo had drunk the wine with the burnt charm in it with not even a trace of a wry look. 'Hey, you've done me all the good in the world.' The purr in his voice made the Nurse dimple once more and toss her head. 'I'll know where to come for any hurts I get.' He took her hand and pressed it to his lips.

As they went back through the palace to the room allotted them, Benno remarked, 'Nurse is on your side now. But did she really help? That doctor's been around, he could be working for anyone, right? *Couldn't* he be the spy here, like Lady Leonora in Borgo?'

There was an unaccustomed touch of impatience in Sigismondo's voice. 'Why hire a man as your spy when you can hire him to kill? Doctors have better means to use than cords or arrows.' The blood had congealed on the side of his scalp under the grey ridge of cobweb, and people they passed turned round to stare again. The hero of the hour, the rescuer of the Duchess, again in the wars?

'Well, the Duke and the Duchess'd be dead by now, wouldn't they, and everybody'd think it just natural. Nurse said he moved on when he'd killed his quota.' Benno gasped of a sudden. 'But the Duke *was* ill, right? Could he have done it?'

He had forgotten to keep his voice down and Sigismondo turned and cuffed the side of his head so that his ears rang and a jolted Biondello let out a minuscule yelp. Sigismondo's face was dark, very different from the smiling one that Nurse had seen.

'No more, Benno. I must have time to think.'

As they climbed the smooth-worn marble stairs to the floor where their room was, Benno reflected that nobody likes to stand as target. Sigismondo must badly want to be out in the city tracking down the man so dedicated to killing him. His master knew what the man looked like even, but finding him in Altamura, well, it could be like jabbing your hand on the needle in the haystack. And then, Sigismondo couldn't rush out for personal revenge, for the Duke was counting on him to protect the Duchess and find his daughter's murderer, and that meant tracing the one who had *hired* the man who killed her. Benno didn't see even Sigismondo getting the information out of this assassin, who didn't seem the type that'd break down and confess if you shook a sword at him. In fact, it was Sigismondo himself who gave Benno the feeling that the man, whoever he was, must be nearly his match. Benno's mind refused the idea that anyone could possibly match him. Anyone who could do *that* could kill him.

Come to think of it, meeting this man at all wouldn't be bright of Sigismondo, wounded as he was. Benno, remembering the arrow quivering in the shutter, thought it might be appropriate to pray to St Sebastian to avert future harm from his master, since it seemed he only had to wait around for it to happen.

Silently, but with moving lips, Benno began to pray.

Chapter Thirty-three

Of high position

Once Sigismondo had left, Nurse bustled about, checking on her charges and giving a routine scold to the nursery maids. They had learnt not to be caught cuddling the ducal children, as Nurse was jealous of affection attracted to anyone else but herself. She cooed over Lord Andrea in his gilded cradle carved with the arms of Altamura, and supervised the settling of the Lady Camilla for a nap before her supper. Then she was busy collecting her basket of things: fine linen towels, swabs of wool, and scented oils. The nursery maids watched her as they hemmed sheets, and they exchanged glances and smiles. Nurse was going to have her daily treat.

It was Tebaldo's treat too. Once a day he could look forward to a little relief from pain, and a little of the comforting and consolation he had never had from the mother who died at his birth – cruel folk said from the shock of seeing him. Nurse was a maternal soul and, in her fashion, a clever woman. She never let Tebaldo see that she pitied him. Her visits were, it seemed, purely practical and intended to relieve the ache from his twisted back, and she never failed to accord him the respect due to his high birth. After her massage, he would sleep well for quite some hours. As he shrank so from people, he was often ignorant, too, of what went on in court and

Nurse's gossip made him feel more in touch. Today she had plenty to tell him.

'I am very glad you came back home safely, Nurse.' Tebaldo was helped by his servant to take off his doublet and shirt and to recline on the couch. He had missed the attentions, and the company, of one of the two people he believed liked him. The expedition to Borgo might have deprived him of both, but he could not wholly deplore it, all the same: it had resulted in the death of Ariana. This was in his mind as he went on, 'I had feared at one time that I might not see you again. Her Grace said to me before she left that the Lady Ariana – the Princess, of course I should say – had requested that you stay with her in Borgo.'

'She was kind enough to do so.' Nurse's tone conveyed the truth: the late Princess had been cruel enough to want to part the Nurse from her adored nurselings simply to look after her own selfish whims. 'Her Highness believed I could add to the comfort of her life.'

'As you do to mine.' Tebaldo closed his eyes, feeling his muscles, always tensed against pain, relax and some of the ache melt into warmth. 'You would have been an irreparable loss to me.'

Not spoken between them was what ought to have been a greater loss, that of the Princess herself. Nurse wiped her hands and uncorked another bottle, letting the scent of lavender fill the small book-lined room. As she worked the oil into the palms of her hands, she brought up a topic she knew Tebaldo never tired of. 'Her Grace's health is improving, thank God.' She did not add, no thanks to her physician, because she did not need to. Few people had a lower opinion of physicians than had Tebaldo, who since birth had been their victim; examined humiliatingly again and again; pummelled; stretched; put in steel corsets; hung from beams; and, of course, for the state of his general health in his debilitated condition, bled, purged and given nauseous draughts, from infancy until the time he could refuse. Nurse did not expect him to say Amen to her gratitude either. She, and a few others close to him, knew that Tebaldo did not believe in God. It was another reason she pitied him: to be so afflicted and to have no consolation! She was comfortably sure, though, that beyond this life God would forgive him and an angel meet him with a pair of wings that would make up for all the suffering he had undergone here below — if her prayers had anything to do with it!

As she massaged the oil into his shoulders, she remembered the visitor she had just been talking to. 'His Grace owes much to Sir Sigismondo.' She was unable to resist the boast: 'He came to me for his hurts not half an hour ago.'

Tebaldo was silent, but she did not connect his silence with her subject, nor with the sudden tension in his muscles.

Many rumours concerning the Lord Tebaldo's past had circulated in Altamura when he first came here with his cousin Violante on her marriage, but it was soon decided there was nothing intrinsically interesting in a young man few people ever saw and, apart from a revival of rumour when he was courting Lady Giulietta, scandal had not bothered with him. No one had even troubled to suggest that his absorption with knowledge and old books concerned the Black Arts, a theory which his bodily appearance might reasonably have suggested. He was a disappointing subject. Nurse, in any case, discounted what she heard. People were always unkind about a cripple . . . She worked her way down the wasted muscles of the crooked spine, talking as she went. How lucky they were that Sir Sigismondo had been there to save her Grace! Here, unexpectedly, Tebaldo had something to say, in a dry tone.

'He was not able to save the Princess.'

'And he still doesn't know who murdered her.'

Both of them were silent now, busy with their thoughts. Tebaldo, gently rubbed with a linen towel to take off any excess oil, was first to speak.

'Tell me more about it. Did he really suspect you?'

She smiled confidently. 'For a little, perhaps. But my digestive drink was on the table, untouched. She had already drunk the sedative that made it easy for the strangler to approach. None could think I might have supplied both.'

Tebaldo regarded her bent head, the pleats on her starched cap, as she did up his doublet's laces. His gaze was thoughtful. 'And you say this Sigismondo has not discovered who employed the strangler? Might he be concealing what he has found? He could be holding back if the one concerned were – of high position.'

Nurse adjusted the gilded lace symmetrically in its knot, opened her mouth to speak, and was prevented by a tap on the door and the entrance of Tebaldo's servant, apologising. He thought his master would wish to know that Master Polidoro Tedesco, with some of his pupils, was asking if his lordship would allow them to examine one or two manuscripts in the library, according to the permission already granted in their exchange of letters.

'So soon?' From Tebaldo's face one could tell that for him the arrival of strangers would always be too soon. Nevertheless, pride in the library, and his duty towards its treasures, prevailed over his desire to hide from the world. Nurse, as she curtseyed, thought what a shame it was: his face, though pale and drawn, was as beautiful as his cousin Violante's in its own way.

With one hand on his stick and the other on his servant's shoulder, the cripple went to meet the philosopher.

Chapter Thirty-four

An agent had arrived

'He might be anywhere, looking for you. Looking *at* you.'

It was near to spoiling Benno's appetite, though not quite. The dish of scrambled eggs with cheese and herbs was nearly empty. Sigismondo had not eaten his share but sat brooding, turning his winecup in his fingers, facing the to-and-fro of the street. Other customers on the benches outside the inn were busy with their dinners and the even more serious business of drinking; they could not afford the delicate savouring of fine vintages but they could manage to blur the labour of the afternoon.

'You sound like a preacher, Benno, talking of Death.' Sigismondo had roused himself and was smiling, but Benno reinforced his intent with a nod.

'I *am* talking about Death. Shouldn't we stay in the palace? Surely he can't get into the palace? I mean, he had to use an arrow—'

'Hey, isn't it heresy to suggest Death doesn't visit palaces? Princes would be glad if you were right. No, Benno, it's a question of choice.'

Benno waited, rubbing a crust of bread round the dish before cramming his mouth with it. Sigismondo had already given his bread to a wizened child tied up in rags, who had been crouched patiently on the cobbles at the street corner.

'Choice?' Benno spoke indistinctly. 'You mean you can choose not to get killed? But then what're we doing sitting out here when the assassin's just missed you?'

'Choice, Benno. If I choose to stay safe, I may be endangering those I've undertaken to protect.'

The Duchess, Benno thought, with a touch of resentment. He's saved her life three times already, can't he leave it to her own guards in her own palace? He got wounded taking her from that bandit's lair. He can't be expected to stand up as a target for the strangler again. If he's killed, will it help the Duchess?

He spoke through the last of the bread. 'Seems to me it's a lot of trouble for nothing.' Sigismondo's interrogatory hum provoked Benno to add, 'And if you caught him he wouldn't talk, would he? He's not going to say, oh, so-and-so hired me.' He clicked his fingers to call Biondello who was making friends with the ragged child. Little dogs can make big meals for the starving. 'Don't know why you bother.'

Sigismondo laughed and poured himself some more wine. 'It's the question of my life.' He drank deeply. In the evening light, gilding heads like a blessing, his had more surface to glow. Benno noticed that the arrow's graze had darkened and could barely be seen in the shadow. 'I should go to more philosophy lectures and see if I can find the reason. Though I think I do it for fun.'

Benno could believe this. Sigismondo certainly wasn't risking his life for money; enough rewards from grateful dukes and princes had come his way already for him to live in the grandest style if he wished. Also there was usually a light-hearted confidence in his master's approach to risks and Sigismondo seemed, at the moment, in low spirits. Benno supposed, or even hoped, it was just because of his wound.

The whole business of finding the strangler was baffling. After all, he could be a hundred miles away by now. The Princess might have died because someone had hired an assassin on account of a personal anger with her, like young Tristano, or even Lord Tebaldo. Equally possible, someone wanted revenge on Duke Ippolyto, as the exiled brothers Malgardo had, those experts with the slingshot. One of them, as Sigismondo said, could have escaped the chase, could have alerted the bandit Rodrigo that the Duchess was suitable prey; perhaps that same one was now in Altamura taking potshots at the man who'd killed his kinsman. After all, Sigismondo hadn't actually seen the man with the bolas here in Altamura.

All the same, Benno was glad to notice that his master was wearing the mastiff's collar.

'I must felicitate your lordship on the augmentation of this library since last I saw it. The manuscripts here are a tribute to your learning.'

The flattering words were in Polidoro Tedesco's usual brusque manner, but still they surprised the young men dutifully grouped round him, who were more accustomed to hearing the great abused in their absence and, to their faces, accorded little respect. They supposed, therefore, that scholarship deserved tribute whatever rank the scholar enjoyed. This crippled lord, whose eyes avoided theirs as if to avoid the comment he might see there, was hardly a fit object for ridicule; every chivalrous instinct was against it. Onorio Scudo, the sturdy blond, had even made an effort to help the poor young lord to his chair before the servant intervened. Onorio was always giving too much to beggars and once risked his life to save a drowning kitten. His awed praise of the manuscripts, fetched out and spread on the tables for them to view, was a reflection more of his admiration for Polidoro than his understanding of the texts. He watched smiling as Polidoro took the magnifying glass proffered by the library servant, and bent over a parchment, while Tebaldo shyly disclaimed the compliment.

'All these are a tribute to the learning and liberality of his Grace. My part is only to see that his commands are carried out. His agents travel all over Europe. I merely decide which of the manuscripts they bring back are worthy of his Grace's interest and keeping.'

'And how well his Grace has chosen. Here is a Statius, a Marilius, a superb Lucretius. Someone told me there is a complete Thomas Aquinas, a complete Albertus Magnus. What treasures! Does his Grace specialise in any particular branch of learning?' Polidoro, leaning over an illumination, had spoken with such apparent enthusiasm that it brought a response from Tebaldo, whose pale face had flushed.

'Concerns of state force his Grace to leave much of the choice to me. I try to collect over a wide field.' Tebaldo gestured at some manuscripts by his elbow, and grimaced as a muscle complained. 'We have quite a few in Greek − most of Sophocles, Pindar and Menander. Some works on medicine, Latin from the Arabic . . . Avicenna. Dante and Boccaccio, of course. A few comedies of Plautus. We are adding all the time.'

'Are you not afraid of forgeries? I hear they are only too common; and with so many noble patrons competing for manuscripts, it is not surprising.' Polidoro caressed the binding of a volume of Cicero, *De Oratione*, as he closed it.

'There is a risk but I believe I have come to know when a piece is doubtful.' Tebaldo glanced suddenly, quickly, round the faces watching him and was disconcerted to find that he knew one, Tristano Valori; just the sort of young man, his own age, with whom he would have liked to be friends had things been different. Ariana had treated him badly too. 'Something about the parchment, perhaps, even about the man who offers it for sale . . .'

'How fortunate is his Grace in possessing you. Some princes care for nothing but French chivalrous romances, some will not spend on books at all. This printing too; I fear it will vulgarise books. I have heard the Duke of Urbino declares he would be ashamed to own a printed book.'

'We have only one, it is true, a Lucretius printed in Latin, merely a curiosity. His Grace employs five copiers full time, and I have found two *scrittori* who can copy Greek.' Tebaldo, expanding in justifiable pride, and feeling that he was talking to people who could appreciate the value of what he said, managed a smile that included Tristano Valori, and was suddenly encouraged to see it answered.

Polidoro spoke. 'Two *scrittori*? The Duke of Urbino employs thirty. But then I am told he has already spent thirty thousand ducats on his collection. The Duke of Altamura has as much to spend, I dare say, but his Grace never put learning before all else.'

The sneer in his voice was familiar to most of his listeners. Tebaldo opened his eyes wide and wondered if he had imagined it. No one had told him, indeed few people told him anything, that Polidoro had at one time the honour to be tutor to the young Lord Ippolyto before his accession. The bitterness, sounding like personal experience, went unexplained. To cover an awkward silence, Tebaldo turned with tentative daring to the philosopher's pupils.

'What works do you like to study best? Your master asked to see the Cataline and the Sallust, and they're being brought now. Do you, too, prefer the satirists?'

He was looking at Tristano, but it was the young man whom Benno had christened Ratface, Atzo Orcagna, who replied. 'We admire their stand for liberty, my lord. They mock those who do not see the chains that bind them; who fancy that Church and state are fond fathers; who do not see what tyrants and hypocrites these really are.'

He spoke with a flourish, but his fellow pupils heard only their master's words repeated without the biting energy they were accustomed to. Onorio Scudo, impelled by vague feelings that it was impolite to talk of tyrants to a man so closely connected to one, offered what he meant as an apology. 'Not all tyrants are wicked, my lord, and some religious are sincere. My confessor is one.' He nodded at Tebaldo seriously, his blond locks bobbing at his shoulders. Polidoro clapped him on the back with more force than kindness.

'We are not here to waste his lordship's time with tales about the confessional. His lordship will excuse us,' he indicated the clerk who had carefully deposited two books on a table near the window, 'if we study what we have come to see.'

Tebaldo was quite sorry to see them withdraw to the table and stand round while Polidoro opened the first book and, reading, began an exposition in a low tone. He had almost been conducting a conversation with people his own age about the very things which interested him most – the dreadful grip in which the worldly tyrants of the Church held the poor and ignorant, and the need to free the mind of preconceived ideas that justified such authority. Perhaps it would be possible to talk to Tristano Valori another day. After all, he appeared at court. The difficulty lay in having to appear there himself, a thing he had not done since Giulietta, at Ariana's instigation, made him a laughing-stock.

Another thought gave him pause: Tristano had declared love for Ariana, and so he must be either a fool or her dupe. Tebaldo preferred to think the latter.

While Polidoro expounded Cataline, and Onorio's eyes were swimming with tears from repressing his yawns, a servant interrupted Tebaldo's thoughts, coming to murmur in his ear. An agent had arrived, not one of those Ippolyto himself employed but a stranger, who wished to sell a manuscript acquired in south Germany, a very valuable one. Would his lordship see him?

As Tebaldo, who preferred such transactions to be carried on in private, made his cautious, deliberate preparations to remove to his little study, the agent waiting to see him amused himself in looking all round. One of the *scrittori*, passing him on the way to relieve himself, thought the fellow might well be inquisitive about so splendid a library. He could not have been in many such.

In this he was correct. The man known to some as Pyrrho had not had occasion to carry out his commissions in libraries hitherto and, as a professional, he was interested in entrances and exits. As he glanced round he hummed a love song, one that had haunted him for days.

239

Chapter Thirty-five

An appointment with destiny

Brunelli had done his homework thoroughly; not for nothing was he called, among other things, a perfectionist. He had studied the plans of the library, as delivered to him by the Duke's clerk of works, until he had them by heart and could see them in the mind's eye. Now was the time to examine the library itself, to get the feel of the space, the distribution of light, the areas beyond it into which the extension should go. He set off confidently through the palace, having quite forgotten – having scarcely listened to – warnings about not disturbing the Duke's cousin, Lord Tebaldo. The Duke had not thought to mention that he intended to break the news of the imminence of the, hitherto theoretical, improvements to the Lord Tebaldo himself and he did not for a moment suppose that his new architect would anticipate this. Had the Duke in fact mentioned it, Brunelli would have seen no sense in it and no respect for the Duke's intentions would have stopped him from bursting into the library unannounced as he did.

He entered by a side door close to Polidoro and his pupils, who turned to stare at him, and crossed the marble floor to survey the windows, look down at the river and across at the houses. The angle of light was excellent; the houses were distant by the river's width and

241

respectfully more squat. Once the windows were enlarged, he would have exactly what he envisaged. He spat out of the window, narrowly missing the boatman waiting at the watergate steps below, and took his ferrule from his belt to measure the sill and the embrasure's depth. As he worked, jotting down figures on grubby tablets also hanging at his belt, with a stick of charcoal in a tarnished silver holder, he sang, loud and off key, the same song Pyrrho had been humming. It was beginning to be popular that year, a sad ballad of two lovers who died in each other's arms, victims of a cruel husband's jealousy. Brunelli did not notice when the boatman below took up the refrain with a much better idea of the tune.

The combined noise was too much for the group studying Cataline. Polidoro rolled up the scroll and turned away. His pupils were surprised that he did not bid the uncouth intruder to be silent, but Polidoro had seen Brunelli's face and manner as he passed. Every teacher comes to recognise the hopelessly intransigent, the ones blind to authority, and sensible teachers do not challenge them; there are other strategies if necessary. Here, Polidoro merely instructed the servant to convey his thanks to Lord Tebaldo, his trust that they might on a future visit see more of the library's treasures, and then led his young men to the door. Onorio, who had been watching Brunelli with absorbed interest, happily hummed the ballad in time with the sonorous rendering from the watergate below.

Brunelli, who had never known they were there, was equally unconscious of their leaving. Satisfied with the windows, he turned to pace his way to the further wall, where the extensions were to begin. His attention on his feet and on counting aloud, he was surprised on emerging from between two tall bookcases to hear rustling, scratchings and angry murmurs like a disturbed hive all around him. He paced on, counting, to the wall and turned, scowling, to meet other scowls.

Men concentrating on copying Latin and, still more, on Greek, do not take kindly to someone counting loudly and prepared to push between their desks. Mistakes cost trouble, careful scraping of vellum, tedious and discouraging work. Several copyists as well as one *scrittore* had already blotted their copybooks at the apparition of the counting architect. From the wall, his back to an alcove and a marble bust of Apollo, he glared at them.

'You'll have to go. All of you. I can't have you here.'

That the extension was also meant to provide more room for the copyists was ironically lost on Brunelli. All he saw was a gaggle of penpushers who were in the way.

One of them, a *scrittore* who had just ruined an epsilon in the Ethics of Aristotle, now by reason of his superior salary spoke for them all.

'Lord Tebaldo will not permit any such thing. Ask him.' He gestured towards the door between the bookcases; and Brunelli, not a man to waste words or time, stamped over and flung the door open.

'They'll have to go, that lot of scribblers. If the Duke wants the library extension, they'll have to go.' Brunelli, faced with the pale young man with the hunched shoulder and the tall one beside him, addressed the one sitting down. He would be the one with authority.

Both men concealed their reaction to Brunelli's pronouncement because they were both accustomed to showing no emotion. Tebaldo automatically repressed complaint and would not reveal his horror at the chaos into which his life would be thrown. Pyrrho had already had to repress anger that his plans had not allowed for the presence of a bunch of scribblers in the library, and now he did not let himself smile with triumph that the obstacle was perhaps to be removed after all.

'Everything shall be as his Grace wishes,' said Tebaldo, a little faintly. The man beside him was satisfied that the wretched cripple had signed his cousin's death warrant.

'Your Grace must write in strong terms. It is totally on account of Duke Vincenzo's negligence in not ridding his lands of the brigand Salazzo that her Grace was nearly lost to us.'

Bonifaccio Valori spoke truth, although not a truth that Duke Ippolyto cared for. Sigismondo had assured him Salazzo was dead, but men who had witnessed the capture, the humiliation of the Duchess, were still alive and beyond his grasp. There had already been a rumour that Vincenzo was recruiting some of the leaderless band into his own guard, when in decency he should be hanging them for their part in the abduction. Then, some of Salazzo's men were insisting he was alive and would return to lead them again. Violante would not speak of him, and that in itself told Ippolyto enough; Vincenzo had all too much to pay for.

'You shall write the letter, Bonifaccio, and we will consider it.' Ippolyto hesitated. 'If it should come to war—'

'Prince Galeotto would support us, your Grace. The treaty is signed and ratified.'

Ippolyto did not answer. Galeotto was an object of contemplation no pleasanter than Salazzo or Vincenzo. While he did not really believe Galeotto to be involved in Ariana's death, obscurely, he held him responsible, and all Galeotto's grotesque attempts at grief augmented this feeling. Besides, war with Vincenzo would involve his city and his state in waste and suffering for which Galeotto's support would not compensate.

'What condottiere is free?' he asked all the same.

This was an all-important point. The wrong condottiere lost not only the money paid to him but also the war, which meant possibly one's state and one's life into the bargain. Ippolyto turned to the tall man in black standing silently by, and Valori put the question on his master's behalf. Discreetly phrased, it came to an enquiry whether Sigismondo, a soldier of fortune, a mercenary, knew of any captain who could succeed in providing a threat to Venosta. Vincenzo was not a man to be easily frightened and if he really intended war – and the building of the fort was a glove thrown down – then he had very likely already negotiated with a condottiere himself.

Sigismondo had no immediate help to offer. The great Scala was dead, by Sigismondo's own hand as it happened. Gatta, with a long list of successes to his credit, was not available, enjoying at the moment a cosy berth and less inclined to risk his men. Il Lupo was rumoured to have finished a profitable little war in the south and might be ready to sell his sword again, but he was a long way off. There were others, but – Sigismondo did not put it into words but Ippolyto and his counsellor both had the impression that diplomacy was still a better bet than any of them. Venosta was rich, Vincenzo unpredictable. An elegantly turned letter might avert a smoking city.

Valori engaged to draft the letter, and Sigismondo took his leave. Ippolyto turned with relief to consider a more civilised matter, the extension to the palace library.

Orders were here for workmen to be hired, materials bought. Brunelli was insisting on Carrera marble for the work. Ippolyto put to the back of his mind the knowledge that if war with Vincenzo did come, not only would the new library never be built but the palace itself might be destroyed. He gave orders that the marble should be from Carrera. As he signed the last paper and the secretary, bowing, took the desk away, a servant arrived with, appropriately, a message from the library. Ippolyto read Tebaldo's note with interest.

'A complete Quintilian! Lord Tebaldo writes that he has never heard of one until now, yet he believes the manuscript to be genuine.'

'A great asset to your library.' Valori's large face creased into smiles. He, too, was happier with peace than with war. 'Has Lord Tebaldo purchased it, your Grace?'

'No. The price is such that he wishes me to see it first. Yet if he believes it to be genuine, there can't be much cavil as to the cost. A complete Quintilian!'

'Does his lordship mention its provenance?'

Ippolyto reread the letter. 'South Germany. The agent who found the manuscript is to return with it tomorrow.' He thought for a moment of the audiences and engagements on hand and then turned to the library servant. 'Say to the Lord Tebaldo that I shall come to the library at eleven tomorrow. Let the agent attend us then.'

The servant, bowing, withdrew. Not he, nor Valori nor the Duke knew that an appointment had been made with destiny.

Chapter Thirty-six

What can go wrong?

There were no courses at Salerno or Padua, where Master Valentino had attended, which taught a physician how to deal with the great. That was a technique which Master Valentino had with extreme rapidity picked up for himself and, of course, it varied from one great person to another, as he had never made the mistake of being tamed into becoming one man's personal physician. The *réclame* of a travelling consultant, one who could be called on in an hour of need, was far greater. It meant higher fees, and also the pleasure of having his natural curiosity indulged in the observation of different courts and manners.

The Venostan court was like every other court in one respect: the sudden appearance of a celebrated physician to attend its Duke created rumours that Vincenzo, long credited with a morbid interest in graves by those who fancied he roamed by night as a werewolf, might at last be wavering on the brink of his own. Yet Master Valentino had visited here before, and the Duke had then neither appeared in need of his services beforehand nor altered in energy and activity afterwards. Some at court were convinced that Master Valentino was a spy; certainly he had opportunities every spy would envy.

Few would have envied his position at the moment,

bent with his ear to Duke Vincenzo's chest and with the Duke's black and burning gaze fixed on his furred cap a few inches away.

'Well? Is there any difference from last time?'

'Your Grace, I have not finished the examination.'

Surprisingly, Vincenzo suffered the rebuke, even smiling slightly as Master Valentino shifted his head, applying his ear to another part of the Duke's chest, and at the same time tapping it sharply here and there with bunched fingers.

'Cough, if you please, your Grace.'

Vincenzo obliged, blowing the fur of the cap awry. Master Valentino straightened up and lifted one of the Duke's hands as though to kiss it, but instead examined the nails with care.

He had a further request. 'Would your Grace be so good as to walk to the door and back?'

Vincenzo obediently got off the day bed and, watched in fascination by his page, who had not before had the chance to see his Duke take orders from anyone, walked to the door and back. Master Valentino, too, watched keenly. Vincenzo's harsh breathing was audible over the buzzing of bees in a pot of marjoram on the windowsill, and the doctor nodded.

'Very good, your Grace. I can now prescribe.'

At the doctor's signal, the page summoned the assistant waiting outside with the case of medicines. As Master Valentino selected the distillations, Vincenzo sat down with a touch of precipitation on the day bed and asked, in that voice of grated glass, 'You think I am going to die?'

The doctor permitted himself a sardonic smile or, one might say, a more open expression of the sardonic that was inherent in his face and nature. 'Your Grace, I know

you are. But then so am I, and this child here,' the page
looked first offended and then horrified, 'but only God
knows the time. If your Grace takes my medicines and
avoids too much exertion and excitement or an excess of
wine, the Angel of Death will be forced to delay for many
years.'

He spoke to an augmented audience. The Duchess
Dorotea had appeared silently in the doorway behind her
husband. Dressed in black velvet as though she already
mourned the loss of him, she stood with her back spear-
straight and her hands folded before her, the pale face
between the dark braids as composed as ever. Vincenzo,
evidently aware of her presence, turned to look at her,
and she moved forward, acknowledging the doctor's bow
with an inclination of the poised head.

'All shall be done as you direct, Master Valentino.
How long can you stay with his Grace?'

Master Valentino, having measured out his digitalis,
paused with another vial in his hand, considering. 'Not
long, your Grace, I fear. Although the Duchess of
Altamura is recovering, I have promised to return there
shortly.'

'You shall be well lodged in Venosta as long as you can
stay.'

The Duchess was above all a practical woman. She
supervised the taking of the medicine by her husband,
directed a page to conduct Master Valentino to the room
allotted by the chamberlain, and with her own hands
closed the shutters as Vincenzo lay back again on the
cushions. She placed a hand for a moment on his
shoulder, with no alteration in her calm, and withdrew to
her apartments. She did not return to her embroidery
frame and the wall-hanging on which she had reached the
scarlet stitching of Marsyas' flayed skin, draped

negligently like a coat from his shoulders while a triumphant Apollo wielded the knife. She opened her desk and drew a sheet of finest prepared vellum towards her – one does not write to princes on less. This was not a letter, moreover, to entrust to the prying eyes of a secretary. She dipped the quill and, supporting her hand upon an ivory slip, she began.

'Dearest cousin, we have not yet written to ensure you of our sympathy in your grief . . .'

If grief was itself approaching Duchess Dorotea, she was preparing for its pangs.

And if the great were suffering in Venosta, those in Altamura were not being spared. Little Lord Andrea started to kick and scream while his sister was being washed and dressed for the day. The nursemaid hurried to pick him up, fearful that Nurse, occupied with braiding the Lady Camilla's hair, would scold if the screams continued, but all her cuddling and soothing had no effect. Nurse abandoned the braids and came to take her princeling in her arms. At the noise, both Ippolyto and Violante, on their morning visit to the nursery to admire their offspring, the hope of Altamura, came to try parental cooing. The screams stopped abruptly and they smiled at each other as Nurse laid the baby down; but then stared in horror as the small body stiffened and bent backwards, turning blue in its gold-embroidered silk.

Nurse did not hesitate. She snatched up the baby in its mortal spasm and thrusting aside the Duchess ran out of the room, pulling off the silk smock and tossing it away as she ran. Duke and Duchess stared at each other in paralysed fear, as the nursemaids set up a violent shrieking to compensate for their helplessness. And

250

Master Valentino was in Venosta!

No need for the Duke and Duchess to speak. Their child, their heir, was dying and his nurse had gone mad. After that first frozen instant they ran, Violante picking up her skirts and flying after the madwoman. Crazed with grief, she might do anything − fling the child from a window into the river, beat its head on a wall . . . Ippolyto followed, maids and pages streaming after.

One flight of stairs down and through a series of rooms the nurse ran, to the laundry; the child's clothes littered the floor on the way, a page who had tried to stop her was still on all fours. She burst into the great echoing room with its cacophony of shouts, songs, beating-sticks, splashes, cascading water and the huge activity half visible in the steam. She scattered laundry maids from a trough and dipped her elbow into the water full of shirts; the next moment, the baby was plunged in among the linen just as Violante and the Duke erupted into the room and peered through the saturated air in search of their abducted son. In Ippolyto's mind was the thought that Nurse had been with his daughter in Borgo, and that crazed women after a death had been known to turn against all that was most dear to them. It was at this moment that he saw through the swirling clouds the Nurse in the act of drowning his son.

Violante got there first, strong-arming the laundry maids aside with more force than even Nurse had used. She slipped on the wet floor and fetched up against the trough.

'*What are you doing?*'

Nurse turned a beaming face, running with tears and perspiration and water, and showed the baby, whose head she was supporting as he lay in the hot water, no longer blue but a healthy pink, kicking his legs and

251

crowing. Violante, smiling too, picked up her son regardless of the water that soaked her sleeves and poured down the front of her satin skirts. She was pressing kisses on her son's chest and rounded stomach, on his knees and cheeks and brow when Ippolyto reached them.

'Look!' She thrust the child into its father's arms to the ruin of gold brocade. 'He's alive! He's well!' She turned to Nurse, who was now sobbing with delayed shock, the sound echoing in the vaulted ceiling and throughout the wide chamber. Work was slowing to a halt as more and more of the women came to realise that something extraordinary was going on. The girls at either end of a long sheet they were wringing stopped like statues. Beyond them, women with kilted petticoats tramping sheets in a stone trough had halted their song and stood still.

'What did you *do*?' Violante demanded, embracing her.

'Oh your Grace, it is thanks to Our Lady. She put it into my head what I'd seen as a child, a baby in a fit being put in hot water. I saw in my head as it might be Our Lady Herself ducking that child. She showed me I was to come here and here it was She brought Lord Andrea back to life.'

Ippolyto, his son strongly kicking in his arms, handed the child to the Nurse again, glad to acknowledge his debt to her, instrument of his son's rescue, and glad above all to give thanks to the Virgin Mary who had taken pity not only on his son, his wife and himself but on Altamura too. A duke with no heir is at the mercy of plotters, of enemies of whose existence he had proof enough. His impulse of gratitude became a decision.

'I shall go to the Church of the Annunciation to give

thanks to Our Lady at once. We shall have a Mass of thanksgiving said.' Who knew by what neglect of religious duties he had incurred the disasters that seemed to have rained on him of late? He had not properly given thanks for the restoration of his beloved wife. The saints who had saved her must wonder at his ingratitude and might refrain in future from troubling with his affairs. The Duke's theology was based on a strong understanding of duties and favours.

'I shall come too.' Violante looked up from kissing her son's small fist, with which he had been intent on remodelling Nurse's nose. 'We'll go together and thank Our Lady. I have so much to thank Her for.'

She did not glance at the Nurse, who knew what the Duke did not. That morning, Violante had confided in her that her worst fear was over: her next child, whenever God chose to send it, would not have a bandit as its father. Violante glowed with relief and joy.

Ippolyto hesitated. 'The risk to your health? Master Valentino was very firm, almost his last words as he left were that you should stay within doors and rest. When he returns, he will say whether an excursion outdoors will be safe.' The word reminded him of another man's warning. 'And Sigismondo. Did he not advise against venturing out into the city?'

'We'll send word to him so that he may come after us. And we'll take guards. What can go wrong?'

This question was not to get an immediate answer. For the moment, all went as the Duke commanded. The Duke informed Valori where he was going and why, and the captain of the palace guard was summoned and told that his men would surround the Duke and Duchess as far as the tiny church of the Virgin of the Annunciation in the square behind the palace. The Duchess refused a closed litter for so short a distance. A page was sent to find and inform Sigismondo. No one, least of all the Duke, remembered to tell Lord Tebaldo that the Duke's visit to the library to examine the manuscript must be postponed. Indeed, the agent carrying it had already arrived at the river stair beneath the library windows.

Chapter Thirty-seven

The voice of Il Toro

The page sent to find Sigismondo and tell him to follow the Duke and Duchess to the church failed to find him. He looked diligently but, probably misled by his impression of Sigismondo as a slayer of bandits, had no thought of looking in the library. Besides, Lord Tebaldo never saw anyone if he could help it. There were the agents who brought manuscripts, the copyists and *scrittori*, and the Duke on his occasional visits to inspect and admire acquisitions. Even then, as everyone knew, the Duke came alone so as not to disturb Lord Tebaldo. Naturally, the page did not think to seek Sigismondo in the library.

It was Biondello's doing. The servant who had been helping his master on with his best doublet and combing his hair ready for the Duke's visit had left the door of his study ajar, and Biondello, who was a dog of as much active curiosity as had his master, noticed this. Benno was chatting to Sigismondo as they strolled through the anteroom on their way to their lodging, and Biondello checked on this with a glance before veering aside.

Tebaldo looked away from a dispirited consultation with the hand mirror to meet the intelligent gaze of an animal that would not judge him by his looks. Hunting dogs repelled Tebaldo by their size, ferocity and clumsiness; he always feared one would knock him down, and then everyone would laugh or pretend not to; and he could hardly keep the kind of dog ladies kept, small enough to hide in a sleeve, because that too was laughable. Here was one just as small, rather dirty and, with its one ear, no more perfect than he was.

Benno always experienced panic when Biondello disappeared, even though he was unlikely to be stolen in a palace where most ladies would insist on their dogs having the full quota of ears. He was saying to Sigismondo, 'You know how we got Biondello from Poggio's village, well, Poggio as good as admitted he got him off a lady at court to sell and then he got stole from him again and lost his ear. Poggio says his old mother fed him daisies when he was a baby to stunt him so he'd do for court. Would they do that to dogs?'

He turned to survey the stunted dog and found him missing.

Tebaldo's servant, anxious to shoo away the obnoxious little cur pawing at his master's embroidered shoe, was told to go, and Tebaldo lifted Biondello up, hardly noticing the pain that shot through his shoulder muscles. Biondello, ready to be friendly where he sensed genuine goodwill, bestowed a generous lick on Tebaldo's chin. His infancy had been made up of more kicks than cuddles and he was still keen to get as many of the latter as he could. Benno, casting about like a dog himself, heard the amused tone of a man speaking to a small animal and, as the servant came out, caught a glimpse of Biondello kissing a stranger inside the little room.

'Beg pardon, sir, is my dog bothering you?' Once Benno was inside the room − a long, narrow room with bookshelves, a desk, and an odd-shaped couch − he recognised the young man in the fine brocade. Although older by a few years, he was the same, with the same melancholy eyes. Benno made his bow. 'Lord Tebaldo! You was ever so kind to me once — back in Rocca, about burying a dog.'

Tebaldo, who had long forgotten the episode, clasped Biondello to his chest as though he suspected this dog too was scheduled for interment. The man he did recognise, with no pleasure at all, was the one who now appeared in the doorway behind Benno.

'Sigismondo . . .' It was more horror than surprise. Nurse had informed him of Sigismondo's presence in the palace and the reason for it, but he had confidently expected there would be no occasion to meet. All his life he would be haunted by painful memories of his father's death in Rocca. Here was Sigismondo to remind him.

Somehow he clawed his way to his feet, letting Biondello drop and scattering the manuscripts before him over the floor. Sigismondo, while Benno fielded the dog, was quick to retrieve the scrolls and leaves.

'*De Genealogica Deorum*,' Sigismondo was glancing at a scroll as he restored it to the table. 'What a beautiful copy, my lord. And you have Greek manuscripts too; this is one I was shown by Andronikos Kallistos in Florence, I believe.'

'By Kallistos himself?' Tebaldo was amazed. This bravo in black leather could recognise Greek and Latin, talk to scholars? He leant awkwardly on the table and stared.

'I was fortunate enough to meet him and, later on, Manuel Chrysolatas and Demetrios Chalcondylas. All were in Florence at the time. I understand that Greek, and the teaching of it, is better appreciated there than anywhere.'

'Here at Altamura we have also a centre of learning,

257

though we are not the size of Florence. Why, my servant can read Latin to me — even though Greek is beyond him.' Was he trying to make excuses to this creature?

'My lord, I have been astonished to learn what has been collected here. The Prince-Bishop Gioffré, Abbot of Borgo, was telling me only last week of the reputation this library has already required. A manuscript of Pliny, one of the best — is that so?'

'The Duke's agents bring back many fine things.' Tebaldo, making a gesture to convey the wide extent of both the search for the works of learning and the nature of their contents, caught sight of the silver brocade of his sleeve and recalled at once for what occasion he was wearing one of his grander doublets. 'We are shortly to acquire a complete Quintilian, sir, which his Grace comes to inspect presently.'

Tebaldo hoped, firstly, that the man would be impressed — had enough knowledge to be impressed — and, secondly, that he would take the hint and go before Ippolyto arrived. Audiences with the Duke were always private and the presence of even someone he knew made him uncomfortable. It was not pleasant that the man had come closer and was looking at him keenly. He was looking him in the eyes, not giving the slightest glance at his body, yet Tebaldo inwardly drew back.

'A complete Quintilian, my lord? That's indeed a rarity. May I ask where your agent obtained it?'

'From an abbey in South Germany, he tells me.' Tebaldo was anxious to get rid of the man and his questions and, if answers would do the trick, he was willing to supply them. 'Our own agents have not penetrated that area much and this man is new to me.' He looked hopefully towards the door. Surely the page would arrive to announce the Duke's coming?

'You have the manuscript here? Might I be allowed to see it?'

What a nuisance the man was, and how disturbing despite his impersonal manner. It was essential to keep one's temper and not let him see how rattled one was by this interrogation. Tebaldo gripped the marble rim of the table and reached for his handbell. 'No, sir. The agent would not let it out of his hands. He is bringing it for his Grace to see at eleven this morning.'

As Tebaldo spoke, so did the bell of the cathedral chiming the hour, the deep notes rolling along the water beyond the window. 'It is eleven now, my lord. Does your agent come by the river?'

Such tedious, irrelevant questions! This last was answered by Tebaldo's servant, appearing in answer to the handbell. 'My lord, the man Pyrrho has arrived at the watergate. Shall I show him into the library or is he to wait in the anteroom?'

'The library, the library.'

This order provoked the strangest response of all from Sigismondo. Without a word – with only a gesture to Benno – he followed the servant and, turning as Benno came out, took the key from the inside of the study door and, shutting the door on the astonished Tebaldo, locked it on the outside.

There was no one in the anteroom. Benno, gaping for once in a completely unstudied way, saw Sigismondo draw his sword as he went into the library.

Facing them was the space from which Brunelli had banished the copyists with their desks and bookstands. The ink-stained marble floor stretched towards two bookcases, joined by a wide arch, that divided this section from the library proper, with its shelves, bookcases, cupboards, tables and reading stands and a cushioned couch. Two tall glazed windows looked over the river at the far end, one with a lower casement open against the folded shutter. In the nearer, deserted area the light came from clerestory windows high under the ceiling.

Sigismondo looked for a way of securing the main doors from the anteroom and found none.

'Stand here, Benno. If anyone comes, say the Duke orders that no one enters.'

Benno, even in these his most decent clothes, did not look like a palace servant or a figure of authority. His face and bearing were incorrigibly unkempt. Sigismondo touched his shoulder and said, 'Do your best.'

He shut Benno out and took up a position on the near side of one of the dividing bookcases, a position of ambush, sword ready. An agent coming into a library he expected to find populated by a duke and a lord might well walk on through the arch to find out where they were, or to check on the empty space yesterday full of busy writers.

The door from the water stair was by the windows. It opened, and a servant spoke. The door shut. Soft footsteps crossed the floor. There was quiet. Something was put down on a table − a book, a portfolio − and then the footsteps, hardly audible, retreated towards the window; paused there; a foot swivelled on the marble and the steps came forward.

The main doors were flung back. Brunelli, sweeping Benno aside with one arm, strode in. What he saw, framed in the arch but still a few yards from it, was a scholar in a grey loose tabard and, slightly crouched by the archway's shelves on this side, an armed ruffian. He pointed accusingly and said, 'What the devil are you doing here with a *sword*?'

At once the scholar's left arm flung up, he ducked out of the tabard in the same movement and wound his arm in it. His right hand now gripped a long dagger.

Brunelli stood astonished at the effect of his words.

His advantage lost, Sigismondo sprang forward and was through the arch and engaging Pyrrho. Stripped of one advantage by Brunelli, he yet had a sword against a dagger. Pyrrho evaded, used his tabard like a Roman gladiator's net to entrap Sigismondo's blade, flailing and flicking, as Sigismondo drove forward. Pyrrho was fast, and agile. As they moved, as he backed and feinted, his whole look one of concentration, he took in that Sigismondo's left arm did not follow and balance his manoeuvres. He gave a brief, tight-lipped smile. He whipped his tattered garment at the sword and jerked it towards him but the blade slid free.

Brunelli saw a street bravo attacking a scholar, whom he had luckily warned of the ambush, a scholar surprisingly quick with his weapon. The architect's natural belligerence led him to look about for a means of joining in the fight.

Pyrrho, backing, came up against the marble table, sat back and swung across it. Sigismondo leapt onto it and struck downward. An hourglass flung at him by Brunelli missed its moving target and shattered against an opening door beyond, opposite and twin to the water-stair door. Tebaldo had made his difficult way the length of his study to be greeted by flying sand and slivers of glass. He drew back only for a moment. He could hear steel, and the erratic slap and pad of feet, and harsh breathing. As he came in, he found that the combatants were at the far side of the room and he stumbled to his table, seized the handbell there and furiously shook it. No one came. Somewhere in the palace confused shouting resounded.

261

He saw that the fighting men were Sigismondo and the agent Pyrrho, whose grey cloak whirled with a sound like a great bird's wing. Pyrrho kicked a stool at Sigismondo, who avoided it but lost his stroke; Pyrrho slipped away round a reading stand to feint from the far side and come back with a dangerous blow on the near side. Driven from that, with a cut on the shoulder, he jinked away in time to avoid being driven into a corner.

Tebaldo was distraught: at any moment the Duke would be here, alone and unarmed.

Brunelli had snatched a large thin volume from a shelf and, holding it by both sides, advanced on Sigismondo from behind. Benno yelled a warning but, as he spoke, Pyrrho launched a large celestial globe on a wheeled stand at Sigismondo. He sprang aside, the globe trundled rapidly on and caught Brunelli amidships, carrying him backward, the folio leaving his hands and slamming to the floor while Brunelli rode on the globe until it struck the wall. Biondello, peering from behind the books on the lowest shelf, withdrew.

Still the fight went on. Tebaldo rang his bell, amazed that no one came, bewildered by events.

Brunelli toppled from the globe, but was inert only for seconds before he scrambled to his feet and laid hands on a library ladder propped against the shelving. Still the adversaries circled and fought, engrossed, implacable. As Brunelli raised the ladder and whirled it towards Sigismondo, Benno jumped for the free end, took hold and bore it down and they wrestled for it.

Tebaldo had seen bouts of swordplay between young courtiers, full of taunts, dancing steps and fancy passes. This was silent; a burst of action, vigilant circling, deadly combat again. He leant on the table, ringing his useless bell so hard that the handle broke and case and clapper rattled to the floor. The Duke would be here! And this Sigismondo, whose face he could now see, grimly intent, must have come to seize the Quintilian for some unknown competing prince. Tebaldo cried out for servants, for aid. Where had everyone gone? Suddenly Brunelli and the ladder, propelled by a desperate Benno, hurtled against the table, pitching Tebaldo to the floor. At the same moment a terrible clangour broke out in the city, a strident metallic din reverberating up the river, its brazen noise intensified by the high walls: the double-beat of the tocsin, the bell called Il Toro.

Pyrrho vaulted the marble table, was at the open window. Sigismondo had nicked his brow and his face and tunic glistened red. He put a foot on the sill and leapt outward. Sigismondo, at the window in the same moment, looked down. No splash could be heard, or any other sound but the tocsin's voice, the urgent raw bellow.

Benno had forced the ladder down over Brunelli's shoulders, trapping him between rungs. He sank to the floor under its weight, shouting inaudibly. Sigismondo beckoned Benno with an imperious arm and ran for the door. They had never heard Il Toro until now but they both knew what the terrible sound meant. The city was in danger.

Chapter Thirty-eight

Liberty!

When Bonifaccio Valori heard the Duke state his intention to give thanks for the miraculous recovery of his son, he at once sent word to his own son: he could not now go with him to view the estate he was thinking of buying. He told the servant to mention the church by name; his son just might get his head out of the clouds and do the acceptable thing by attending.

Now, crossing himself before the altar in the little church of the Virgin of the Annunciation, he turned to see if Tristano had, by any remote chance, had the sense to come. Naturally, all those at court who'd heard of the Duke's impulsive decision had impulsively left their own pursuits to follow him. A courtier does the right thing at the right time and now was the right time for a special devotion to the Virgin. And there – Bonifaccio was as pleased as he was surprised – there was Tristano at the back. The boy had come so much under the influence of that anti-clerical Polidoro Tedesco that he had avoided going to church at all. Even more surprising, here were Tristano's friends Atzo Orcagna and Cola Borsieri, who must have used their elbows effectively to be at the front; yet here they were, their eyes fixed attentively towards the altar. And here, demonstrating how they had reached their place, came that handsome young clodpoll Onorio

Scudo, pushing his way, smiling, apologising, catching his feet in ladies' skirts, edging between shoulders, until he was next to his friends and only a foot away from where the Duke knelt on the steps leading up to the chancel. This little church was almost like a theatre, with the altar raised high, as on a stage. Some clergy were still hurrying in, adjusting vestments, caught out by the Duke's impetuosity, taking their places on the wings either side of the steps. Valori was unsurprised that his son had not followed Onorio; his son was too sensitive to people's opinion to make such a brash movement.

The Mass began. Valori lowered himself carefully to his knees. The position was difficult for a man of his bulk. To distract himself, he set his mind on why he was here. If the little Lord Andrea had died in that fit, one visible advantage Altamura had over her immediate neighbours would have died with him: Borgo had no heir – Galeotto had married Ariana in the hope of sons; both he and Vincenzo had only daughters. Duchess Dorotea's sons had died. Altamura had a son, and a duchess who might well produce more . . . Valori gazed approvingly at the back of the Duchess's head, at the blonde braids wreathed with pearls under the black gauze veil. Duchess Violante, for all her passionate temperament and occasional interference in matters of state, was an asset to Altamura.

How great an asset he had as yet no idea.

The Mass proceeded. The courtiers fell to their customary fidgeting and whispering, eased their knees, looked about them. Those crowded in at the back without room to kneel had the best view of the Duke and Duchess. Those in front were forced to show proper concentration. Valori, aware of his own attention wandering, noticed the intensity of Polidoro Tedesco's students, their gaze unmoving. Here were young men in the grip of an experience beyond themselves. It was astonishing. Had they undergone a change of heart? Had the finger of God touched them?

The finger of God would have had to give Onorio a sharp dig. He had raced through the street in happy pursuit of his friends, who had so inexplicably rushed off when old Valori's message about the church arrived, and now the morning's wine and the steady chanting of the priests were having their effect. He tried hard to attend, but his eyes slid shut. His head began to droop.

For once his friends were not looking after him, to prevent him from becoming conspicuous in a public place. They were about to do that themselves.

Onorio's chin had reached his chest when the priest raised the Host and the bell rang, signalling the Elevation; and not that alone. In the midst of the rustling as everyone present crossed themselves, Onorio jolted awake, lost his balance and fell headlong, one hand seizing the Duke's ankle to steady himself. Simultaneously Atzo beside him leapt forward, knife in hand, shouting 'Liberty!', found Onorio on all fours in his path and fell over him, losing the knife which jangled on the steps. Cola, however, better placed to overcome the obstacle of both bodies now sprawled and kicking, surged past them and aimed his knife at the Duke, shouting also 'Liberty! Death to the tyrant!'

Luck was not with Liberty. The Duke, startled at the hand on his ankle, recoiled and turned, saw what seemed to be a tumbler's act with a knife and a failed somersault and two entangled young men, but was slow to understand. The Duchess by his side was not. The instant the knife left Atzo's hand she drew her own and was on her feet, thrusting herself in front of her husband.

Perhaps Cola Borsieri had not intended to kill the Duchess, only the Duke – perhaps he failed to see her as a tyrant, perhaps could not strike a woman. It made him hesitate, for him fatally. The Duchess struck before he could. If Cola had been looking for liberty, he might not have thought his own soul would win it so soon. He too fell, his weight bearing the Duchess backwards into her husband's arms. An assistant at the Mass, a young priest with fiery eyes, had run down the steps with the tall processional cross, jewelled, on a carved pole, and he held it in front of the Duke and Duchess, as if in interdiction to repel tyrannicide.

Shrieks and shouts echoed throughout the church. Onorio had got to his feet and helped Atzo up without at all knowing what had gone on. He stood amazed while Atzo thrust him away and, after a desperate glance at Cola dying on the marble steps, turned to escape.

The guards at the main door had heard the noise and appeared; swords were out; all was confusion. In this confusion Atzo might have got away but, as with so many, women were his undoing. As he ducked and twisted, running for the side door to a narrow alley and the hope of freedom, he stumbled among the skirts of women who still knelt. His foot slid on satin and he was in the hands of the Duke's guards advancing through the throng.

Bonifaccio Valori, taking in swiftly that the Duke and Duchess were unharmed, frantically scanned the chaos before him for his son. These two were his son's friends, these young murderers. God protect the boy! Was he involved? Was he with them? Dear God! If he were, not all his father's influence could keep him from a dreadful death.

Chapter Thirty-nine

The lure

'The Duke is dead! They've killed the Duke!'

People were shouting it in the streets as they ran towards the church. Sigismondo cut through the crowd and Benno, pounding behind him, thought: my master must be furious. Fighting that man in the library – and how did he know that man was going to be there? – while the Duke was getting murdered somewhere else . . . How far was this church? Who could have killed the Duke there? Was the library business just meant to draw Sigismondo away from accomplices in the church? And the assassin in the library had got away – again.

He caught up with Sigismondo in the church doorway, making way for a man being carried out by the palace guard. Blood pollutes, Benno thought, as Sigismondo exchanged words with the guard. They can't let the poor Duke die in the church. Then he took in the way the guards were handling the man, head swinging, arms dangling helpless, and now they threw him down. The fine clothes were not a duke's clothes.

A priest in vestments came out and crouched by the man. Sigismondo had gone inside the church and only by pressing close after him could Benno get in. 'Your Grace, are you hurt?'

The Duke was not looking in the least murdered. He

269

was pale, certainly, and he was clasping his wife's hands in both of his but, as he told Sigismondo, he had escaped unhurt, 'Thanks to Our Lady. Where were you, Sigismondo? At such a time? I sent to tell you to follow us here.' There was reproach in both their faces. Oh, typical, Benno thought, they go out when you've told them it's dangerous and then expect you to put on wings like an angel and be there to rescue them from what they've got into.

There was no hint of an apology in Sigismondo's reply. 'My reason waits for your Grace's greater leisure. Who are the villains of this attempt?'

The Duke indicated three young men in the hands of his guards. All appeared dazed by their misfortune. Benno had a shock at seeing Tristano Valori, never more like a stricken fawn, and Onorio, who looked as if he had been presented without warning with a mathematical problem of some complexity. The third was another of the philosopher's pupils, their friend Ratface. He, unlike the other two, had actually drawn a knife on his Duke. His ravaged face showed his thoughts: not only had he failed, but there were terrible consequences for the attempt, consequences he might more heroically have faced if he had succeeded. Every head of state had torturers in their employ, some with ingenious minds, and he had just supplied them with an opportunity to exercise their talents. Atzo Orcagna knew his death would be public and frightful and that he would long for it before it finally came.

How much were the others implicated? Tristano Valori and Onorio Scudo had been arrested because everyone knew the friends did everything together. These same ingenious officers of the Duke would find out how deep they were in this conspiracy. Bonifaccio Valori might have the influence to save his son, or his enemies might accuse him of being implicated too.

People round the Duke, some of his courtiers, were urging him to show himself in the city, to reassure the people, clamouring outside, that he lived, that he was neither dead nor on the point of death. The captain of the palace guard was not so sure. Who could tell what accomplices were abroad? Had these villains a band of rebels to back them in the city? What could be more likely?

Nobody was surprised, though few were pleased, when the Duchess took the initiative and turned to Sigismondo for his opinion. The deep voice was unhesitating.

'I agree with the captain, your Grace. There's too much danger in the city at this time.' Benno had a nasty vision of the flying bolas. 'If your Grace returns now to the palace, word will certainly spread that all is well.'

A large man, swarthy enough to be a Moor, here intervened. His men, he said, brought no reports of any uprising in the city, nor had the lookouts on the city towers seen any sign of advancing armies. The murder of the Duke, if it stemmed from the ambitions of some greedy neighbour, had been timed badly if it was meant to accompany invasion. Benno fancied this speaker to be chief of police, a post in which no one was ever popular. He looked as if he knew what he was talking about.

They were moving. The Duke was taking Sigismondo's advice. The guards formed a knot round the Duke and Duchess, the captain with drawn sword in front, Sigismondo and the chief of police behind. Even a man with the best aim in the world, with arrow, slingshot or bolas, would find it hard to penetrate that cluster.

The court streamed after them, full of loud congratulations and low-voiced gossip. No one spoke to

Bonifaccio Valori who had been kept from his son as the prisoners were hurried out by the side door under heavy guard. The mood of the crowd being what it was, cheering the Duke with deafening force, they were in greater danger than the Duke was.

They were spared, therefore, the sight of their friend Cola, now dead at the foot of the church porch. The guards saw no need to preserve his body from the crowd and were not concerned if he were pulled in pieces a little ahead of the executioner's job. Crowds in this state need an object of vengeance and here was one to hand.

Benno, who bumped into some fiercely laughing Altamurans brandishing a bit of Cola, hurried on, feeling sick, a hand on Biondello inside his jerkin for comfort. What puzzled him was how the conspirators had thought they could get away with it. How had they planned to persuade this crowd that it was a good idea to have killed their Duke?

The Duke had his own questions to ask. In the small audience room, he dismissed all but his wife and Sigismondo, and put the first of them, one he had already asked without answer.

'Where were you when I sent for you?'

'No message reached me, your Grace, in the library. I was there because you were expected to visit Lord Tebaldo at eleven.'

Ippolyto's face briefly showed that he had forgotten this entirely; and though a duke, he was human; guilt made him angry.

'What was the need for you to go there? Do I need protection from a . . .' there was a brief hesitation, 'from my wife's cousin?'

'No indeed.' The deep voice was smooth in answer. 'It

272

was because I realised that your Grace's life was in danger that I stayed there.'

This needed a bit of replay. Both Ippolyto and Violante were visibly listening to Sigismondo's words in their minds. Ippolyto became impatient. The shock of near-death had left him out of mood for mysteries.

'The danger was in the church! How should it be in the library?'

Sigismondo hummed, a long, cynical sound, a bee with no opinion of the world. 'Hey, those young men in the church, your Grace, were *amateurs*. The man who came to kill you in the library was *professional*.'

The Duchess cried, 'Tebaldo!'

'He was not after Lord Tebaldo's life, your Grace.'

'A man — to kill me in the library?' The Duke leant forward and the Duchess involuntarily copied him, both of them staring at Sigismondo.

'Certainly. He knew you would be there, and that you would be alone because Lord Tebaldo shuns company.'

'But I was to go there to see the manuscript. Who could know that?'

'The man who provided the manuscript.'

Ippolyto looked blank. It was Violante who spoke, and she was angry. 'Do you accuse my cousin?'

Sigismondo, bowing, raised apologetic hands. 'Your Grace, no such thing. Lord Tebaldo could not have had the slightest idea that the man who brought the manuscript you were to see had been hired to kill you.'

'Then how did you know it?'

'I recognised what manuscript it must be when Lord Tebaldo told me of it.'

'You'd seen it already? I was told it came from Germany.'

'From the monastery at Lübeck. I had not seen it, your

Grace. Prince Gioffré, the Abbot of Borgo, told me of it – the only complete Quintilian, and found in that monastery. I did not think there could be two such.'

The Duke's amber eyes, the Duchess's blue, continued to watch the man before them. 'Still I do not understand what made you see harm in it.'

'Because, your Grace, that manuscript, that only complete Quintilian, was purchased from the monastery at Lübeck some months ago.'

'And so?'

'The agent who found it brought it to Duke Vincenzo, who purchased it for his library at Venosta. He paid, the Prince-Bishop told me, many thousands of ducats for it. Evidently he thought them well spent if it lured you to your death.'

Chapter Forty

The promise

'Vincenzo.' The Duke's surprise was such that he said the name without expression. 'He sent the Quintilian, then, in the hands of his assassin.'

'His informers must have told him it's your Grace's habit to visit Lord Tebaldo alone, and to inspect any outstanding manuscript he thinks you should buy. This one in particular would require the sort of outlay your Grace would have had to sanction.'

'His informers! I'd like to know . . . But this assassin,' Violante's eyes sparked excitement, 'he's dead? You killed him all among the books?'

Sigismondo's face darkened. 'No, your Grace. When the tocsin sounded, he escaped. He'll be in the city now.'

Ippolyto struck his hands on the carved snarling lionheads that were his armrests. 'He can't get out, then. The gates close when the tocsin rings. We will search every house, every building. My chief of police will find him out. Oh, Vincenzo shall pay for this.'

He looked round for a familiar face, someone on whose advice he was used to rely; and then grimaced as he remembered. Bonifaccio Valori, because of his son, was under house arrest. There were other counsellors, but Ippolyto had depended so long on one man's wisdom, caution, shrewdness, experience . . . The

275

deprivation was keen. Valori had been a rock. It could not be possible he was implicated.

Venosta. He brought his mind back to the immediate urgency. Where could he find a condottiere to fight for him if he went to war against Venosta?

'Your Grace, if I might suggest?'

The Duke looked again at Sigismondo. This man was a rock, one against which the most violent waves had smashed and left no mark – for the moment Ippolyto forgot Master Valentino's report on Sigismondo's wound and the bandages he could not see. This was the man who had rescued Violante from a fate he would not yet permit himself to consider.

'Sigismondo. Suggest what you wish.'

'That your Grace does not show Duke Vincenzo that you are aware of his enmity. That you send to him only to announce your escape from assassination in the church, that he may rejoice with you.' The deep voice had a bubble of amusement and Violante laughed for the first time and clapped her hands.

'Yes! He shan't know till *we* take our revenge. We will plan that so finely—'

'My daughter, Ariana . . . Was that, too, Vincenzo's work?'

Sigismondo's dark eyes became grave. 'I believe so, your Grace. It was the same man I fought in Borgo who came to the library.'

'But why? I have done no harm to Vincenzo. He cannot be acting from ambition or he would have had an army at my gates waiting to hear of my death.' Ippolyto struck the arm of his chair again. 'This is pure evil! To have my poor daughter murdered. To attempt my life.'

'Also, your Grace, to send to Rodrigo Salazzo to inform him how close her Grace would be passing to his mountain lair. He must have sent word to him, perhaps as soon as he heard of the destruction of his fort.'

Violante suddenly laughed at the memory; she was still exalted at her husband's escape. He, however, was frowning. 'My daughter died before that. He had no reason to decree her death.'

Sigismondo's shrug was a little one-sided. 'Some men are born malign. It takes little to stir up the evil in such a nature. Your Grace will not have forgotten that Duke Vincenzo's offer of his own daughter's hand was refused by Prince Galeotto in favour of the Lady Ariana.'

'Why did he not take his revenge on the Prince and not on my child?'

'Mm-m . . . Perhaps, wishing to ally Borgo to Venosta, he hated to see it allied with Altamura. And again, I expect he had in mind to ruin any alliance with you beyond repair. The Lady Leonora, a Venostan agent, not only saw to it that the Princess took a sleeping draught, and signalled to the murderer when it had taken effect, but also made it seem that the Prince himself had strangled your daughter.'

'How? How did she do that? You told us nothing of it.' Ippolyto's frown was carving grooves into his handsome face.

'By stealing buttons from his sleeve − not hard to do, in an embrace − and, when she was alone with the drugged Princess in the pavilion, forcing them into the bracelets the Princess wore, to make it seem they had lodged there in the heat of her struggles.'

'Those bracelets which he also gave Lady Zima.' Violante's tone made clear how she would have dealt with the stupid insult.

Her husband took her hand automatically as if to soothe her, before asking, 'All this, is it connected with

277

those young traitors just now in the church?'

Sigismondo's hum was almost regretful. 'I believe, your Grace, that Duke Vincenzo knew nothing of them, that he was counting on this man Pyrrho to settle the matter. No prince has to look far for traitors, your Grace, and young men were ever fools. Your chief of police has sent to arrest their tutor; of course it is conceivable that he was in Vincenzo's pay.'

Ippolyto's frown was now thunderous. 'They shall all be questioned. We shall come at the truth.' He paused, finding himself looking around again for the familiar face, the illuminating counsel, and said, in sudden pain, 'How could Valori betray me? He helped me quell a worse uprising when my father died. I thought of all men *he* was loyal.'

'Your Grace may find him so.' Sigismondo spoke quietly and with conviction. 'Neither he nor his son may be involved, despite appearances. May I beg your Grace not to be too swift in judgement? To leave all in prison without questioning until time shall show more? I have found often that to do nothing forces others to do that which makes all plain. The cat that waits at the mousehole will catch the mouse at last.' Sigismondo, looking blandly at them, so sleek with his shaven head and gleaming black leather, resembled a patient cat quite enough to make both Duke and Duchess smile, however reluctantly.

'It shall be so. My torturers can wait; their instruments won't rust.' Ippolyto paused. 'You counsel prudence and delay. I am not to challenge Venosta, not to punish those who try to murder me. In turning the other cheek in so Christian a fashion, are we also to wait to see if the assassin who escaped you returns to give himself up?'

Ippolyto saw the flicker − was it anger? − in the dark

eyes, but there was no trace of it in the cool reply.

'That matter I ask your Grace to leave in my hands. I promise you that before the city gates open again, either Pyrrho or I will be dead.'

Chapter Forty-one

Ready for anything?

'He's got to be found, hasn't he?' Benno did not really expect an answer, and he got none. They had come back to their room through a palace buzzing with excitement and rumour, courtiers hurrying to discuss and explore each other's experiences of the morning, rejoicing that the Duke had been saved and that the villains responsible were either dead or waiting for their proper spectacular punishment.

Benno wondered how happy everyone would feel if they knew that another assassin, far more important and likely to succeed, was still alive, well, and free. Even with the city gates shut so he couldn't leave, how could he be found among so many! Outside the Duke's room during Sigismondo's audience with the Duke and the Duchess, Benno had overheard the courtiers' speculation of all kinds, but no word of what had happened in the library before the tocsin sounded and he and Sigismondo had raced out into the streets. They had passed Lord Tebaldo's servant hurrying from downstairs to answer the handbell the poor lord had rung before he was dashed to the ground. Sigismondo had called to him to run to his master who needed help. Benno hoped that Lord Tebaldo hadn't suffered more damage than he already had; his frame was not built to take knocks. Then there was Brunelli, whom he had last seen shouting vituperation, his shoulders wedged in the library ladder. As Benno had put him there, it would be best to dodge any meeting with him in future.

'Better not go near the window again.' Benno, approaching cautiously, pushed the shutters to against the heat and light outside, so that only on the coffered ceiling did the ripple of gold from the river float in pale discs. The rest of the room lay in cool shadow, a relief from the relentless glare and glitter outside. Even the city noises – the cries of children playing, streetsellers, the braying of a recalcitrant donkey, a cock crowing and the screams of birds quarrelling over the fishguts on the rocks almost opposite – seemed to be muted in the blaze of noon as Altamura prepared for its siesta.

There was luxury this side of the river. The *maestro di casa*, however much the palace might be simmering with animated gossip about the failed assassination, kept a tight rein on his underlings and was mindful of the Duke's guests. First a boy had arrived with a can of hot water for the majolica basin on the tripod, then shortly after two more came with a flagon of wine, a covered dish of cold meats and another piled with peaches, melons and grapes. Knives might flash in the Church of the Annunciation but palace hospitality should not be found wanting. Benno, whom excitement had never yet robbed of appetite, ate eagerly, but observed that his master, after washing away the sweat and dust of the morning's exertions, sat on the bed with head down, brooding, a piece of chicken uneaten in his hand, on which Biondello, a few polite inches away, focused with complete concentration.

Suddenly Sigismondo came to life. He put the piece of chicken in his mouth, to Biondello's visible disappointment, took a cup of wine, drank, and seemed disposed to ask questions himself.

'Tell me, Benno: what would you do if you wanted to evade arrest?'

No thought was needed about that one. 'Hide,' Benno said instantly. Sigismondo nodded.

'If you'd tried to kill the Duke, where is the least likely place they'd look for you?'

That was harder. Benno finished his cup before he answered, and when he did it was tentative.

'*Here?*'

Another nod. Sigismondo was smiling. 'Who'd expect you in the palace, particularly if you'd been seen to leave?'

Benno recalled Pyrrho's dramatic exit, how he had stepped so swiftly to the window, stood poised there for a moment and then vanished. He must have swum across to the other shore and disappeared into the city's turmoil, among people rushing about like ants disturbed and the relentless bellow of Il Toro overhead. The idea of his being nearby made Benno acutely nervous. He actually lowered his hand with a peach in it. 'But – in the palace? Everyone knows everyone, don't they? The servants'd spot a face they didn't know right away, even if he'd stole someone's livery.' Benno was anxious to prove his case, but Sigismondo shook his head.

'You don't have to be seen if you're hiding, Benno. Hey, this man's a professional. I have to ask myself, what would I do if I were Pyrrho? There are ways to get into a palace – into any place that has to be serviced daily. I'd come in carrying something. People don't ask questions if you look as if you know what you're doing.'

This was an old lesson to Benno and he nodded.

'Then . . . mm'm . . . I'd find a place quite quickly

where I could lie low until my opportunity came.'

'Opportunity?'

Sigismondo laughed, and held out his cup to be filled. From across the river came the sound of dogs barking as men directed by the chief of police went from door to door enquiring about all strangers in the city. 'Opportunity to kill the Duke. Hey, the man's been paid to kill the Duke, so much down, so much to collect when the job's done. If he doesn't accomplish it, he doesn't collect, but also he loses his reputation. Would you hire a man who'd failed?'

Benno was silent. Surely the Duke was safe in his own palace? Particularly if Sigismondo were to warn him of Pyrrho being there in hiding . . . Benno glanced quickly into the shadows, into the corners of the familiar room. Absurd. If Pyrrho were there, Sigismondo would be the one who'd failed and in fact by now they'd both be dead.

Curious, how he wasn't cheered up by that.

'There, my lord, you'll find that more easy.' Nurse put the stopper in her vial of scented oil and stowed it among the others in her basket. Tebaldo, who hated a servant to see the Nurse's ministrations, managed to pull the sheet up by himself. Manoeuvring onto his back again, he accepted her help in propping himself against the silken bolsters with their drawn-thread work and tassels. There was a look of faint surprise on his face.

'You know, Nurse, it *is* more easy.' He looked up at her with the sad eyes she found so heartrending. 'It's been easier to move since this morning when I fell. Something in my back seems to work differently. Of course it aches still and you tell me I'm covered in bruises, but that deep pain I've always had − it's gone.'

Her face blossomed in a delighted smile. 'I've not prayed in vain then, my lord. Such a terrible thing, this morning! The palace has scarce heard about it yet, they're all babbling about his Grace's escape in the church. The Virgin and the saints have been at work this day, no doubt of that, my lord.' She beamed still. She was looking forward to describing to her friends what had happened to Lord Tebaldo in the library. True, he had been his usual reticent self, and she would not dream of retailing anything that would make him seem undignified, but she had gathered that a man who acted as one of his agents had been attacked by Sigismondo, apparently for no reason, and there had been a fearful fight interrupted only by the tocsin – whereupon the agent had plunged into the river and Sir Sigismondo had run from the room. Nurse, while marvelling at the tale, could tell him that Sigismondo had returned from the church guarding the Duke and Duchess, 'And I am sure he would never attack anyone who's not a villain. Could it be your lordship was deceived in your agent?'

Tebaldo had been silent. He did not know what to think, in fact, and was reluctant to impart his feelings even to her. The brutality of the fight in the library, until now a haven of refuge for him, had conjured up scenes from the past in which Sigismondo had also figured, and which disturbed him profoundly. At the same time, something had changed in his thinking as it appeared to have done in his body. Violence could not after all be banished from life. Perhaps it should be confronted. He had lived with nightmares for so long; perhaps it was time to wake up.

'Who are these young men who tried to kill his Grace?'

'Lord Valori's son is one of them, and the word is that his father sent to tell him when the Duke was leaving for the church, so he and the other traitors would know where to go. Who'd think one so beautiful could be so evil? His father, now, his father must have put him up to it.'

Tebaldo had time to contemplate once more the idea that beauty is equated with goodness and that it was no wonder he himself was shunned; and Nurse had gathered her belongings together and was settling herself with folded hands for a bit of gossip more when a tap came on the bedroom door and, in the absence of a servant, she went to open it.

'Your Grace!'

It was the Duchess herself, with no one to keep her company except a rather unusual lady-in-waiting in black leather. Nurse dropped her curtsey to the Duchess and gave the benefit of her dimples to Sigismondo.

'How is Lord Tebaldo? Is he able to receive us?'

'Cousin!' Tebaldo had nothing wrong with his hearing and could pick up a whisper at a distance. 'Come in! I've but just heard of your escape,' he went on as she came into the room in a rustle of taffeta; he stopped short when he saw who was with her. Sigismondo had given the Nurse one of his broadest smiles, not necessarily reassuring to a young man of a nervous disposition; but now Violante, with her scent and jewels, was between them, bending to kiss Tebaldo's cheek.

'And I'd but just heard of *your* escape, cousin. Were you much hurt? Are you worse?'

Her concern soothed him. 'Strangely, cousin, I seem rather to be better.'

She clapped her hands. 'God has watched over us all today.' Tebaldo copied her sign of the cross as Sigismondo did, and with less than his usual cynicism. It might really be Divine intervention which had left him feeling stronger, less twisted. Violante went on, 'Sigismondo has been telling us of the assassin who brought the manuscript, and who meant to kill Ippolyto when he came to see it.'

'I was deceived, I fear. I truly thought the manuscript to be genuine.'

Sigismondo came forward. 'It was, my lord. You were not deceived in that. It was the agent who was false. May I enquire where the manuscript is now?'

'I ordered it should be locked in my desk.' Tebaldo, even when thrown down in what seemed like a fight between madmen, had not lost his consideration for books, more real to him than were most people. You did not leave a complete Quintilian lying on the floor, and his first thought on being helped up off it himself had been for the manuscript. The thought that it could be a forgery had tormented him — could his discernment, his knowledge, be so far wrong? And now he managed to include Sigismondo in his goodwill, and returned the smile. Violante pressed his hand and bent to kiss him again, her long plait with its pearls falling forward softly onto his neck.

'We must not tire you; Ippolyto has sent for Master Valentino to return from that viper Vincenzo's court,' she glanced round and saw Nurse, ears no doubt as eager as her eyes were wide, 'but more of that later. Ippolyto comes to see you tomorrow, he promises—'

'I shall be up by then. If his Grace comes to my study,' Tebaldo gestured towards the door in the corner, giving onto the hoist that lowered him from bedroom to study, 'I shall be there and will show him the Quintilian.'

'The spoils of war,' remarked Sigismondo, amusement in his tone. 'His Grace will not now have to pay for the manuscript.'

They left Tebaldo looking happier than Violante could remember ever seeing him.

Benno was waiting for his master outside and, as the Duchess swept on her way, Benno's jerkin suddenly erupted into barks. Sigismondo caught and righted the Nurse's basket in time to prevent the phials of different oils falling out and, after she had been supported by his strong right arm while she got her breath back, a process that was not to be hurried in such circumstances, she was able both to admire Biondello — still untypically bursting with barks and surveying the ceiling — and to excuse him.

'Rats, that's what it is. Any dog would want to be at them, and there's rats even in palaces. Plenty of spirit, that one, though there's rats almost his size to be found. Just now, in Lord Tebaldo's chamber, I heard one scuffling overhead, but it stopped when I spoke — cunning, rats are.'

'That's something we must never forget.' Sigismondo was genial, pressing the nurse's hand to his lips. 'I am much beholden to you,' and as she glanced at him in surprise, he added, 'my head, thanks to you, has mended quickly. Soon I shall be ready for anything.'

His next kiss was on her cheek and provoked a small scream and a smaller slap. Nurse was well pleased when she set off for her domain, the nursery, and her good temper was not even ruffled by meeting on the way the architect Brunelli, who confronted her with a scowl. She had heard from Lord Tebaldo's servant that he'd had to be cut out of a library ladder that morning, and what he'd been up to, to get himself in such a fix during the fight, she did not enquire. Such was her good mood now that, before he could speak, she ventured to offer him arnica for his bruises.

'Devil take arnica! What *I* want is that bearded halfwit in the filthy jerkin. Have you seen him?'

'How should I know where such a one is?' she retorted, and so temporarily averted an encounter that Benno would not in the least have enjoyed.

Brunelli might be looking for Benno; the man everyone else was looking for was not, as Sigismondo had said, where everyone was looking.

Nuto Baccardi had not been surprised when men of the police came to ask after his lodger. He described Lorenzo Corsini — which was perhaps his real name, he would not be surprised if it was not — as villainous of face, with sly eyes. Nuto's wife said he was aristocratic of face, with an observant gaze, but both agreed he had a mole at the corner of his mouth, which seemed to settle the question for the police. The man was wanted for the Duke's justice, and everyone knew what that meant. Nuto's wife had great faith in the police and was sorry to think she would next see the handsome stranger with a rope round his neck. With any luck, though, he might be up for worse than a mere hanging and then she could contrive to be in the forefront of the crowd — might even be the last person he saw!

Stefano Cipolla, on the other hand, was not one to confide in the police. The stranger had paid good money for a room over the river that made even the police hold their noses and they were not even saying why they wanted him. The bow and pack that had lain there were gone. The police did not get to hear this, however, because no one offered Stefano money and he was not going to part with any commodity, such as information, for free. He also withheld the information that only that morning he had met the man they sought — with the

mole, that is – on the stairs. Stefano had been running
down the stairs to answer the tocsin like a good citizen,
and the man coming up was soaking wet. His landlord
would have liked to know why, but the man had an air
that discouraged curiosity. Of course his being soaking
wet explained why he was running away from Il Toro
instead of towards it. He'd been the ideal lodger, Stefano
did not tell them; no complaints. It would be hard to
replace him.

The lodger, alone in the house, had been swift to strip
his wet clothes, wring them out and wrap them in his
pack, putting on dry ones. The bow he abandoned to the
river; a pity, but an archer in the mob that was filling the
streets in answer to that hoarse reverberating roar might
be too much noticed. This was a time to blend with the
crowd. If the cry of 'The Duke is dead!' gave him the
impression that he was out of a job in Altamura, that he
had no more to do but wait the chance to leave when the
gates were open, then the shrieks of joy following the
discovery that the Duke still lived altered his programme.
This he was already planning as, with the crowd, he flung
up his cap and cheered the Duke on his closely guarded
return to the palace.

Although the day was still bright outside, it was dim
where he settled his things round him, his pack on which
to rest his head, bread and sausage to eat, wine to drink,
the razor-sharp sword in its battered leather scabbard at
his hand, a more familiar friend to him than any man had
ever been. Now it was only a matter of waiting and he
was used to that.

Chapter Forty-two

A step that could be fatal

If Pyrrho was waiting, so was his employer, for news of him and the success of his mission. Vincenzo's wife, his courtiers – he had no friends – all observed that he took no comfort from his usual pleasures. Master Valentino had some time ago advised him to give up hunting, as exercise increased his breathlessness and the pain in his chest. While for a period he had sat in a chair and had the game driven in front of him to be pinned down while he came over to despatch it personally, he had now given up so weak a satisfaction. It had always been the excitement of the chase, the pursuit of something unlikely to get away, which he had enjoyed. Without that, the infliction of death lost some of its charm.

His engraved gems had lost their interest too. He had heard almost with indifference of Prince Galeotto's purchase, for a large sum, of an onyx intaglio of Herakles subduing the Nemean lion, a piece from the collection of a Roman cardinal for which he had himself been offering. On the other hand, the news that Brunelli, who had escaped attempts to eliminate him in Venosta, was now said to be redesigning Duke Ippolyto's library, brought only a smile to Vincenzo's thin lips. With any luck Brunelli would be literally on the spot when Ippolyto died; even were he nowhere near, he would be once again without a job and a patron.

Master Valentino was in attendance on the Duke when the envoy from Altamura was announced. He had been taking Vincenzo's pulse and felt it race before the wrist was snatched away.

'Show him in at once.'

Vincenzo absorbed immediately that the envoy was not in mourning. The envoy did not fail to notice that the Duke had a doctor – he knew Master Valentino – at his side and that he looked not only like a werewolf but a sick werewolf. He bowed profoundly, concealing his smile.

'Your Grace. Greetings from Duke Ippolyto. He calls on your Grace to rejoice with him on his providential escape from murder, in which his assailant was killed—'

The envoy got no further.

Duke Vincenzo had risen, taken one step forward and fallen on his knees before the envoy as though begging him to deny his message, to say something completely different . . .

Master Valentino was at the Duke's side in an instant, but he had been forestalled by the enemy all doctors fight. Duke Vincenzo, if he had ever been a werewolf, was now a dead one.

'That's funny sort of writing.'

Benno had been very interested when Sigismondo asked a page for paper, pen and ink. He had watched, fascinated, while his master mended the quill to his satisfaction, and now he peered over the broad shoulder to watch him writing. He liked to see his master make the inexplicable signs that meant words. He knew he could never make anything of them, but this time he was quite sure they looked different from normal letters. Sigismondo hummed as he wrote, and said 'You're an expert?' Then as he finished and sanded the letter from the silver shaker on the writing-board, he added, 'But you've good eyes, Benno. It's Greek.'

Benno wondered if every language had different shaped writing, and if his master knew them all. However, getting one answer meant he didn't dare ask the question it called up. To whom would his master write in Greek? It crossed his mind that it might be Polidoro Tedesco, but then surely he'd already been arrested?

Sigismondo called the page and held out the note. 'For the Lord Tebaldo. Give it into his hand.'

Benno understood the need for this insistence. Servants of the crippled lord would be likely to protect him from being bothered when he wasn't well, and put the note by until they judged him well enough to deal with it. Benno, with experience of being stopped at people's doors, wondered if the page would be able to insist against the lord's servant if he refused him . . . More interesting was what Sigismondo had to say to him. He'd seen him, with the Duchess, not half an hour ago, so why hadn't he said it then and *why say it in Greek*?

Sigismondo was slipping his arm from his sleeve, and accepted help in removing his doublet. Benno watched as he lifted his bandages to look underneath, and was alarmed in case his master's wound was worse. The fight with Pyrrho this morning couldn't have done it any good. However, when Sigismondo raised his head he was smiling.

'Hey, don't start the prayers for the dead yet. What I told Nurse was true: it's knitting well. And I gave Pyrrho something to remember me by – he'll want to return the favour.'

A cold feeling touched Benno's spine as he thought of what Sigismondo had said: Pyrrho was likely to be somewhere in the palace. Mightn't he come through the door this minute?

The door opened. Benno went tense and stopped breathing. Even Sigismondo had his hand instantly on his sword. Both had to adjust their stare to the right level.

It was Poggio, wearing an ingratiating smile.

'Thought I'd come to see how you are.' The small black eyes took in Sigismondo's bandages and the broad hand relinquishing the sword. 'Expecting enemies, then? Don't look in too good a shape if I'd been carrying an axe.' Poggio was grinning as he sidled round the door and shut it behind him. 'Want me to lock it? Could always climb up from the river, though, couldn't he?'

Benno had to stop himself from rushing to bolt the shutters.

'You've come to tell us something,' remarked Sigismondo, holding out his doublet for Benno to help him on with the sleeve. 'Tell us your gossip first, and then you can carry your report on me round the rest of the palace.'

Poggio scrambled himself up onto the bed beside Sigismondo, and sat surveying them both with a grin that rendered his eyes nearly invisible. 'Things have been buzzing like an upturned hive all day. I missed the bit in church,' his mouth took on a grotesque downward curve, 'should say my prayers more often . . .' His eyes brightened. 'But I was there when they brought the traitors back here for prison. The state they were in, after the crowd'd thrown things! Could've made an omelet of their hair alone. If they're not fed in prison they can get a

294

meal off their clothes — not that there'd be time for many meals before the gallows, I'd think.' He stopped swinging his legs and put his head on one side, regarding Sigismondo, waiting for questions.

Sigismondo obliged. 'Have they arrested Polidoro Tedesco yet?'

Poggio flung up his hands. 'Funny you should ask. But silly me, you'd guessed. Oh yes, the Duke's men went for him and what did they find? He'd gone.'

'Gone?' Sigismondo raised his eyebrows. 'With the city gates shut?'

'Oh well, he'd left his body behind. Gone to sneer at the afterlife. Took poison, they say, not a pretty sight. Left a letter to the Duke, though, saying it was his glory to have inspired a burning desire for liberty in Cola Whatsisname and Atzo Thingy. Tedesco will be kissing Cola in Hell now, thanks to the Duchess, for all he said he looked to meet them in a better world. A better world's a great hope for a suicide and a gang of murderers, wouldn't you think? Well, that's two down and three to go. Funny, he didn't mention the Valori boy and that sleepwalker Onorio.'

'Perhaps they are innocent.'

Poggio cackled. 'Innocent! Wait till his Grace's questioners have done with them. Men'll damn their souls to Hell sooner than bear another twist of the thumbscrew. Tristano Valori will wish he'd been a bit cleverer at killing himself when Lady Ariana left for Borgo. I was there then; he made a real hash of it. Mind you, I was sorry for him then and I'm sorry for him now but there's nothing anyone can do for him, is there?'

A long, thoughtful hum from Sigismondo was his only answer.

Poggio left, anxious to collect his money on bets laid

about Sigismondo's wound, rumoured to be so bad that he had failed to make it to the church on time. Not long after his going, Benno was entrusted with one of his master's lies. They had come from their room and were entering the anteroom outside the library.

'Go to the Lord Tebaldo's room. Tell his servant to inform Lord Tebaldo that the Duke has arrived to see him and is waiting below in the study.' Benno, setting off, wondered how Sigismondo knew where the Duke was; as he climbed the stair, Biondello leaping at his side, he glanced down and saw his master turn the handle of the study door and go in, reaching behind him to take his axe from the back of his belt.

Rejecting the idea that Sigismondo had run mad and suddenly decided to murder the Duke himself, he came to the conclusion that, with Pyrrho in the palace, nothing could be more sensible than to take an axe into any room when you didn't know who was inside.

He delivered his message and, although the servant gave Benno's splashed and drabbled jerkin a shocked stare, he repeated the message to Lord Tebaldo, who seemed upset as he called out, 'So soon? Help me to dress – I shall be keeping his Grace waiting.'

Benno hurried back downstairs. His insides told him that something particularly nasty was going to happen. Sigismondo had looked so calm, so intent, his head slightly on one side as if he listened, when he went into the study with the axe gleaming in his hand. Yes, there was trouble. Could his master know that Pyrrho was in the study already?

As it happened he was not.

Sigismondo went the length of the room to the door screened by a tapestry curtain, that led to the library.

The room was filled, in the summer evening light, by

the chiming of bells all over the city for evening Mass, the tenor jangle from the Church of the Annunciation, just behind the palace, rising above the rest as if in special celebration of the Duke's happy escape within its walls that morning. Almost imperceptible among this joyous noise was a far softer one, hardly more than a mouse might make, a small creaking from behind the door in the opposite corner. Lord Tebaldo's hoist was making its journey down from above.

The hoist came to a halt. There was enough pause for a man to lever himself from the chair bolted to the hoist platform, and the doors opened.

The evening sun glittered on his jerkin like discs of light from the river's reflection on the ceiling, and slid in a gold gleam down his drawn sword as Pyrrho stepped out. That same instant the sun flashed on a thing cleaving the air. From the shadow of the library door curtain Sigismondo had sent his axe to meet Pyrrho.

Opening the study door, Benno stood paralysed at what he saw inside.

Pyrrho's heart should have been cleft in two by the axe that struck his chest — but he had come prepared for emergency. A quilted jerkin sewn with steel rings, work of a master armourer of Milan, had saved his life before this. Winded, with two ribs broken, gasping, he reeled back against the shelves holding Tebaldo's own books. A shower of scrolls and portfolios, jolted from their pigeonholes, bombarded Pyrrho as he fought for his balance and his breath.

Sigismondo wasted no regrets on his axe. He tossed the sword waiting in his left hand into his right, and leapt to strike Pyrrho's head as he supported himself on the shelves. As the sword swept down, Pyrrho flung himself sideways and the blade parted a long vellum scroll falling from the tottering shelves. In the moment the sword took to descend, Pyrrho seemed to have life pour into him again, so that Sigismondo, wheeling in recovery from the stroke, found his enemy had got Tebaldo's desk between them, across which his sword hovered ready to meet Sigismondo's. Pyrrho's face, a gold mask in the shaft of low sunlight, showed no fear, anger or pain, but in the sudden quiet as the bells stopped, his harsh breathing sounded like tearing silk.

Benno himself had almost stopped breathing. Should he run for help? But his standing orders were: don't interfere in a fight.

Sigismondo moved, a step that would bring him within sword's length of Pyrrho, a step that could be fatal for either. As he stepped, he slipped. A paper from the shelves drifting underfoot proved a treacherous surface.

Benno heard a shout of terror but did not know he had shouted. For a second, Pyrrho's attention divided, to check the figure in the doorway. His sword's sweep deflected and fell, not on Sigismondo's neck bent before him, but on the edge of the desk, prising off a strip of inlay and splintering the top. Sigismondo, on one knee, was rising, but Pyrrho leapt on the desk with dreadful agility and wrenched his sword free. Another blinding flash in the sun and Pyrrho whirled the sword high for the stroke that would split Sigismondo's head. Benno started forward in anguish at the same moment that Sigismondo rose. Pyrrho's sword was descending but Sigismondo brought his up with all the force of his rising and pierced Pyrrho's throat. Benno was to see that face in dreams, fierce in disbelief as life left it.

Sigismondo stepped back. Pyrrho crumpled and sprawled on the desk, arms hanging, sword spinning in a great parabola across the floor. No more harsh sounds, just Sigismondo steadying his breathing, and the dull drip on the reddening floor.

Chapter Forty-three

The complete Quintilian

'We are glad,' said Prince Gioffré, Abbot of Borgo, giving his ring to be kissed, 'to see you here alive after so many reports of what has happened in Altamura since we last saw you.' He looked keenly at the face as Sigismondo rose. A pallor, he thought; news of the wound was not exaggerated. 'I am told you are the cause that others are alive today. His Highness showed me the letters from Duke Ippolyto which name you as the saviour of his life and state.'

'My lord,' Sigismondo's voice was amused and he shrugged, 'you know that nothing is as simple as it sounds. I could say that his Grace's life was saved by a young man who fell asleep at his prayers, and then by rats in the roof. The grace of God and Our Lady gave it to me to do as I did.'

The Abbot crossed himself and said, '*Gratias agimus Deo* . . .' The heat of the day was past, and sounds of quiet talk came from the courtyard, with the shrill of cicadas.

'You've been fortunate indeed, Sigismondo. You've achieved much. Prince Galeotto is much pleased that all possibility of blame for the terrible death of the Princess has been lifted from him. It is the Duke Vincenzo who must answer for his sins now at the Judgement Seat. The

Devil walks everywhere, even in high places.'

Especially in high places, Benno thought. He had been kindly permitted to come into the room and stand by the door while his master had audience of the Abbot. If you ask *me*, that Duke will find himself quite at home in Hell . . . Benno surreptitiously rubbed a bruise on his rear on the doorjamb. Brunelli had finally caught up with him, very suddenly, outside the audience chamber at Altamura. Although he now realised he had taken the wrong side in the fight in the library, the architect was not the man to forget an injury. Luckily for Benno, he had been booted into the arms of Sigismondo, emerging from an audience with the Duke and he, glittering with the Duke's chain, had given Brunelli sufficient pause to permit of explanations. Sigismondo had forborne to say that if Brunelli had not given away his ambush of Pyrrho in the library that first time, a great deal of trouble might have been saved all round, even to Pyrrho. Instead, the meeting had ended with drinking, in an Altamuran tavern, to the library extension; which looked as though it might be one of Brunelli's commissions that would get to be completed.

When Benno had attention to spare from reminiscence, he found that Sigismondo and the Abbot were considering Hell.

' . . . and those misguided young men! What blasphemy to attack their Duke in church, and at the raising of the Host. I fear they will pay a terrible price, in this world and the next. Dante puts all traitors with Judas in the ninth circle of Hell.'

'Perhaps, my lord, they will obtain forgiveness sooner than will their tutor, who confessed to setting them on.'

'What cause could he have for such wickedness—'

302

There were suddenly raised voices from the garden and the Abbot moved to the window, opened the shutter fully and stood there a moment, looking down, his hands tucked in his sleeves. There was immediate silence below. He turned and came back, his feet soundless on the tiled floor. 'A learned man, who must be acquainted with the Scriptures, with the works of the sages . . .'

Sigismondo's hum was voiced, derisory and prolonged. 'He believed himself a Socrates, leading the young to revere truth. In fact, he was a bitter man, like Duke Vincenzo, seeking personal revenge.'

Benno became alert. This he hadn't heard. The Abbot moved to the wooden stool behind his desk, and with a gesture invited Sigismondo to take the cushioned bench which he did, and continued. 'His Grace told me, when they reported Tedesco's suicide, that the man had been his own tutor in his youth. This I already knew, but not that he had been beaten on Tedesco's orders, savagely, for his mistakes; nor that, when he became Duke, he ordered Tedesco a flogging to pay him for the injuries to his pride that he could not forgive.'

The Abbot looked briefly to Heaven and shook his head. 'Oh, my son, what lack of charity pride brings. One cruelty begets another and so it goes on. Not for nothing are we told how Lucifer fell through pride . . . So he taught his pupils to hate tyrants when he hated only the man who had humiliated him?'

'Mm-mm, it's easy enough to confuse your motives.' Sigismondo watched as the Abbot extended a hand and opened a small cupboard in the panelled wall behind him. 'A great deal of evil is done for the best.'

The Abbot, smiling, poured wine into plain pewter cups and handed one across to Sigismondo. 'Philosophy! When I taught you in Paris you were among the best minds of your time; but you looked for other solutions to life's puzzles even then.'

Benno, expanding his nostrils to catch the delicious fragrance of the wine, would dearly have liked to hear more about his master's mysterious past, but Sigismondo was not to he drawn. In companionable silence, he and the Abbot drank.

'Prince Galeotto is to be congratulated, I hear. Is the ceremony to take place here or in Venosta?'

'His Highness has asked me to say the Nuptial Mass for him in the cathedral at Venosta, when the time comes. He does not wish to offend Duke Ippolyto by too hasty a marriage, after his last wife's sad death.'

Both men were silent again. The courtyard emptied, or at least the voices were gone and only the sound of hoes chipping at the earth accompanied the cicadas. The proposed marriage of Prince Galeotto to the widowed Duchess Dorotea had taken the world by surprise, yet it served the convenience of both admirably. The Prince wanted an heir; the Duchess was still young and had proved her fertility with the children she had borne to Duke Vincenzo. True, only daughters had survived, but Galeotto's sons might not lose heart so readily after first sight of their father. Besides, his need for an heir was now less urgent, Venosta being virtually his own.

Duchess Dorotea – though this was known to few – had made the first advances, in her stately manner. Vincenzo might have entertained illusions of making a recovery; she had none. After a long consultation with Master Valentino she had begun her secret correspondence with Galeotto. She would now have a husband far more amenable to control, and on the marriage would acquire what Vincenzo had failed to get when he offered Galeotto their daughter. She would bring Venosta as her dowry, but would get Borgo into her hands. Thinking about this, she had ordered the Masses for Vincenzo and calmly set herself to finish her tapestry of the flaying of Marsyas. It should be her present to the groom.

'Duchess Violante is recovered?'

Sigismondo's smile was warm. 'Master Valentino declares she is in better health than ever.' He did not mention the chain of gold and rubies, work of a master jeweller, which the Duchess had put round his neck, nor the kiss she had pressed on his cheek. The look she had given him as well might have made Ippolyto jealous had he seen it.

The Abbot leant to fill Sigismondo's cup again. 'I heard the physician Valentino is by some held responsible for hastening Duke Vincenzo's death at his wife's instigation.'

'Hey, every doctor who attends a great lord and can't cure him must expect to be so traduced, and every wife as well. There are doctors who withdraw from cases they can't cure.' Sigismondo drank, and added, 'Master Valentino told me in confidence, on his return to Altamura, that the day after Duke Vincenzo's death, he opened his door to find tributes of flowers from grateful citizens of Venosta.'

The Abbot gave an unexpected bark of laughter. He turned his cup in his thin fingers and glanced at the man opposite. Sigismondo's face and bearing were serene, untroubled by all that had happened since they last met.

'This assassin – Pyrrho, you said? That must have been a man to strike fear to the heart. What you said of him entering the study recalls to me what Virgil says—'

'Vestibulum ante ipsum primoque in limine Pyrrhus
Exsultat, telis et luce coruscus aena,'

Sigismondo quoted, and wagged his head, marvelling. 'I might have remembered that and taken it for a sign. Stand on the threshold he did, and glitter too—'

'*Qualis coluber*,' put in the Abbot.

'*Precisely* like a snake. That particular snake, though, had his scales made by Missaglia of Milan — I know his work — and they saved his life. For a moment.' The hum that followed this remark was valedictory, almost regretful, one professional saluting another. 'I had a Mass said for his soul . . . It was unlucky for him that he did not know his employer was dead and there was no need for him to carry out his task.'

The Abbot sighed. 'He killed for gain. He will need many prayers in Purgatory. But those foolish young men led into sin by their tutor — have they suffered the Duke's justice?'

'One was killed, as you know, by the Duchess herself, whom no man easily daunts — ' Remembering Rodrigo Salazzo, Benno hoped the Duchess wasn't getting a taste for stabbing people — 'and the one who was his fellow conspirator was hanged before the palace in Altamura yesterday. The others, Tristano Valori and Onorio Scudo, were judged innocent of the plot and the Duke freed them, restoring Bonifaccio Valori also to his position of chief counsellor.'

'It was unthinkable that such a man could be disloyal,' the Abbot said, 'and although over and over it has been found that the unthinkable is true, we may rejoice that both father and son were exculpated.'

Sigismondo bent his head in agreement, and then clicked his fingers suddenly, causing the Abbot to raise his eyebrows, and Benno came hastily forward with the portfolio he had been nursing. At a gesture from Sigismondo, he laid it on the table before him, bowed and drew back to his observation post by the door.

'What is this, my son?' The Abbot regarded the portfolio, leaning forward in polite interest.

'Duke Ippolyto wishes to show his gratitude to God for his escape from death, my lord. This is the manuscript you told me of, that Duke Vincenzo acquired for Venosta. Your telling me of it happened to save his life in the end. I was able to catch the assassin because he believed Duke Ippolyto was coming to see it.' Sigismondo spread his hands and laughed. 'How grateful I ought to be for my education. Pyrrho was hiding in the roof above Lord Tebaldo's room and could hear what passed below. I could not ask Lord Tebaldo aloud to pretend Duke Ippolyto was coming to his study to see the manuscript, but I sent a message to him in Greek which his servant could not read. Pyrrho, deceived, did as I expected and came down the ropes from the roof to his lordship's hoist and thence to the study. Where I was waiting.' Sigismondo smiled and pushed over the portfolio. 'His Grace wished you to accept this for the abbey library here in Borgo, in memory of Princess Ariana.'

Reverently, the Abbot opened the portfolio and gazed at the complete Quintilian. The cover, vellum beautifully inscribed with gold letters, bore a scar across it as if from a wound: Pyrrho's blood, seeping into the desk, had stained it and been scraped away.

The Abbot had opened the cover and was regarding the first page with absorption when a discreet scratch at the door heralded a monk with a message. A man was below seeking Master Sigismondo very urgently. He had come more than a hundred miles and would tell his errand to no one but the man he sought.

Benno, following Sigismondo from the room where

they left the Abbot oblivious of all comings and goings, wondered where they would have to travel now and what they would hear. He hoped to see no more assassins and no more libraries. Until now he'd had little acquaintance with books but he began to consider them as dangerous objects.

He picked up Biondello, rotund from feasting in the abbey kitchens, and set off happily into his future.